MEG ANNE BRIGHTON

Silence of the Loons

Murder in Maury County

Cover art by Book Cover Zone.com

This novel was inspired by a true story. It constitutes a work of historical fiction inspired by events that occurred in Maury County, Tennessee. The names, characters, and incidents presented in this narrative are entirely the products of the author's imagination. Any resemblance to actual individuals, living or deceased, events, or locations is purely coincidental, with the exception of "Big Bill" Thomason. The Wallace/Fautt trial represents a factual event that transpired at the courthouse in Columbia, Tennessee, around the year 1923.

First edition

ISBN: 978-0-9973819-3-1

This book was professionally typeset on Reedsy.
Find out more at reedsy.com

Dedicated to my beloved ancestors.

"The loon cried out as if calling upon the god of loons to aid him."

Contents

Preface

Maury County, Tennessee 1919

Priscilla Powell had always believed her life was ordinary. But her mother said it wasn't because they were fortunate enough to live in their family's Civil War-era home, nestled against the backdrop of Duck River. A portrait of normalcy, Priscilla's life was quietly extraordinary, surrounded by the lore and mystery of her home's past inhabitants. Her mother's antiquated beliefs, her sister Amanda's modern beliefs, and the detailed stories of ghostly sightings recounted by her siblings had shaped her childhood.

Priscilla herself had yet to encounter these spirits, even when she'd stayed up half the night sleeping on the plank floor stained with the blood of a Confederate soldier. With a grounded nature and a life colored by antebellum ghost tales, Priscilla is the bridge between the mundane and the mystical, ready to uncover the secrets in the echoes of the past while dreaming big and always wanting more out of life than what her sisters had settled for: marrying and becoming homemakers.

She wanted none of it. Her genuine passion lay in the great outdoors—nature, especially the birds. The marshes held a special place in her heart, serving as her sanctuary to observe the Great Egret and the swift Peregrine Falcon as they engaged in their instinctual displays of survival. Her favorite bird was the mysterious loon, whose haunting call sent shivers down her spine.

Change was in the air; she sensed her life teetering on the brink of the unknown. Something perilous loomed on the horizon, and at the tender age of fourteen, she pondered the complexities of survival. Her father was gravely ill, and her mother, naturally inclined toward matchmaking, was determined to arrange a marriage between her and her cousin, Lee Dodd—a man eleven years older, infamous for his dual occupations as a gunslinger and moonshiner.

Any other girl might have succumbed to the pressure and married Lee, but Priscilla desired more from life, so she fled.

Acknowledgments

I would like to thank the Maury County Archives for providing the book *Born Old in Sin,* which featured several stories written by Bob Duncan about Big Bill Thomason, one of the main characters in my book. I also appreciate the Facebook group *"I Remember Mt. Pleasant, Tenn., Way Back When,"* which helped me connect with several cousins who contributed valuable information. Lastly, I acknowledge Virgil Stewart for sharing pertinent information regarding homicides in Maury County, Tennessee.

Running Away

Maury County, Tennessee, 1919

At fourteen, Priscilla Powell felt the world's weight pressing down on her as she sprinted across the sunlit field, her worn carpetbag clutched to her chest. The bag held only a few changes of clothes, just enough to sustain her on this uncertain journey. She had slipped out the back door after realizing she had to escape her tumultuous situation with Lee Dodd before it escalated. Her simmering resentment had boiled over, and she could no longer endure the suffocating atmosphere of her home. She wanted more from life and had one thing on her mind: fleeing an arranged marriage orchestrated by her matchmaker mother.

By chance, she spotted a milk truck rumbling down the gravel road. With a mix of trepidation and excitement, she hitched a ride, enjoying the cool breeze on her face as they sped into town. Bees attracted by the fresh smell of sweet, creamy milk swarmed into the open milk truck, distracting her from her worries. As usual, the driver dropped her off at the drugstore, where she'd shared many happy times having ice cream with her sister, Amanda.

Priscilla threw her shawl over her head to protect her identity. She hurried across the bustling street, weaving through Tin Lizzies and horses, her destination clear in her mind — Belle Barker's saloon, where she hoped to find a job and perhaps a hint of adventure.

Her heart thumped as she peered through the grimy window with trepidation and intrigue, landing on a figure that matched her sister's description of a "woman of the night." The woman, Belle, wore a striking off-shoulder red satin dress that clung to her curves, shimmering under a smoky haze. Her blue eyes, outlined with mascara and thick lashes, locked onto Priscilla's with a blend of curiosity and suspicion. She raised an eyebrow. "What do you want, little girl? You're too young to be here."

Priscilla fought to steady her trembling voice as she struggled to tear her gaze away from the captivating woman standing before her. With her bold crimson lips and an aura of confidence, Belle was unlike anyone she had ever encountered. A knot of fear in her throat caused her to stammer. "I...I need your help. My sister told me you assist girls with nowhere else to turn."

Belle's brows creased. "Meet me at the back door," she replied in a low tone. "I can't let you enter through the saloon—it would stir up too much gossip."

They made their way to the kitchen, filled with the rich aroma of spices and the faint sound of voices from another room. Priscilla pulled her shawl around her tight as she settled on a small, worn chair at a rustic wooden table. A flicker of hope sparkled in her eyes as Belle placed a chilled soda and a glass brimming with ice before her. Thirsty and grateful, Priscilla took a long gulp, the bubbly sweetness washing over her parched throat, offering a brief respite from her worries.

Brushing a tendril of auburn hair from Priscilla's face with surprising tenderness, Belle said, "Everything will be all right, dear. What in the world has happened? You look scared."

"I'm only fourteen," Priscilla stammered, "and my mother is trying to force me into marrying an older man. I might buy a train ticket to New York if I could earn enough money. My sister lives there; she's a dressmaker." She lowered her gaze. "One thing is certain—I can't marry Lee Dodd. People say he beat his first wife."

Belle raised her brows, intrigued. "Lee Dodd? I can't believe your mother would consider such a match. Lee's my best customer, a cunning card player, and he's been with all my girls."

Priscilla's look of confusion betrayed her naivety. "He never said a thing about it. What do your girls do here?"

"They perform favors for my clients for money," Belle said casually.

"What favors?" Priscilla asked.

"You're too young to understand," Belle's voice was filled with concern and warmth. "This environment isn't suitable for a girl your age, but I can't bear to send you away. You can help in the kitchen. In return for your work, I'll provide you with three nourishing meals daily, five dollars a week, and you can sleep on a small cot in the storeroom just off the kitchen."

A deep wave of gratitude washed over her. Though her situation was modest, it was a far cry from the dismal fate of an unwanted marriage to her cousin or the bleak prospect of wandering the streets penniless and alone. In the kitchen, a lively whirlwind of sounds and scents enveloped her; the air was thick with the aroma of herbs and spices, while the rhythmic clatter of pots and pans filled the space.

Jake, the cook, was a robust man with a commanding presence, his voice booming as he barked orders to the bustling kitchen staff and complained about the sweltering heat. Still, there was a warmth in his manner that kept the atmosphere lively and engaging. Priscilla focused on her tasks, always with a quiet determination, scrubbing vegetables, peeling potatoes, and chopping herbs. She kept her head down while her ears remained attuned to the kitchen's lively chatter and clanging sounds, absorbing every detail of this vibrant world around her.

Three days later, she peered through the splintered cracks of the kitchen door, her heart racing as she gazed into the main hall of the saloon. The low, smoky ceiling hung heavily overhead, casting a murky shadow over the animated crowd of gamblers and drinkers below. Flickering lanterns on the wooden tables emitted a warm, dim glow that danced along the surfaces, creating a cozy yet mysterious atmosphere. The rich aroma of whiskey intertwined with the pungent scents of sweat and tobacco, wrapping around her like a thick veil. The air was thick with boisterous laughter and lively chatter, louder and more raucous than usual. In a cozy corner, a group of men raised their glasses high, their faces flushed with exhilaration as they laughed, toasting to their fortunes and camaraderie.

Priscilla's breath caught in her throat as she spotted the leader of the pack, none other than Lee Dodd, with his tall frame and charming smile that could disarm even the toughest opponent at the card table. His brothers, Gilly and Jack, stood like devoted guard dogs, ready to follow his every command. Every inch of their presence exuded confidence and danger, drawing fear and fascination from the patrons like a storm brewing on the horizon.

Lee slammed his hand on the table, causing his brothers to erupt into uproarious laughter. Priscilla watched in awe as a deck of cards danced between his skilled fingers, captivating the patrons. "Well, I'll be damned," Lee exclaimed, laying down an Ace, King, Queen, Jack, and a 10, all of the same suit. His opponents grimaced as he gathered piles of chips and a gold nugget. Lee never lost, and the only man who'd ever accused him of cheating lay dead in Spencer's Cemetery.

The hair raised on Priscilla's arm at their brazen rowdiness—so different from how they acted in front of her parents.

A harlot noticed the glint of a gold nugget. Draping her long legs adorned with black fishnet stockings around Lee, she joined in his boisterous laughter and sly innuendos.

"Game's over," he announced, cashing out his chips to the dealer and pocketing the cash and the gold nugget. "Looks like I got myself a distraction," he said, moving to a table in the shadows and pulling the girl onto his lap.

Priscilla watched in fascination as Lee kissed the girl roughly. Her hands seemed busy under the table. He grabbed her long, flaming red hair adorned with a feather, and the feather fell onto the floor. Priscilla noticed a subtle shift in Lee's gaze; his dark eyes held a glint of predatory darkness that hinted at a ruthless nature beneath his charismatic facade. It felt as if he wanted to hurt her. A shiver ran down Priscilla's spine, leaving her feeling vulnerable as she backed away from the door. Curiosity pulled her back as Lee hoisted the girl over his shoulder like a sack of potatoes and climbed the steps.

Priscilla stepped away from the door, her stomach churning from what she'd witnessed. Her sister had warned her about men like Lee—charmers who could use and abuse you without a second thought, then discard you like a piece of trash.

She busied herself to erase the scene from her mind. Her hands moved quickly as she scrubbed the kitchen counter with a rag. She focused on the task, trying to steady her nerves and push away the gnawing anxiety in her stomach.

Jake noticed. "It's clean," he said, taking the rag from her. "Unlike what you saw through the door."

Priscilla turned beet red. "I was curious."

"Curiosity killed the cat," he said with a serious expression. "Sit for a while. I'm going to make you a big ham sandwich with pickles. You need to eat—you're working yourself to death, girl."

"Better not. I don't want Belle to catch me slacking off. She has enough to worry about without adding me to the mix."

Jake placed the sandwich in front of her with a soda and a glass of ice. "You more than earn your keep." He raised an eyebrow. "Belle told me you're on the run."

"Sort of," she responded, a hint of frustration lacing her voice. "I don't want to get married at all, but my mother has taken it upon herself to arrange a marriage for me with my cousin, Lee Dodd." She took a long swallow of her drink.

"You're in a tough spot. Lee Dodd is dangerous."

"That's why I left," Priscilla said, savoring the last bite of her ham sandwich. "My sister Amanda is a dressmaker in New York and was supposed to send me money for a train ticket. When I didn't hear from her, I lost hope and left. Lucky for me—Belle took me in."

"Belle took me in, too. It's been over twenty years—she's a good woman."

"Um... what did you do, Jake? Were you running too?"

"Yes. Everyone in this place is running from something." A shadow crossed his weathered face, marked by troubled times and the effects of whiskey. "I killed a man," he admitted without so much as a flinch.

Priscilla's eyes widened, leaving her speechless.

Jake's brows furrowed. "There's no justice in this country. Our lawmakers are corrupt; I knew I would never receive a fair trial, and I ran."

Priscilla winced. Shielded from the harsh realities of life, she never dreamed she would sit across from a murderer. "What was your life like before you fled?"

"I was a schoolteacher," he said. "A student came to school with bruises. When I questioned her, she told me that her father was beating her. One day, she arrived at school with a black eye and a broken arm, and I went to her house and confronted her father. I only wanted to talk to him, but he got rowdy and told me to stay out of his business, saying he'd do what he pleased with her. I saw 'red' at the thought of what he'd done to her and what he might do. I beat him within an inch of his life, and then he fell, causing his head to hit a rock. I didn't intend to kill him." He paused, gazing upwards. "Do you know anything about hangings and mobs?"

Priscilla shook her head. "They hang people?"

"Sure do. You feel like a scared rabbit when the mobs chase you. I caught the first train out and ended up in Maury County."

Priscilla pushed her plate away, a chill running through her from the cold realities of life, even though it was a hot, muggy day.

Later that night, the saloon grew louder and more chaotic. Belle shouted out orders, her voice booming to keep everyone in line. The sound of glasses breaking and men shouting filled the air. Fights broke out, sending tables and chairs flying. The bouncer came to get Jake to assist him.

"Go to the storeroom and stay there," Jake ordered. "I don't want you getting caught in the crossfire." In the short time he'd known Priscilla, he'd developed a soft spot in his heart for her. She reminded him of his daughter, whom he'd lost long ago. But he couldn't bring himself to think about her or his wife.

Priscilla took a deep breath and returned to her small cot, her mind racing with thoughts of survival. Soon, everything quieted, but the noise and excitement had left her riled. Unlike the soft, inviting featherbed she adored, Priscilla tossed and turned on the narrow, unforgiving cot. It was her third night away from home, and it wasn't getting any easier.

She stared at the barren ceiling of the gray, windowless room, the flickering glow from the oil lamp casting dancing shadows across the walls. The warmth of the lamp's light was a poor substitute for the comfort of her room, which had handmade quilts and her dog, Tiny, snuggled next to her. The walls of the storeroom closed in, stifling and isolating. A wave of profound homesickness washed over her, tightening her chest.

Visions of Lee lingered in her mind, and a shiver crept down her spine. She wondered if all men had a Jekyll and Hyde persona. The daunting web of deception he had created made her wonder if she could ever trust again. The scene of Lee with the prostitute replayed over and over in her mind. Part of her wished she'd never seen it, but another part was glad because it confirmed what she'd known. She pulled the frayed coverlet up to her chin, missing the warmth and safety of her home. The life she'd once had with her family seemed distant, and she somehow knew those days were past, and it was up to her to make a new life.

Priscilla longed for those days when she was carefree and her sisters doted on her like a princess. "I hate you, Mama," she muttered under her breath. "It wasn't enough that you robbed me of my childhood — you're cheating on my father with Sidney right under his nose while he's on his deathbed."

She remembered the day *her mother threw her to the wolves* as if it were yesterday. It was to be her first outing with Lee, but she ran away.

Dressed in a white, low-waisted, light cotton frock that Amanda had sewn, she had sat bored. The dress was the height of fashion, draping loosely around Priscilla's developing form. Hormones raged, and the injustice was too much for her to bear. Leaving through a side door, hoping to make a break for the river, her plans changed when she saw her mother on the lawn harvesting dandelion greens. She took off down the gravel road.

Hitching up her dress, she ran, the wind whipping through her long auburn hair and unraveling a blue ribbon. The ribbon soared into the endless blue sky, making her follow it with her gaze. She yearns for freedom and wishes she could fly.

A black Model T soon interrupted the peaceful scene, leaving a trail of dust in its wake. Her mouth turned downward, and she came to an abrupt halt. Lee slowed down and pulled up beside her. His expression carried an air of amusement. "Might you be my cousin, Priscilla Powell?" he drawled.

"I am," she replied in a haughty voice.

"If I'm right, we planned an outing today." His words held a teasing tone as he pulled over.

Lying there, she pulled the coverlet tighter. *She knew it had been a mistake to get in the car with a man she didn't trust, but he had been charming, and like a fool, she'd climbed into the front seat. Her cheeks burned, remembering how she had cringed when she saw her black shoes, once shiny, now caked in dust. She feared her Mother and knew she now had two reasons to be in trouble: running away and getting dirty and sweaty.*

She couldn't help stealing a furtive glance at Lee as the car bumped along the gravel road. Despite his chiseled features and good looks, she remained guarded. His jaw twitched, betraying his disinterest. The faint smell of whiskey clung to him like a second skin. She recognized it all too well, as her family kept a bottle of medicinal whiskey in the pantry. The sound of the Tin Lizzie's loud whirring drowned out any potential conversation between them.

A noticeable chill lingered in the air as the car pulled up to their two-story brick house, encircled by a pristine white fence. She leaped out of the car and dashed toward the house, almost bumping into her mother, who was drying her hands on her apron.

Priscilla had eavesdropped at the screened window, pleased by Lee's apparent discomfort as he explained his reasons for not wanting to see her again. Apparently, he had little patience for a sulking child. "She's too young," he had said. "I suppose she's afraid of me—maybe she heard rumors I beat my ex-wife."

Priscilla's muffled laughter was the only sound in the saloon. She could not contain herself, and her laughter brimmed over into the musty pillow used to muffle the sound. She'd won over her mother. That's what she'd thought. Fannie had apologized and used every excuse imaginable for her inappropriate behavior: She was nervous. It was her first time alone with a boy. Give her another chance—she'll warm to you.

"When pigs fly," Priscilla said under her breath. *Her mood turned sour when she remembered how her Mother had prodded him to go to the dance, using her father's fiddle playing to draw him.*

"It's time the family got together for some fun," she said in a sugary voice. "You

always were my favorite nephew, and it would do my heart good to see you and Priscilla dance tonight."

Priscilla had made a face. She had a sinking feeling in her stomach at the thought of dancing with an old man—her cousin. Her mother's persuasiveness had changed Lee's mood; he was smiling a dazzling smile that complemented his tanned face.

"I can't remember the last time I danced," he said.

Priscilla rolled her eyes, her mind shouting that she would not dance with Lee Dodd if he were the last man on earth! Just when she thought her mother couldn't keep up the charade any longer, she said, "Vinnie said you signed the divorce papers. You can celebrate tonight." She took a breath and continued with an exaggerated flowery tone, "I only wish I had more girls to keep you company. I married off most of them." She raised her brows. "It's a sign of good breeding. Every man in town wishes they could marry one of my girls. I raised them right—by the word of God. And they're excellent housekeepers and cooks."

A look of surprise crossed Priscilla's face at her mother's blatant lie. She'd never lifted a finger because her older sisters treated her like a princess. Her mother complained that she was a hopeless dreamer and spent too much time in the marsh, drawing and painting pictures of the birds. She'd never made a meal—not even a cookie. She was relieved when a smile tugged at Lee's lips.

"I'm sure," he said, with a hint of doubt. Even Lee was aware of his aunt's penchant for over-exaggeration and persuasion.

Priscilla poured herself a glass of iced tea and gathered her dog, Tiny, before retreating to her room. She lay down on the colorful patchwork quilt, feeling confused, something she had never experienced when her sisters were home. The hint of discord in Lee that told her his mother had pushed him to date her. She felt a smugness convinced her haughty behavior had deterred him. As exhaustion took over, Priscilla drifted off to sleep with Hilda, her beloved doll, clenched in her arms, and Tiny curled beside her.

That evening, Priscilla had braced herself for the usual scolding about her inappropriate behavior. However, no reprimand was given as they passed the biscuits around the table, followed by succulent pork chops, steaming turnip greens, and creamy mashed potatoes. Her grandmother's cherished white ceramic gravy boat, all the way from Ireland, was treated with the utmost care.

Priscilla pushed her food around with her fork, tuning out her mother's melodic voice as she asked about David's day at work. The mundane routine of daily life bored Priscilla. Tonight, she thought her father looked tired. Sending messages at the telegraph office in Mt. Pleasant wasn't exciting unless notable figures visited—like the President of the United States, Woodrow Wilson, once did. Priscilla could still remember her mother's excitement that day, clapping her hands and eager to hear every detail of their conversation.

Priscilla's fork pierced the tender pork chop on her plate, dread overshadowing her appetite. Eventually, her mother would mention that she had fled from a date with Lee earlier that day. But as the minutes ticked by, her mother said nothing about it. Breaking the silence, Fannie announced, "Daddy's playing the fiddle tonight at The Old Red Barn. Wear something pretty and polish your shoes. It will be fun."

The forced enthusiasm in her mother's voice grated on Priscilla's nerves. At fourteen, she was tired of being treated like a marionette controlled by her mother's wishes.

Priscilla tested them with a deliberate tilt of her head and steady composure. "I'm not in the mood for the fiddle tonight."

The tension in the room became almost tangible. Her mother's gaze flickered towards her father, laden with exhaustion.

"I would appreciate your presence tonight, Priscilla," her father intoned in a deep voice reminiscent of Sam Elliott. The sound echoed through the spacious dining room, reverberating off the elegant crystal chandelier and wallpapered walls. "Your cousins will be there."

She squinted her nose, clenching her jaw tightly to hold back any retorts. The twitching of his thick gray mustache told her she had struck a chord. She knew better than to argue with her father, his stern demeanor leaving no room for negotiation.

He drummed his fingers on the worn cherry table. "You don't get out enough, Priscilla. All of your sisters have married and left home, except Amanda. And who knows how much longer she'll remain? It's high time you ventured out and made some new acquaintances."

A loud clang resounded through the quiet dining room as she dropped her fork onto her plate. "Daddy, my cousins are the biggest hell-raisers in Maury County. You can stick a fork in me, but I'm not going."

Priscilla's toes curled tightly inside her shoes. She'd sinned again, talked back. She noticed the familiar intensity in his gaze—the same fiery passion he possessed while delivering sermons of hellfire and brimstone from the pulpit. As the assistant pastor, his fervor often instilled fear in her.

"Priscilla, you can pick your friends, but you can't pick your kin. Remember that Christ died for us," he said. "Whoever turns a sinner from the error of his way will save him from death and cover many sins."

Priscilla mustered every ounce of courage within her to speak up. Her voice emerged shaky and small, audible over the clinking of silverware on plates. "That's not what Amanda claims," she said, steeling herself for the backlash that was sure to come. "She insists we must distance ourselves from our cousins to protect our reputation. They are devils, and God knows they are as wicked as sin."

Fannie's eyes widened in disapproval, her stern expression revealing her deep-seated beliefs. "Do not take the Lord's name in vain, and stop listening to your sister," she reprimanded. "We are God-fearing people doing what is best for you."

As her father's cough escalated into a forceful hacking, Priscilla recognized she dared not push the matter any further. Her stomach was knotted with frustration and anger as she pushed her half-eaten plate away and exited the kitchen with heavy footsteps. Her family's disapproval seemed to crush her from all sides.

Amanda's absence from the dinner table only made it more difficult because they focused solely on her. She knew Amanda was with John, and it was only a matter of time before she left. She disregarded her mother's empty threats. The only person whose words resonated with her was Amanda, who had never deceived her.

A New Beginning

Priscilla remembered the day *her mother threw her to the wolves* as if it were yesterday. It was to be her first outing with Lee, but she ran away.

Dressed in a white, low-waisted, light cotton frock that Amanda had sewn, she had sat bored. The dress was the height of fashion, draping loosely around Priscilla's developing form. Hormones raged, and the injustice was too much for her to bear. Leaving through a side door, hoping to make a break for the river, her plans changed when she saw her mother on the lawn harvesting dandelion greens. She took off down the gravel road.

Hitching up her dress, she ran, the wind whipping through her long auburn hair and unraveling a blue ribbon. The ribbon soared into the endless blue sky, making her follow it with her gaze. She yearns for freedom and wishes she could fly.

A black Model T soon interrupted the peaceful scene, leaving a trail of dust in its wake. Her mouth turned downward, and she came to an abrupt halt. Lee slowed down and pulled up beside her. His expression carried an air of amusement. "Might you be my cousin, Priscilla Powell?" he drawled.

"I am," she replied in a haughty voice.

"If I'm right, we planned an outing today." His words held a teasing tone as he pulled over.

She knew it had been a mistake to get in the car with a man she didn't trust, but he had been charming, and like a fool, she'd climbed into the front seat. Her cheeks burned, remembering how she had cringed when she saw her black shoes, once shiny, now caked in dust. She feared her Mother and knew she now had two reasons to be in trouble: running away and getting dirty and sweaty.

She couldn't help stealing a furtive glance at Lee as the car bumped along the gravel road. Despite his chiseled features and good looks, she remained guarded. His jaw twitched, betraying his disinterest. The faint smell of whiskey clung to him like a second skin. She recognized it all too well, as her family kept a bottle of medicinal whiskey in the pantry. The sound of the Tin Lizzie's loud whirring drowned out any potential conversation between them.

A noticeable chill lingered in the air as the car pulled up to their two-story brick house, encircled by a pristine white fence. She leaped out of the car and dashed toward the house, almost bumping into her mother, who was drying her hands on her apron.

Priscilla had eavesdropped at the screened window, pleased by Lee's apparent discomfort as he explained his reasons for not wanting to see her again. Apparently, he had little patience for a sulking child. "She's too young," he had said. "I suppose she's afraid of me—maybe she heard rumors I beat my ex-wife.".

Fannie had apologized and used every excuse imaginable for her inappropriate behavior: *She was nervous. It was her first time alone with a boy. Give her another chance—she'll warm to you.*

"When pigs fly," Priscilla said under her breath. Her mood turned sour when her Mother had prodded him to go to the dance, using her father's fiddle playing to draw him.

"It's time the family got together for some fun," she said in a sugary voice. "You always were my favorite nephew, and it would do my heart good to see you and Priscilla dance tonight."

Priscilla had made a face. She had a sinking feeling in her stomach at the thought of dancing with an old man—her cousin.

Her mother's persuasiveness had changed Lee's mood, for he was smiling a dazzling smile that complemented his tan face. "I can't remember the last time I danced," he said.

Priscilla rolled her eyes, her mind shouting that she would not dance with Lee Dodd if he were the last man on earth! Just when she thought her mother couldn't keep up the charade any longer, she said, *"Vinnie said you signed the divorce papers. You can celebrate tonight."* She took a breath and continued with an exaggerated flowery tone, *"I only wish I had more girls to keep you company. I married off most of them."* She raised her brows. *"It's a sign of good breeding. Every man in town wishes they could marry one of my girls. I raised them right—by the word of God. And they're excellent housekeepers and cooks."*

A look of surprise crossed Priscilla's face. Another blatant lie. She'd never lifted a finger because her older sisters treated her like a princess. Her mother complained that she was a hopeless dreamer and spent too much time in the marsh, drawing and painting pictures of the birds. She'd never made a meal—not even a cookie. She was relieved when a smile tugged at Lee's lips.

"I'm sure," he said, with a hint of doubt. Even Lee was aware of his aunt's penchant for over-exaggeration and persuasion.

She poured herself a glass of iced tea and gathered her dog, Tiny, before retreating to her room. She lay down on the colorful patchwork quilt, feeling confused, something she had never experienced when her sisters were home. The hint of discord in Lee that told her his mother had pushed him on the date. She felt a smugness convinced her haughty behavior had deterred him. As exhaustion took over, Priscilla drifted off to sleep with Hilda, her beloved doll, clenched in her arms, and Tiny curled beside her.

That evening, Priscilla had braced herself for the usual scolding about her inappropriate behavior. However, no reprimand was given as they passed the biscuits around the table, followed by succulent pork chops, steaming turnip greens, and creamy mashed potatoes. Her grandmother's cherished white ceramic gravy boat, all the way from Ireland, was treated with the utmost care.

Priscilla pushed her food around with her fork, tuning out her mother's melodic voice as she asked about David's day at work. The mundane routine of daily life bored Priscilla. Tonight, she thought her father looked tired. Sending messages at the telegraph office in Mt. Pleasant wasn't exciting unless notable figures visited—like the President of the United States, Woodrow Wilson, once did. Priscilla could still remember her mother's excitement that day, clapping her hands and eager to hear every detail of their conversation.

Priscilla's fork pierced the tender pork chop on her plate, dread overshadowing her appetite. Eventually, her mother would mention that she had fled from a date with Lee earlier that day. But as the minutes ticked by, her mother said nothing about it. Breaking the silence, Fannie announced, "Daddy's playing the fiddle tonight at The Old Red Barn. Wear something pretty and polish your shoes. It will be fun."

The forced enthusiasm in her mother's voice grated on Priscilla's nerves. At fourteen, she was tired of being treated like a marionette controlled by her mother's wishes.

Priscilla tested them with a deliberate tilt of her head and steady composure. "I'm not in the mood for the fiddle tonight."

The tension in the room became almost tangible. Her mother's gaze flickered towards her father, laden with exhaustion.

"I would appreciate your presence tonight, Priscilla," her father intoned in a deep voice reminiscent of Sam Elliott. The sound echoed through the spacious dining room, reverberating off the elegant crystal chandelier and wallpapered walls. "Your cousins will be there."

She squinted her nose, clenching her jaw tightly to hold back any retorts. The twitching of his thick gray mustache told her she had struck a chord. She knew better than to argue with her father, his stern demeanor leaving no room for negotiation.

He drummed his fingers on the worn cherry table. "You don't get out enough, Priscilla. All of your sisters have married and left home, except Amanda. And who knows how much longer she'll remain? It's high time you ventured out and made some new acquaintances."

A loud clang resounded through the quiet dining room as she dropped her fork onto her plate. "Daddy, my cousins are the biggest hell-raisers in Maury County. You can stick a fork in me, but I'm not going."

16

Priscilla's toes curled tightly inside her shoes. She'd sinned again and talked back. She noticed the familiar intensity in his gaze—the same fiery passion he possessed while delivering sermons of hellfire and brimstone from the pulpit. As the assistant pastor, his fervor often instilled fear in her.

"Priscilla, you can pick your friends, but you can't pick your kin. Remember that Christ died for us," he said. "Whoever turns a sinner from the error of his way will save him from death and cover many sins."

Priscilla mustered every ounce of courage within her to speak up. Her voice emerged shaky and small, audible over the clinking of silverware on plates. "That's not what Amanda claims," she said, steeling herself for the backlash that was sure to come. "She insists we must distance ourselves from our cousins to protect our reputation. They are devils, and God knows they are as wicked as sin."

Fannie's eyes widened in disapproval, her stern expression revealing her deep-seated beliefs. "Do not take the Lord's name in vain, and stop listening to your sister," she reprimanded. "We are God-fearing people doing what is best for you."

As her father's cough escalated into a forceful hacking, Priscilla recognized she dared not push the matter any further. Her stomach was knotted with frustration and anger as she pushed her half-eaten plate away and exited the kitchen with heavy footsteps. Her family's disapproval seemed to crush her from all sides.

Amanda's absence from the dinner table only made it more difficult because they focused solely on her. She knew Amanda was with John, and it was only a matter of time before she left. She disregarded her mother's empty threats. The only person whose words resonated with her was Amanda, who had never deceived her.

The Dance

That night at the dance had been a rude awakening, one where she faced the cruelty of life.

Priscilla faced her friend and dance partner, Cooper Williams. At only seventeen, he radiated youth with his fiery red hair and freckles. As the caller's instructions rang out, their practiced grace and skill led them around the old red barn's wooden floor. The women's vibrant skirts swirled and fluttered, revealing glimpses of delicate white petticoats beneath. Laughter and music filled the room, creating a scene straight out of a storybook.

Cooper's blue eyes smiled and beckoned to her as he spun her around. Priscilla felt warmth and new emotions, remembering the day he bought her an ice cream cone and their ride on the Ferris wheel at the county fair. While hesitant to label them as dates, her heart fluttered at the possibility of something more between them.

Priscilla watched her father, lost in his music, as the fiddle rested under his chin. With effortless finesse, he played lively melodies honed from years of practice. Her sister caught Priscilla's attention and shared a subtle nod, directing her gaze towards their mother and Aunt Vinnie, who huddled together on the sidelines, separated from the boisterous crowd by an invisible wall of whispered secrets.

Priscilla noticed her mother's foot tapping in time to the energetic jig, a silent sign that their shared confidences were especially scandalous. At that moment, the festival seemed to come alive with music and laughter.

Vinnie's serious face and furrowed brows showed her concern for Fannie. "Spinsterhood," she warned, "is a dangerous road for any woman."

She studied Fannie's features, noting how she hadn't aged despite her circumstances. "You're still beautiful, like your mother—a true Georgia peach." Vinnie glanced at Sidney Taylor and sniffed, doubting his moody demeanor.

Fannie eyed the well-dressed man, a wealthy widower. She sighed. "Sidney was David's choice, but he doesn't want children in our marriage. I've found husbands for all my daughters, except Amanda and Priscilla. Amanda plans to strike out on her own as a dressmaker. But Priscilla is difficult. She's refusing Lee's attention." Glancing over her shoulder, she whispered, "David has three months to live from black lung disease contracted in the mines years ago. Once he's gone, I'll have nothing. I'm tied to Sidney for financial support; otherwise, I might end up in a workhouse."

"David was a Civil War veteran; you are eligible for a widow's pension," Vinnie said.

"It isn't enough. The house needs repair. My expectations cannot be high. I feel fortunate Sidney will have me."

Vinnie's eyes locked onto Sidney's brooding figure, her face contorting with concern and disapproval as she thought of his lack of decorum and disregard for children.

"Please, do not tell Jerome," Fannie said. "It could incite a feud, and Sidney would withdraw his support."

"What about Priscilla? Does she know of your plan and that David is dying?"

Fannie twisted her shawl. "No. David swore me to secrecy. There's been much upheaval with her older sisters getting married and moving out. She's a bit of a rebel and ran away the other day when Lee was supposed to take her on an outing."

Vinnie nodded, her coiffed hair swaying. "As I recall, you were a bit of a rebel when you were younger. You were a Georgia peach and still are. Why are you settling for that old prune of a man? I couldn't do it." Her eyes roamed to Jerome, conversing with his friends. "Now there's a man. I still love him as much as I did the day we married, and maybe even more. He's a hunk of a man—tall and muscular and sexy as hell." She giggled like a schoolgirl. "As soon as he hung his pants on the bedpost, I got ..."

Fannie heaved a sigh. "I know Vinnie...you got pregnant. You've told the story a hundred times. You were lucky in love, and I settled for a coal miner who was a widower with six children." She dropped her eyes. "I have no regrets. My children were my life and are my legacy. When I reach those pearly gates in heaven, Saint Peter will know I'm worthy."

Vinnie's lips held a hint of snideness. "You are so damned self-righteous," she said in a low voice. "The truth is—you've sinned just as much as the rest of us. And there is living proof in this room. A testimony to your unfaithfulness." She shot Fannie a haughty look. "You never loved David, and you don't love Sidney. My God—you have a chance at life and love—why are you doing this?"

Fannie clenched Vinnie's arm, causing her to wince. "If you dare breathe a word of this, I will never speak to you again." Engulfed by jealousy, her lips were a thin line. "You've always had everything I don't—money and a husband you adore, while I've had to pinch pennies. I've stayed up into the wee hours of the night, sewing dresses for my girls so that they might look respectable. I've raised David's children and eight of my own. And I'm not looking for love at this point in my life. Sidney can give me what I need the most—security."

Vinnie raised her brows. "And your daughter is the only thing standing in your way of marrying him. Priscilla is the most stunning girl in Maury County and all of Nashville." She took a sip of red punch, her brows furrowing in thought. "I wouldn't pin your hopes on Lee. He said he'd prefer to pay your bills rather than spend time with a spoiled brat."

Fannie's mouth gaped in shock. "Lee would turn up his nose at Priscilla? She is my prize. When she walks into the room, all heads turn. After marriage, she will overcome her shortcomings—and learn the domestic side of marriage." She straightened her spine. "My daughter is stunning and an artist. Imagine how beautiful and creative our grandchildren will be."

"It's true, but Lee is a proud man. There's no chance he will marry her. He told me he wanted a woman, not a girl."

"Nonsense," Fannie said. "I'm a matchmaker. I know what I'm doing. They are the perfect match. You'll see… give them time."

As Sidney approached, Fannie's face lit up with a smile. He made a graceful bow and asked, "Fannie, may I have the honor of this dance?"

"Of course, Sidney." She gripped his arm as they walked away. "Please excuse us, sister," she said, glancing back at Vinnie with a look of superiority.

The fiddler's bow flew across the strings, his fingers a blur as he poured his soul into the music. His wife twirled and spun with a man poised to take his place, their feet tapping in time with the lively melody. The music continued for hours, each note building upon the next until it reached a climactic peak. And then, just as suddenly as it began, the music halted.

"Daddy!" Priscilla cried, alarmed by her father's sudden loss of control. Rebecca held her back as he collapsed into a nearby chair, exhausted and covered in sweat. Their mother tended to him with a cool cloth, while the atmosphere in the room shifted from lively to heavy with worry for their father.

"Let me go!" Priscilla exclaimed, her voice trembling as she tried to twist out of her sister's iron grip. Her heart raced with fear and a deep sense of urgency. "I must see my father."

"He's very sick," Amanda replied. She tightened her hold on Priscilla, trying to calm her down. "You'll only make it worse by going there."

Priscilla's mind swirled with conflicting emotions. Fear for her father's health, anger at being held back by her sister, and a desperate longing to be by his side. But she knew Amanda was right and stopped struggling against her. Riddled with grief and misplaced guilt, Priscilla dashed out the door into the cool night.

Lee and his grandfather stood side by side, their frames lean and chiseled. Their sharp features, square jaws, and piercing dark eyes set them apart from the crowd of average-looking men. Lee's grandfather held a mason jar filled with homemade moonshine, its amber liquid gleaming as they spoke. The faint scent of corn whiskey lingered around them. Lee took a long sip, fully aware of the consequences that the jar could bring.

Lee shook his head, his expression grim. "I don't think he can last much longer."

"He's tough," Jerome Milton said, his tone grave and heavy with concern. He ran a hand through his hair, eyes fixed on David, who was pale and drawn. "But I believe your Uncle David has just played his last tune."

"Priscilla is out there all alone, crying," Big Bill said, rushing in from outside with his brother Gillie. "You should do something, Lee."

"I've not finished my drink," Lee drawled in his deep Southern accent, taking another sip from his glass. He winced. "I don't handle hysterical women very well. I'll wait until she calms down."

Gillie's voice held a hint of hurt. "I tried to comfort her, but she told me to leave her alone. She's never liked me. Thinks she's better than I am."

Big Bill pushed out his chest. "Well, if you don't go out there, I will. Uncle David is dying, for God's sake - maybe not right this moment, but anyone can see he can't last much longer." The urgency in his tone was apparent, matching the tension that hung thick in the room.

In raging frustration, Lee bellowed, "Where are the women, for chrissake? Her sisters should look after her!" His brow furrowed, and his hands clenched as he continued, "I like my women laughing, not crying."

"She's only fourteen," Big Bill said in a low, calm voice. "She's as innocent as a lamb—not your type." His jaw was clenched. "The trouble with you, Lee, is that you can get women but can't seem to keep them." The tension between the two men was palpable as their conflicting views on how to treat and protect women clashed.

"I can keep them," Lee said with a clenched fist. "But I don't want an iceberg. And I'm tired of Mother and Aunt Fannie shoving her down my throat." He shrugged. "Why the hell are you all looking at me to do something? I didn't ask for this."

"Stop your bickering," Jerome Milton demanded. His eyes scanned the nearby crowd, filled with disapproving glances. "I promised Vinnie we would all be on our best behavior."

Gillie's brows furrowed into a deep frown. "People always seem to stare at us, Pa. They say trouble follows us wherever we go."

Jerome let out a hearty laugh, revealing his amusement. "They're just jealous. We're better-looking and have more money. We can take them all on."

Gillie looked at the jar of moonshine in Jerome's hand with disgust. "If I drank enough moonshine, maybe I'd believe it, too."

"That's because you're a coward," Big Bill quipped, grabbing him and holding his head under his arm while rubbing his head hard with his knuckles. "Where did you get this red hair, boy? You're not like the rest of us; you're the only one who runs from a fight."

Gillie jerked out of Big Bill's hold. "Mama said not to fight. It always leads to trouble."

Big Bill patted his cheek — too hard. "Do you always do what Mama says?" he goaded. "You'll never be a man if you do."

"I'm not a coward. I don't enjoy fighting." He showed his fearless cockiness to his hulking brother when he shot back with a snide grin. "I'm Mama's favorite, and you're a piece of shit."

Big Bill's dark eyes turned wild as he reached for his younger brother, but Jerome stepped between them. "Stop. Why do you always do this? Can't we get along and have a good time?"

Gillie smoothed his shirt. "Y'all stay in here and fight. I'll give it a go with Priscilla since Lee doesn't want her—even though she hates me." The twinkle in his eye showed that he still held onto hope for winning over the unattainable beauty.

"You're never going to find a girl," Big Bill goaded. "You're too ugly."

Gillie flipped him off and strode towards the door with a swagger.

Lee's dark eyes held a flicker of jealous anger. "You stay away from her. She needs a man—not a boy."

"I have youth on my side," Gillie boasted. "I don't have to be stronger— I have more endurance. Women love running their fingers through my curly red hair." His blue eyes danced as he gave the ultimate insult over his shoulder. "Good luck, old sport. I've never had to pay for it."

After a while, Lee walked outside. Gillie was nowhere in sight, but Priscilla leaned against a majestic Southern Red Oak tree, sobbing, her tears glistening in the moonlight like diamonds on her cheeks. Her long auburn hair cascaded down her back, and a white ribbon in her hair contrasted with the darkness of the night.

Lee softened. He placed his hand on her shoulder to comfort her. Maybe it was the moonshine, but he felt a spark, and the warmth of her trembling body, which he felt through his fingertips, made him believe that there could be something. She looked vulnerable, and her full lips looked inviting. He reassured her in a measured voice, "Everything will be all right. Your father is just worn out from playing the fiddle."

Priscilla shook her head, tears streaming down her face. "My sister told me the truth," she said in a cracked voice. "My father is on his deathbed, and my mother is already looking for a new husband."

Her words hung heavy with uncertainty and fear, leading Lee to believe he might have the advantage. He took another swig of moonshine, undressing her with his eyes as he admired her porcelain skin and the pert swell of her breasts straining against the tight bodice of her dress. Memories of his time as a POW in France haunted him, intertwined in a web of pain and suffering. Amid it all, one bright spot shone: the French girl he had met lingered in his thoughts, her face etched into his mind's eye. He would never see her again. He needed someone. Hope sparked at the thought of winning Priscilla over, making her his, perhaps, if he were kinder to her.

Amanda interrupted his reverie, pulling Priscilla from him with a fierce glare. "What are you doing out here in the dark with my sister? She's only fourteen. You need to stay away from her."

It jolted Lee back to reality. He raised his hands in protest, feeling like a helpless pawn caught in the crossfire between two opposing forces. "I'm just trying to help."

Amanda's words dripped with venom. "You can help by keeping your distance from my little sister," she warned, her voice low and dangerous. The protective fire in her eyes blazed, daring anyone to challenge her warning. Her little sister's safety was her top priority, and she would do whatever it took to keep her out of harm's way.

It seemed brutal, the way Amanda had attacked him. He'd only been trying to help. Priscilla turned her head, her tousled auburn hair cascading over her shoulder as she met Lee's piercing gaze. "I'm only a girl," she lamented, casting her eyes downwards before continuing, "and I shouldn't be with someone like you." Being with him felt dangerous and forbidden, like tiptoeing through a minefield.

Lee wore a wounded expression, cut to the core because it was true. She was only a girl, and he required more. He tipped the jar of moonshine, finishing it. The memory of Priscilla's softness and beauty lingered in his mind.

Amanda gripped Priscilla's hand as she pulled her along, weaving her way through the crowd, hurrying to put as much distance between her and Lee Dodd as possible. She'd seen the lust on his face.

Priscilla coughed when she breathed in the air, thick with tobacco and cigarette smoke. Amanda gestured at a solitary table in a shadowy corner, and Priscilla sank into a chair.

Amanda's hand trembled as she reached for a cigarette and lit it, the flickering flame casting an eerie glow on her face.

Tear tracks marred Priscilla's face as she pleaded with Amanda. "Promise me, no matter what happens, you won't leave me behind. I cannot stay with Mama any longer. She plans to marry me off to Lee Dodd. My gut is telling me it's true."

As Amanda took a deep drag from her cigarette, tears threatened to spill from her eyes. She exhaled, trying to suppress her emotions. How could she tell her sister that she had no choice but to leave her behind? It was cruel—more than a girl should have to endure on an evening meant to be carefree and fun. Finally, she mustered the courage to say, "I'm so sorry, Priscilla, but I can't take you with me. John won't allow it. He says we'll never make it if we bring you along. We'll have to work hard. It's a tough business."

As the words rumbled off Amanda's tongue, the blood drained from Priscilla's face. She turned ghastly white. Dread and loss encompassed her. "I promise I won't be any trouble," she said with glassy eyes.

Amanda turned a deaf ear to her plea. "I'll send you money and pretty dresses and send for you as soon as we're established. I promise."

Pricilla shivered. It was catastrophic that she had landed in a snake-pit, right under the nose of Lee, the man she feared more than anyone else. She buried her face deep into the musty, hard pillow, overwhelmed by her emotions. Her gut revealed what Lee had tried to conceal: the man was a danger to society and women. But with the truth came the cold, hard reality that the person she had trusted more than anyone else had abandoned her: the letters, money, and dresses never arrived. The pain was almost more than she could bear.

She drifted off to sleep as the day's exhaustion washed over her. Tomorrow was another day—a new beginning.

Belle Stages Priscilla's Death

Priscilla sat perched on an upturned crate in the kitchen, knees drawn to her chest, her mind burdened with heavy thoughts. The gentle warmth emanating from the cooking fire enveloped her in a cocoon of comfort, offering comfort in a manner words could not. The boisterous sounds from the saloon drifted through the thick wooden door, with the laughter and clinking of glasses providing a constant backdrop to her thoughts.

It had been days since she had run away from home and her mother's relentless matchmaking pursuits. The entire town was searching for her, and Belle took her aside. "Lee and his brothers are ruthless," Belle said, her voice low and intense. "They will turn this town upside down looking for you and won't stop until they've found you. Staging your death is the only option. Fetch the dress you wore when you left. I'll have Jake take it to the river, muddy it, and throw it over a log."

A wave of guilt washed over Priscilla as she retrieved the beautiful dress Amanda had made, now her death shroud. The thought of her family believing her dead weighed on her heart as Belle put the dress in Jake's withered, trustworthy hands. It hit Priscilla like a ton of bricks as he stuffed the dress in a flour sack and hurried out the back door.

"Don't fret," Belle said. "It's only a dress. You have your whole life ahead of you and will have many beautiful dresses. We have to make it look real."

That night, she dreamed of her cozy wallpapered room, comfortable feather bed, and her dog, Tiny. She awoke with her teeth chattering and feeling dread. Pulling the worn quilt up to her chin, she fought her homesickness.

The next evening, the sheriff and his deputies arrived at the saloon with stern expressions, their lanterns casting dark shadows on their faces. "The whole town is in an uproar about the Powell girl," the sheriff said. "She caught a ride with the milk truck driver who said he'd dropped her off at the drugstore, but she didn't go in the drugstore, and she's been missing since," the burly sheriff said as he scrutinized the saloon.

Belle didn't flinch, pointing them toward the river. "The talk around town is that the girl jumped off the Sandy Hook Bridge because her mother was pressuring her into marriage with Lee Dodd." A smile curved on Belle's red lips as she added, "If that's not a reason for a girl to jump, I don't know what is. The screams coming from the hills at night aren't cougars; they're from women being beaten by their husbands. Everyone in town knows Lee beat his first wife."

The sheriff sneered. "It's none of my concern if Lee beat his first wife. What matters is finding the Powell girl." His dark eyes bore into Belle hard. "They found the dress she wore on a log in the river, but all this talk about her jumping off the Sandy Hook Bridge means nothing without a body. Are you sure you haven't seen her?"

Belle put her hands on her hips, her expression haughty. "The bears and cougars have got to her by now."

The sheriff's nostrils flared. "Since when did you become an investigator?"

"I'm saying what everyone knows," Belle quipped. "The Powell girl is dead. The dress is proof. You're wasting your time here; you should be at the river."

"Horse shit," he growled, sweeping a chair aside, causing it to topple. He strode away, with his deputies following. He and Belle had a tumultuous history since criminals frequented her saloon, and a gold nugget could buy a hearty meal, a hot shower, and a haven for weary souls on the road. Those hardened criminals would go to great lengths for her favor.

Ignoring his angst, Belle set the chair upright.

"He's in a foul mood," one of Belle's girls said.

"Idle threats," Belle said, brushing her hands off on her red satin dress. "He knows better than to fool with me."

Priscilla's mouth trembled, her heart pounding. Listening to the charade of her death with her ear pressed against the kitchen door had been disheartening. She jumped as the kitchen door groaned open, and Belle strode in, her figure casting a looming shadow across the room. Priscilla's swollen eyes met hers, and she tried to hide her pain.

"Are you okay?" Belle asked.

Priscilla swallowed hard, feeling like a ghost of herself. "As well as a girl can feel when the entire town believes her dead."

"It's hard, I know," Belle said, her voice filled with compassion, as she steered Priscilla towards a group of women sitting in a corner in the back room. "You're safe here, but must grow up fast—like I did."

Priscilla wiped away her tears and forced a grateful smile. "Thank you, Belle," she said, though her nose burned at the air thick with smoke and the smell of alcohol, adding to the already suffocating atmosphere. She blinked at the women's bright-colored dresses and elaborate feathered headpieces standing out like beacons of light.

"Ladies," Belle announced, drawing all attention to them, "this is Sarah, my niece. She'll be working in the kitchen. Treat her right, you hear?"

Priscilla's ears perked at the sound of her new name: Sarah. She liked it.

The women welcomed Priscilla with genuine warmth and kindness. Among them was a striking, tall woman wearing a green satin dress, distinguished by a cascade of flowing dark curls. "Have you ever tried one of these?" she asked, extending a cigarette and taking a measured inhale before exhaling a plume of smoke into the atmosphere, as though performing a magical ritual that invited Priscilla to cast aside her troubles.

Priscilla's eyes widened, feeling a surge of nervousness. "No, I haven't."

"And she's not going to," Belle scolded. "She's a good girl. Innocent. And I plan to keep her that way as long as she's here."

Another woman, dressed in a yellow satin dress with a feathered headpiece, leaned over and placed her headdress on Priscilla's head. "You'd look good in full costume," she teased, adjusting the feathers to frame Priscilla's face. The other women agreed, complimenting her on her pretty eyes and delicate features.

Priscilla blushed, her shyness making her feel out of place among these confident women.

"Girls!" Belle cried out. "I told you—she's a nice girl, never to be taken into the saloon. Only the kitchen."

Belle's presence was a reassuring anchor in the saloon's chaos. She watched over Priscilla and had her dressmaker create a few age-appropriate, simple but elegant dresses to help her blend in without drawing too much attention. Belle fawned over her, showed her how to tie her hair back with a ribbon, and sometimes had her wear it in a bun.

"You're a natural beauty and must always carry yourself like a lady of great importance—like a princess. Don't pay any attention to the goings on here," Belle said, afraid of the influence her girls would have on Priscilla.

Priscilla was efficient, and Belle soon gave her additional chores. She would creep up the back stairs, stacking towels in the linen closets. The air was different there — filled with floral perfume and musk scents. When she peeked into a vacant room, she could see the elegant red wallpaper and poster bed with a plush spread—so fancy, unlike anything she had ever seen. When she asked Jake what happened in those rooms, he said, "Mind your own business and don't look around for things that do not concern you."

"I'm sorry," she said, realizing that Jake wasn't the one to ask. She would ask Loose Lucy, the most popular of all Belle's girls. Once, she'd even snuck a cigarette with her outside behind a shack. Lucy had laughed and showed her how to hold the cigarette between her fingers. "Just take a tiny puff and don't inhale."

Priscilla coughed as the smoke hit her throat, knowing she never wanted another cigarette. She despised the smoke in the saloon and longed for the marshes and the freshness of Duck River. It was all there—behind her house: the motorboat her father had bought her on her ninth birthday. It meant freedom, and she'd got a little wild that summer, testing her mother's patience when she stayed too long—not coming home until dusk. Hiding her pictures of wildlife under her bed: herons, osprey, and hawks.

She'd taken to sharing her thoughts with Jake. "Have you ever been to the marshes, Jake?" she asked, looking up from scrubbing a pan.

"I live on Duck River," he said. "I was just there yesterday. Caught me a couple of bass."

"Do you think you could take me there sometime? We could go at night."

Jake stared at her in disbelief. "There are wild pigs and water moccasins in the marsh. It's dangerous at night."

She picked up a dishcloth and dried the pan. "I once saw a timber rattlesnake eat a rabbit."

Jake laughed, looking at her with a newfound respect. "I don't think I've ever met anyone quite like you before." He shook his head. "You're on the run, girl—and you can't go back. So, stop thinking about it."

"I can't help thinking about it. It's in my blood—the marsh and the loons." A shadow flitted across her face. "I miss my Pa. The loons listen to my troubles and understand."

A knowing expression crossed Jake's face. He'd been talking to the loons all his life but had told no one.

As the nights wore on, Priscilla observed the people in the saloon through the cracks in the doors and walls. One man caught her eye—a young, handsome blonde with striking blue eyes and a confident demeanor. Friends laughed and talked about their recent escapades surrounding him. His chiseled jaw and disarming smile seemed to light up the room.

Belle observed Priscilla's fascination and remarked, "That's Clint Wilder. At twenty-two, he is a millionaire—he made his fortune panning for gold in California. He comes from a well-off family in Nashville, involved in show horses—on a grand scale."

Priscilla dismissed the thought of him noticing her. She was just a kitchen helper, a nobody in the grand scheme of life. *Why would someone like Clint ever pay attention to someone like her?*

Belle sensed her uncertainties and offered a reassuring pat on the back. "You're Sarah, now. Never doubt your worth; you are better than all of them."

Priscilla took Belle's sisterly advice to heart. "I love my new name. Why did you choose Sarah for my name?"

"My sister's name was Sarah. She was lively and happy. I never thought she could die, but she died of pneumonia when she was fourteen. You remind me of her."

"I'm sorry," Priscilla said, sad about Belle losing her sister but grateful that Belle had opened up about her past.

"I changed my name, too," Belle confided. "My given name was Maddie. Can you imagine a girl named Maddie running a saloon? It had to be Belle." Her eyes softened. "Maddie will always be there, somewhere deep inside of me. She embroidered, wrote poetry, and dreamed of one day having a happy ever after with a special someone."

"What happened?" Priscilla asked.

Belle's tone changed to matter-of-fact. "The man I thought I loved abandoned me. He left in the middle of the night, leaving me both pregnant and penniless. My aunt took me in, but I lost the baby."

Priscilla's eyes glistened. "I'm so sorry. What he did was cruel."

"That's life," Belle replied. "I made a poor choice, placing my trust in the wrong man, just like all my girls." Belle positioned her hands on her hips. "My advice is to be cautious about your life choices."

Priscilla bit her lip, contemplating whether advising such a worldly woman on how to live her life was appropriate. Taking a chance, she said, "Belle, you're still the same girl you once were. You can still write poetry and embroider. There is more to life than this saloon. Pursue what you love as well."

Belle frowned. "My granny always said, 'If you make your bed, you must lie in it.' I made a mistake and must work hard to keep this place going. I don't have time to do the things I did as a girl."

"Your granny was wrong—just like my mother," Priscilla said. "We're free, Belle—don't you see? The beliefs our mothers and grandmothers try to transfer to us are to keep us down. You can have it all, Belle."

"I wish I could believe that," Belle said.

"Believe it," Priscilla said. "There's a wave coming for women, a whole new world. I know because my sister told me. We don't have to settle anymore. "

Belle's blue eyes softened. "You know—you're like a breath of fresh air."

She straightened her spine. "Somewhere along the line, I got blindsided. How is it you're just a child, yet you know so much about life?"

"It's all because of my sister, Amanda. She told me she'd rather dance in the flames of hell than give up on her dreams."

Belle smiled. "She sounds like quite a girl."

"Oh, she is," Priscilla said with a dreamy expression. For a moment, she almost forgot that Amanda had abandoned her.

As she rested on the cot that evening, her mind was abuzz with many ideas and possibilities for the girl she was and who she could become. Amanda dreamed big, and she told herself she would, too. She reflected on *their last night together.*

In the quiet darkness of their shared bedroom, Amanda and Priscilla whispered to each other like they had since they were little girls. Priscilla clutched her handmade patchwork quilt, a gift from her sisters that comforted her at such times. She confessed her deepest fears to Amanda, knowing she would leave for New York in the morning. "I'll have no one when you're gone," she whispered, feeling a sinking feeling in her belly.

Amanda's face was barely visible in the faint light coming through the window as she considered Priscilla's words. "I'll miss you too," she whispered. "But this is my chance to make my dreams come true. John has big plans for us—we're going to design and sew dresses for women of high society, even the governor's wife."

Priscilla couldn't help but feel proud and excited for her sister, even as sadness crept into her heart. "I'm happy for you, but I'll miss you. You're not just my sister; you're my best friend."

"John says New York is a wild city where women are free to be whoever they want. There are women called 'flappers' who do what they want and don't give a damn about what anyone thinks." With determination burning in her veins, she continued, "John has shown me a different world, filled with art and culture and endless possibilities. He's my escape from this small-minded town and its suffocating expectations."

"You will fit right in," Priscilla said. "You're the only one I know who dares to stand up for what you believe. Mama says you'll go to hell for going to New York with John unchaperoned."

"Don't believe a word of it," Amanda scoffed, her eyes ablaze with defiance. "Mama's threats of hell are just a guise to control us, to mold us into replicas of her own outdated beliefs." Her voice dripped with rebellion as she continued. "I refuse to be shackled by the chains of domesticity and subservience, trapped in a cycle of cooking, cleaning, and submitting to unwanted advances. I'd rather dance in the flames of hell than surrender to such a fate."

Priscilla's tone turned grave. "You must live for both of us because I fear my fate is to marry Lee Dodd. Be bold so that I may live through you."

"I'll talk to Mama." Determination laced her voice. "Perhaps one of our sisters will take you in, and once I save up some money, you can visit me. You must keep your mind occupied and excel in your studies. You can be a telephone operator one day. Until then, we will do what women do — write letters and encourage each other. And I will send you beautiful dresses."

As they lay there in the darkness, their hearts heavy with bittersweet emotions, they knew that tomorrow would mark the beginning of a new chapter for both of them.

It was bittersweet when the family went to the train station with Amanda. Her eyes glittered in anticipation. When she boarded the train with John, Fannie muttered, "God save her soul."

Priscilla felt her stomach sink as she bounced along in the horse-drawn carriage on her way home. Amanda was gone, and it seemed that her older sisters had seen the storm coming and married the first man who came along, valuing safety more than romance.

After they arrived home, the house echoed with emptiness and seemed drab and lifeless without Amanda. Shutting herself in her room, she shook her fist at the four walls, dreading being alone with her mother. It was unbearable that week, as she despised the whispers when her sisters came to visit. Snippets of the conversation, as her mother complained to them about her melancholy and her tendency to get lost in thought all the time, told her that her mother was carrying the world on her shoulders.

Priscilla attempted to talk to her father. After she brought him some soup and a cup of coffee, she said, "Daddy, I feel so alone without Amanda, and Mama is pushing me to date cousin Lee. Even though she knows I don't like him." She sighed. "I wish things were like they used to be when all my sisters were home. Back then, everyone was happy."

"Your mother is doing the best she can," he said. "I don't have much longer, and she did well—found good husbands for your sisters. You're our youngest girl, and I wish all your dreams could come true, and I could provide for you, but I can't. I'm dying."

Her eyes glistened, but she couldn't let him see her cry. He was a broken man. She put her hand over his weathered one and shut her eyes, feeling guilty for thinking of herself when her father was dying. They sat in silence for a few minutes. "I guess I was born too late, Daddy, because I want more time with you," she said in a cracked voice.

"Never think that, Priscilla. You were born at just the right time, because I had left the coal mines and was working at the telegraph office, and had time to enjoy you. Fourteen years of blessed happiness," he said with a faraway look in his weary blue eyes. "When I would hold you on my knee, I thought you were the prettiest thing I had ever seen. You are the greatest gift God ever gave me. And don't think because I'm dying that I'm leaving you. On your darkest days, I'll play my fiddle for you—I'll never leave you."

His words were more than she could bear. She lay her head across his chest and sobbed. "I don't want the fiddle," she said, her face set in stubborn determination. "I want you to stay...I'm too young."

"I can't stay," he said. "It's my time. There's a time to be born, and there's a time to die, and I'm not one to argue with the Lord. Don't worry. Everything is going to work out."

"But how?" Priscilla asked, wiping her tears with her hand. "Mama has gone crazy. She's talking to Sidney on the phone about their future together."

When he didn't answer, she looked up, and his eyes were closed. He was sleeping. She frowned. How could he look peaceful when she had never felt such misery?

Priscilla looked up at the ceiling, gray from time, "Let me tell you something, God—you're not fair. I need Daddy here with me. Do you know how much trouble you're causing?"

God didn't answer, nor seemed to care. Her mother was near hysterics and worried after David became too ill to work. She hated the whispers between her sisters and mother about money, her father's gray skin tone, and the coughing and hacking that went on nonstop.

Priscilla grappled with a profound sense of abandonment. Each morning as she arose, thoughts of Amanda consumed her mind. She attended to the monotonous household responsibilities that Fannie ran with precision: washing dishes, sweeping the kitchen floor, and tending to the livestock. Every week, a sister would visit, providing a brief respite from the monotony and allowing her to escape to the marshes. There, she would immerse herself in bird-watching and muse about her future with Amanda in New York, envisioning herself as a telephone operator—a role of significance and purpose. With unwavering determination, she resolved never to become a woman like her married sisters: confined to the routine of packing a man's lunch bucket or ensuring she served dinner on time, lest she risk the threat of a beating by her husband.

She eavesdropped on her mother's conversations; otherwise, she wouldn't know anything about what was happening. During her mother's phone calls to Sidney, she understood she was not to be part of their union. It confirmed Amanda's assertion—her mother intended to 'cast her to the wolves' by arranging a marriage with Lee Dodd. In Priscilla's estimation, that meant being chained to a monster for a lifetime.

Lee Dodd's Shady Past

Lee didn't know when he stepped off the train at Union Station in Columbia, Tennessee, that marriage plans were in the making. He inhaled the familiar smell of horses, manure, and sweat, glad to be home. The sounds of mules snorting, pawing the ground, and whinnying as a group of men traded their prized mules—wheeling and dealing enthusiastically. The mules were like gold, tough and resilient like the people.

Tall and lean, he might have dropped to his knees and kissed the ground, but he was bone tired and knew if he got down, he wouldn't have the strength to get up again. He'd made it back from hell—the battlefields of France, where he'd been captured by the Germans and held prisoner for three months. The war had ended on November 11, 1918, and it had taken five months to get home.

A familiar voice called out to him. When he turned, he got a lump in his throat at the sight of his grandfather and brother across the street. He slicked over his straight, coal-black hair and took long strides to reach them, kicking away the prairie sagebrush. A blanket of dust covered his boots, and he had to dodge a mule-drawn covered wagon that came out of nowhere.

His face filled with emotion as the men approached him. His grandfather, Jerome, dressed in black and wearing a matching hat, walked with a swagger beside his son, Joe, their shoulders brushing against each other. At 6'2", Joe wore a brown suit and vest, his boots dusty with clay. Their expressions revealed what he already knew: that he was gaunt and only half the man he had been when he left on what his mama called the saddest day of her life.

Jerome grabbed Lee in his iron grip, hugging him hard. "What the hell did those bastards do to you? Didn't they feed you at all? You're as skinny as a rail."

Lee's dark eyes were glassy, and his neck was flushed. "I'm fine, Daddy. I'm alive. That's what counts." He offered a wry smile. "They don't cook coon dinners for POWs."

Joe barged in, throwing his arm around Lee. "I've never been so glad to see anybody in my entire life. Everyone's waiting to see you. Mama has a big dinner waiting." His dark eyes looked around suspiciously. "Let's get out of here before trouble starts. There's always some fool who thinks he can outdraw a Thomason." Joe was clear-thinking, unlike his brothers—wild and wily—who wore a chip on their shoulder and enjoyed nothing more than a drunken brawl.

Jerome and his boys were notorious—known to be dangerous — and had a reputation for being the fastest draws in the county. It was all about the 'still' and the feuds that had gone on for years. One of Jerome's sons, William Jackson Thomason, known as "Big Bill," was the meanest man in Tennessee. When he was drunk, he harassed whoever was in his path. Nobody in town wanted to run into him on a Saturday night. Not even the sheriff.

Lee remained silent, too choked up to utter a word. He knew Joe was right, but the war had left him numb. He couldn't whip his way out of a paper bag right now. And the truth was—he never enjoyed fighting—it was something he had to do to live up to his family's reputation. Otherwise, they'd call him a coward.

The three men walked through the crowd, their presence and camaraderie drawing attention. All were 6'2". People stood out of the way to let them pass. Women walked by in long skirts, their hair up, smiling flirtatiously at Joe and Lee, intrigued by their dangerous and powerful personas. They were lean and mean, and their good looks made women swoon. The brothers had never had trouble getting a woman, but keeping them was a problem.

Joe tipped his hat, smiled, and nodded.

A smile tugged at Lee's lips, embarrassed by the scruffy way he looked. He'd lost weight in the POW camp and walked with a slouch. Bayonet scars from the tips of the rifles had replaced his cockiness.

"I hope the hell they didn't take the fight out of ya," Jerome said in a slow drawl. "That's all we've got sometimes, is meanness. I'm not saying it's a good thing, I'm just saying sometimes we need meanness to get us through the tough times."

Jerome was the patriarch who blazed the trail for the family. A pistol was part of his attire, and he went nowhere without it. If someone had a crow to pick with him, they had a crow to pick with his pistol.

Lee stumbled and then caught himself. "I've got a reason to be mean now, Daddy, and I didn't when I left."

"The war is over, son," Jerome said in a low, steady voice. "Let it rest. It wasn't our war; The Civil War was our war—the war we're still fighting."

Lee bit his lip. "I'm not talking about the war, Daddy. I'm talking about Mary Lou."

"Like I said. Let it rest." Jerome's voice was firm. "We don't need another feud, Lee. Let it go, for God's sake."

He led the way to the black Henry Ford car, the "Tin Lizzy." He was proud of his car and the fine clothing he could afford for his family.

Toby, a negro wearing a white shirt, had been standing guard, straining his long neck, anxiously awaiting a glimpse of Lee. The hair stood up on his arm when he saw him.

Overcome by emotion, Lee pushed his endurance, picked up Toby, and swung him around. Toby was a small man, not more than a hundred pounds. He held him in a bear hug and then set him down. "How the hell have you been, Toby? I missed your coon dinners."

Toby was tongue-tied, his brown eyes huge, stunned at Lee's gaunt appearance. Toby rode in the front passenger seat with Jerome, keeping a watchful eye on the eight-mile drive back to the farm. That was his job—keeping watch. Even though he didn't carry a gun, he could scream louder than any man in the county. And when he did, the men would come running. He was loyal to Jerome, who was his protector. Joe had found Toby half dead in the woods from a mountain lion attack. Joe took him home, and the family nursed him back to health. And he'd never left. They were his family. The only family he had, and he felt like he belonged.

Lee and Joe climbed in the back. There were three rifles on the floorboard. "Had any trouble lately?" Lee asked, eyeing the rifles with scrutiny.

"Nah. Just the same old shit," Jerome said, wiping beads of sweat off his brow with the back of his hand. The Feds nose around but are too scared to come up the mountain. The still is in the thick of it, and there are too many mountain lions up there for the Feds to risk their life. A scream from a mountain lion will stand the hair up on your arm. A lot of bears, too." He chuckled. "Feuds aren't any better. The Wallace boys are itching to kill me." Jerome carried the weight of centuries-old feuds and grudges that he'd been born into. That's why he always had to carry a pistol, keep his rifle nearby, and sleep with one eye open.

Joe handed Lee a jug.

Lee took the cap off and took a swig of the 'white lightning,' feeling the familiar burn and kick that came with it. If he drank a little more, he might forget the hell he'd just left.

Joe always seemed to know what Lee was feeling—they were six years apart. He'd always been there to pull him out from under the bottom of the pile when he was a little boy. God knows he'd taken his share of licks—most were from Gilly. But there was nobody meaner than his brother, Bill. They called him "Big Bill" because he was 6'8" tall. It had been "Big Bill" who had taught him how to fight dirty.

"Blind them," "Big Bill," said. "Throw dirt in their eyes, kick them in the balls, then beat the holy shit out of them. And if you lose, I'll beat your ass."

Lee took Big Bill's word as the gospel truth. Nobody wanted to mess with "Big Bill." So, Lee fought dirty, like the rest of them. He'd never picked a fight, but sometimes, he had to finish them.

That night, after a coon dinner and all the fixings with dandelion greens, biscuits, and potatoes, they all went out on the back porch. And in the inky night, taking large swallows of 'white lightning' out of a jar, Lee told them the story about how he'd been captured.

"There were too many," Lee said. "I had ten rifles pointed at me. There was no place to run. They had me by the balls."

"Jesus," his brother, Gillie, said, aghast. "You could have whipped them,

Lee. You're a mean son of a bitch when you get riled. Were you riled, Lee?"

"Hell, no. They scared me shitless. I put my arms up in the air and surrendered." He heaved a sigh and then took another long swallow of the moonshine that eased his pain, wiping away the memory of the war: the smell of putrid dead bodies lying in fields in all positions. The booming sound of the large cannons still rang in his ears. He didn't want to talk about the war, nor did he want to tell them about the fear and dread that came with it. And the demons he had to fight every night. He wondered if the nightmares would continue for the rest of his life.

Lee smiled at a memory. It hadn't all been bad. He'd only seen her twice, but he was sure it was love. Even though the older, more experienced soldiers had told him it was okay to have the company of a woman without emotional involvement, Lee hadn't listened. It was the first time he'd given away a piece of his heart.

Maybe he shouldn't have said anything, but he was feeling looser than usual. "The women in France differ from those around these parts. They dress differently, and they're perfumed."

Joe swatted a mosquito. "You always could get any woman you wanted. Was she pretty?"

"She was a French girl—the prettiest girl I've ever seen in my life—black hair and slender. Skin as soft as velvet. Thoughts of her kept me going while I was in the POW camp. I was going to go back to see her again—and work out something—maybe get married. But they shipped me back to the States before I could get back to her."

"I thought you'd be sour on women," Gillie said. "After what Mary Lou did."

"There's nothing worse," Lee said, biting into a stick of chaw. "But I wasn't the only one who got a 'Dear John' letter. When I left, I had a wife and a daughter, and now I have nothing."

Joe piped up. "She thought you would die there, Lee. So many of them didn't come home."

"Ain't that a bitch," Lee said in a slurred voice. "I lived." He looked up at the sky as if searching for an answer. "I don't give a shit about Mary Lou, but I miss my little girl. Annie was everything to me."

"Got yourself some little brothers and sisters," Gillie said tactlessly. "Guess you could visit them if you want to see a kid."

"Don't tease your brother," Vinnie scolded from the front porch as she rocked back and forth in a creaking rocking chair handed down through the ages. Her voice softened. "Winnie's going to come by and see you tomorrow."

"Ain't that just dandy?" Lee's voice was filled with sarcasm. "I don't want to see Winnie, and I sure as hell don't want to see Jim Fautt. How many babies does she have now?" He set his jaw and looked out over the cotton field with a pained expression. He'd never understood how she could leave the family for Jim Fautt and be a mother to his children when she hadn't been a mother to him.

Joe handed Lee another jar of moonshine. He was the peacemaker in the family and loved his sister, Winnie. His handsome face, weathered by the sun and wind, held character. "Don't be so hard on your mama. She didn't go far, and she didn't take you with her when she got married because Daddy wouldn't allow it." He sat down on the porch step, his dark brown eyes gazing at Lee straight on. "Winnie has had a hard life. Be nice."

"Bullshit! Before I went off to the Army, I would see her gallivanting around town with Fautt and his kids like I didn't exist. It eats at me."

Vinnie lit her corncob pipe and sat back in her rocking chair. "Where did all that hate come from? I'm your mama, Lee. I raised you. You're our boy; Joe, Gilly, and Big Bill are your brothers. That's how it is, and all your belly aching can't change it."

Lee took a swig of moonshine, feeling like a misfit. Knowing he was a Dodd and different from his brothers weighed on him. "I might be able to live with it if the man would look me in the eye. I pass him on the street, and he looks down. Everyone in town knows John Dodd is my daddy. I look just like him."

"Let it go, Lee," Joe said in a firm voice, "or it will eat you alive. Do you think you're the only one shit happens to? It's life. It's like Mama says, you can't change the past."

Jerome took a swig of moonshine. "I spit on the ground when I pass by him in town. Dodd knows better than to come by here." He stroked his beard. "I should have killed him back then. Then you wouldn't have to look at his face. It's like he haunts you."

"Burning down his barn was enough," Joe said. "It wasn't necessary. It takes two to make a baby. Winnie was just as much to fault."

Jerome pointed his finger at Joe and said defensively, "I couldn't just let him get away with it, like I didn't know. The barn was already falling. The only reason I didn't kill him was that his kids wouldn't have a daddy."

Dusk was deepening, and the Darkies' singing echoed over the hills and valleys. Their deep baritone voices soothed Lee.

I looked over Jordan, and what did I see? Comin' for to carry me home? There was a band of angels a-comin after me. Comin' for to carry me home...

Lee closed his eyes, tired of the same old stories—old grudges that had never been put to rest. Gillie had told him he wasn't Jerome's and Winnie wasn't his sister, but his mother. His words had been cutting, almost as bad as the bayonets. He could hear Gillie's taunting voice; something etched the memory in his mind.

"Ever wonder why you don't look like the rest of us?" Gillie spat, his blue eyes flashing as he wiped blood off his lip. Blood that had come from losing after sparring. "Winnie's not your sister; she's your mother. She and John Dodd had a thing going, and she got herself pregnant." He pointed his finger at Lee. "You're a bastard, Lee. A bastard."

Minutes later, Gillie had begged Lee not to tell Jerome. "Daddy will kill me if he knows I told."

Lee looked at Gillie hard. "Shut up, Gillie, you're whining like a girl." Then he went straight to Jerome.

"Tell me it's not true, Daddy," Lee said, fighting tears.

"Son, I want to tell you it's a lie, but I've never lied. It's true. But I raised you, and you're my son, Lee. Not Dodd's. Do you understand?"

Lee bit his lip. It was a shock to learn that Winnie was his mother. Winnie had stayed in the background like a piece of furniture while Vinnie did the mothering. Sometimes, Lee saw Winnie looking at him with a wistful expression; other times, she looked bitter.

Later that night, Lee could hear the sounds of Gillie's screams. Jerome gave him three lashes with a horsewhip.

Vinnie gazed at Lee. His downtrodden expression bothered her. Lee could not let go of his past and now suffered damage from the war. She was proud of her tight-knit family and somehow kept it all together, despite the fighting and feuding both within the family and with the townspeople. When she glanced at Jerome, his jaw twitched. He did that when he was worried.

Jerome was plain; she could have had any man, but she chose him. Vinnie, the daughter of a war hero, Lewis Riddle Powell, was a regal woman. It didn't matter that Jerome's father was a blacksmith and Jerome had grown up poor. He had proved himself by becoming wealthy at a young age. He owned more land than her father, and his business was booming. When he came calling with a box of his best whiskey, her father took notice.

When Jerome courted her, she used her fan to hide her flushed neck. He had a long face but kind blue eyes, and his 6'2" frame and body like steel made her weak in the knees. She loved his Southern charm and how he lifted her into the carriage as if she were a china doll. She knew no man would ever love her the way Jerome loved her, and she said 'yes' when he proposed after only three weeks of courting. Thank God her father said 'yes,' or she would have died of heartbreak.

After their marriage, she found Jerome carried the weight of centuries-old feuds and grudges. He always kept a rifle nearby. She did not know that Jerome was a collector. A collector of people, down-and-out people who worked their farm and tobacco plantation. Some were free Negros who depended on Jerome for their livelihood, and Jerome felt responsible for them. Vinnie had plenty of help and spent her days reading, embroidering, quilting, and writing letters. She supervised the cooking and often made old Southern recipes that her mother had made.

The 'still' and moon shining were their primary source of income, and Vinnie accepted it even though it went against her religion. As the family's matriarch, she knew what to do about Lee. He needed a good woman. Her niece, Fannie, was a matchmaker, and she'd already mailed a letter to her—the ink was hardly dry on the page.

Dear Fannie, Lee is coming home from the war today. Mary Lou left shortly after Lee left for the war and took Annie with her. Lee will need a companion to help get him through this sorrowful time, and I wonder if Priscilla might be available to spend some time....

The Marshes

Priscilla's escape had always been the marshes, and she went there often when she was having conflicts with her mother or when her father's groans were too much to bear.

On this day, she headed deep into the swamp, a dark place—an enigmatic realm where the shadows cast by the trees grow long and menacing in the twilight. It was a bridge between the mundane and mystical, both serene and thrilling, offering a rich tapestry of natural beauty juxtaposed with the thrill of the untamed.

She skillfully maneuvered her modest motorboat through the Duck River waterways, exchanging waves with the fishermen she passed. Suddenly, her heart raced at the sight of a wild pig foraging in the underbrush along the riverbank. She brushed aside the tendrils of her auburn hair, her hazel eyes widening in surprise. A shiver ran down her spine as she recalled her father's tales of feral pigs attacking unsuspecting individuals. Struggling to divert her gaze, she maintained a firm grip on the tiller, guiding her boat into the marshes—her sanctuary, a true refuge.

Although the feral pigs were a menace, they posed no greater threat than her gunslinger cousin, Lee Dodd.

Her mother had accused her of being unruly, believing that marriage would provide the stability she required. However, resolute in her commitment to preserve her independence, she pressed on. Her mind wandered through reflections filled with defiance. *I refuse to become a captive of a man, confined within the walls of a household. She pondered on the remarkable notion that a mere ceremony and a piece of paper could transform a woman into a servant of her husband's whims and aspirations for eternity.*

Being the youngest in a family comprising fourteen children—four boys and ten girls—Priscilla was 'the apple of her father's eye.' Her father, David, had six children with his first wife, and after her passing, he married Fannie, Priscilla's mother, with whom he had an additional eight offspring. Priscilla was exempt from household chores, a privilege granted by her doting sisters. However, circumstances had shifted. Only her sister Amanda and she remained at home. In Maury County, the marriages of five sisters within a year had ignited a flurry of speculation and skepticism among the townsfolk, fueling a wave of gossip. Never in Maury County had there been five marriages in one family within a year.

Priscilla knew the swamp was dangerous, but she'd been going there since she was six years old, and her father had given her the motorboat for her birthday. After that, she felt free. It was getting darker, and a blue heron flew ahead of her as if guiding her. She reflected on how it started. If only Aunt Vinny hadn't sent the letter.

It had started like any other day. In the sweltering heat of the South, like any other self-respecting Southern woman, the morning chores were done, and they sat in the drawing room, fanning themselves and drinking iced tea. The sudden arrival of a letter disrupted their routine.

Her mother, Fannie, rocked back and forth in her rocking chair, her knuckles white as she clutched the letter in her hands. "Sweet Jesus, I cannot believe what has happened." Her face was pale, and her expression was intense as the letter dropped to her lap.

"What is it, Mama?" she asked, looking up from reading a book. She'd sensed the alarm in her mother's voice, and her little dog, Tiny, sensed it too and drowsily gazed up at Priscilla. When she remained motionless, he yawned and went back to sleep. Priscilla's presence was a calming force in the household, a trait mirrored by her loyal canine companion.

Fannie spoke, her eyebrows knitted with concern. "I've received a letter from my sister, Vinnie. My nephew, Lee, has returned home from the war. He's in a state of devastation because, months earlier, his young wife, Mary Lou, left him, taking their daughter, Annie, with her. According to Vinnie,

Lee has depression. She is seeking a companion to help him through this difficult time."

Priscilla glanced at her sister, Amanda, who was busily engaged in embroidery across the room. Amanda, a dressmaker by trade, donned a chic sleeveless drop-waist dress made of cotton. The hue of the garment, reminiscent of a robin's egg, complemented her eyes beautifully. Among all four sisters, Priscilla held Amanda in the highest regard. She wondered if Amanda would volunteer.

Without so much as a misstep in her needlework, Amanda shrugged. "He got what he deserved. I've heard from reliable sources that Lee assaulted Mary Lou. The gossip claims she was eagerly awaiting Lee's departure, eager to begin anew with a man by the name of Davis—an individual reputed to be far kinder and more respectful in his conduct."

"That was malicious," Fannie reproached. "Why would you speak so ill of my sister's son? Vinnie has raised him well. It's nothing but gossip; such rumors are what the town thrives on." Fannie had a particular affection for Lee, who was her most cherished nephew.

With an air of condescension, Amanda rolled her eyes. "Why do you always assume the best in everyone, Mama? They shared these tales over the party line, and my acquaintance, Mavis Hill, who works as a switchboard operator, assures me the rumors are true. I'm quite fond of my Aunt Vinnie, yet it's undeniable that her sons are unruly, and her husband, Jerome, is perpetually embroiled in quarrels and feuds."

A wry smile appeared on Amanda's face as she continued, "The Thomason brothers may be charming rogues, but they're also cunning. According to Mavis, the party line virtually ignites on Saturday evenings following the Thomason boys' visits to town. She claims they flatter the young women until they've had their fill, and then they discard them unceremoniously, as though they were merely a sack of potatoes." Amanda's eyes sparkled with a mischievous glee as she relished the scandal. "The girls refer to them as untamed and mischievous stallions."

"Stop it this instant," Fannie had whispered sharply. "It's merely gossip — unsubstantiated rumors." She twisted her hands nervously. "Lee comes from the Dodd family. By heritage, he has no Thomason blood and bears no resemblance to their character."

"I know well that he's a Dodd. His birth, out of wedlock, led to his being raised by his grandparents. They brought him up alongside uncles, whom he believed were his siblings, and I suspect their malevolent influence has tainted him." Amanda examined her embroidery with a critical eye before she commented, "They claim 'Big Bill' is the most deplorable of them all. He had his way with a girl, refused to marry her, and she jumped off the Sandy Hook Bridge and committed suicide."

Priscilla inhaled sharply, her blue eyes widening in shock. "All because of a man?"

"Not just any man," Amanda said. "It was Big Bill Thomason. He's a giant of a man, and he's got women crazy for him. They swoon when he walks by. They don't seem to mind the rumors that he's killed six men. And I've heard he always gets his way with the women."

"Amanda, cease this conversation immediately," Fannie admonished. "Your sister is merely fourteen years old. She's at an impressionable age."

"I'm old enough, Mama," Priscilla interjected.

With the firmness and heartfelt gravity of someone who recently went through a breakup, Amanda said, "Priscilla ought to be aware of the dangers that can befall young girls. Women need to be aware of potential dangers. The issue in today's society is that women do not communicate enough. Open discussions might shield our hearts from devastation—or even graver outcomes."

"Did the girl who jumped off the Sandy Hook Bridge survive?" Priscilla inquired with burning curiosity. "And what exactly do you mean when you say he always gets his way? Is that how babies are born?"

Amanda set her embroidery aside and clasped her hands in her lap. "I didn't expect to be the one teaching you about the birds and the bees," she reflected. "You learned about pollination in second grade—picture girls as flowers in a beautiful garden and a man as a bee. In spring, the bee pollinates the flowers, and that's how babies are born. However, on Watt's Hill, where we live, the bees often deceive the flowers before they pollinate them." She

51

sighed. "Sometimes, the bee pollinates the entire garden. What I mean is that when a girl believes a man's lies, she may end up conceiving babies, and then those men leave. They fly away to pollinate other flowers."

Fannie's expression revealed her disapproval of Amanda's forthright explanation. "Why do you complicate things like this, Amanda? Why can't you tell her that the stork brings the baby?"

Amanda retorted, "For heaven's sake, Mom, she's fourteen. She deserves to know the truth."

Priscilla scrunched her nose in disgust. "It all sounds terrible—the lies and the idea of jumping off the Sandy Hook Bridge. I don't want a boyfriend, and I refuse to be 'pollinated.' That sounds disgusting."

"Girls who don't like boys end up old maids, and old maids end up lonely. A girl as pretty as you could have any man she desired."

"Being alone is my preference," Priscilla insisted, her usual obstinacy coming to the forefront. "My married sisters aren't happy, Mama. They're constantly complaining about their husbands. They claim they are slaves to their husbands' whims."

Fannie crossed her arms. "You've been eavesdropping again, Priscilla. And whatever you overhear, you must not repeat. Your sisters are fortunate to have husbands to support them. God knows you'll never be able to support yourself. You're always off in that boat, reading or drawing. Money doesn't grow on trees."

Priscilla lowered her gaze. "I'm not stupid, Mama. I don't want to be like my sisters. They aren't truly happy. Doesn't happiness mean anything?"

"She's right, Mama. Times are changing. This is 1919," Amanda interjected. "There's talk of women voting soon. I've also heard that women from Maury County are working as telephone operators in New York. Priscilla is an intelligent young woman; marriage is not an obligation for her."

She turned to her, offering a radiant smile. "We don't have to talk about things like that. You're only fourteen. Let's gather some wildflowers and forget about this silliness."

"Hold on," Fannie said. "My sister Vinnie has asked for one of you to be a companion to your cousin during this turbulent time in his life."

"When pigs fly," Amanda retorted, her laughter echoing as she tossed her head back. "Lee Dodd? I wouldn't go near that man with a ten-foot pole."

"Vinnie requested Priscilla, not you."

Priscilla gasped. "Mother, why are you pretending you don't know that Lee Dodd beat his wife?" Priscilla objected, her crimson complexion betraying her indignation. She stamped her foot in frustration. "Besides, Lee Dodd is not a mere boy—he's a man. Divorced already — an older man, surpassing my age by a decade at the least."

"Your father was significantly older, yet we've enjoyed a blissful union," Fannie countered. "Vinnie has it all arranged. Lee shall retrieve Priscilla this Saturday at 2:00 p.m. They've bought a new Model-T Ford. You may wear your new sun hat."

Aghast, Priscilla found herself at a loss for words. She understood the futility of contending with her mother's wishes, as it would be unseemly. She stood, cradling Tiny, then clasped her sister's hand.

Glancing at her mother, hints of rage flickered in her gaze. She stated, "I'd like to go with Amanda now—to pick wildflowers."

Amanda held Priscilla's hand with conviction. Her gaze was laden with reproach upon Fannie. "Surely you wouldn't do this. It's like casting her to the wolves."

Fannie's posture was resolute. "A woman who cannot secure a suitor is ill-equipped to advise her sibling."

Those words struck a chord, leaving Amanda visibly wounded. With an arm protectively entwined around Priscilla, they hurried away; the door thundering shut behind them.

A red-tailed hawk's sharp, piercing screech jolted Priscilla from her daydream. She searched for the source of the sound in the thick foliage surrounding her. Her gaze settled on a magnificent bird perched atop a towering oak tree before it gracefully took flight. Mesmerized, she watched as the hawk's majestic wings stretched to their full span, easily spanning at least four feet. It was a sight that filled her with both admiration and longing

— to soar above and leave behind the chaos and madness that consumed her life.

Cigarettes and Sodas

Desperation had driven Priscilla to be with Lee. She missed Amanda terribly and would have done anything to escape the house, away from her mother's constant complaining. But once they were alone, she felt bewildered and unsure of how to act. His reputation with women only added to her distress—a divorced, older man who might or might not have beaten his wife. That's what Amanda had said.

As she bounced along in the Model T, her face showed a mix of boredom and slight revulsion. She absentmindedly pulled at a loose thread in her dress, berating herself for accepting his invitation. She knew she couldn't confine herself to that house forever. With Amanda gone, the atmosphere was sheer misery.

She risked a glance at Lee. The subtle twitch in his jaw revealed the inner turmoil he was experiencing, a familiar clue she had observed in her father during troubled times. Assuming responsibility, she felt a sinking sensation.

Her voice quivered in a high-pitched tone as she nervously asked, "Do you have a cigarette?" She believed smoking would lend her an air of maturity and sophistication.

Lee's lips curled into a subtle smile as he reached into his shirt pocket and retrieved a pack of Camels. With a gentle tap, a single cigarette slid out. Priscilla delicately grasped it between two fingers and brought it to her lips. She recalled the one time she had done this before, with her friend Allyson behind the barn, and had vowed never to repeat it. However, she never could have fathomed finding herself in this unexpected situation.

As Lee extended his lighter, she fumbled twice before finally igniting the flame, a look of surprise crossing her face. She quickly puffed and blew out the smoke, fearing it might make her choke. Mimicking the way Gloria Swanson held a cigarette in the movies — delicately between her fingers, feeling a surge of confidence. Her raven hair billowed in the wind as she spoke in a high voice, "I heard on the radio that it's supposed to rain tomorrow," stealing a glance at Lee to gauge his reaction.

His gaze lingered on her with unmistakable intrigue, as though her words had struck a deep chord within him. "Is that true? Do you often tune in to the radio?"

"Yes. We listen to the weather and farm reports; sometimes, Mama lets us listen to music."

Lee flashed a smile, revealing a set of dazzlingly white teeth. "What songs do you like?" he asked.

"Bye, bye, Blackbird," she said, accidentally taking a long drag on the cigarette. Choking, she drew in a long breath, finally recovering.

Lee looked straight ahead, pretending not to notice. "Sing it."

Priscilla snapped her fingers rhythmically and sang, *"Bye, bye, Blackbird... Gonna pack up all my cares and woe..."*

Lee's dark eyes danced. "You have a magnificent voice."

She skewed her face. "Do you mean it?"

"Yes! Sing it!"

She belted out three lines of the song — loud, then halted. "That's all! I'm done!"

"You're so funny," he said, giving her a friendly slap on the knee.

Feeling old enough to be with Lee Dodd, she flicked the cigarette out the car window.

Priscilla felt uneasy as she observed Lee delivering to the drugstore's back door and then quickly driving to the front. She resisted the urge to ask questions despite her curiosity. With a stiff gait, she walked alongside him towards the soda fountain at the back of the drugstore. Taking a seat on a vibrant cherry-red stool, she cast a sly glance over her shoulder, hoping to escape the attention of her friends.

Lee sat down beside her and asked, "What kind of ice cream do you like?"

She gazed at the menu as if it were the first time she had seen it. In truth, she had been coming in with Amanda every two weeks when Amanda got her paycheck. They never changed the menu, and she always got the same thing.

The soda clerk, Billie Joe, leaned forward. "Do you want your usual, Priscilla? Two scoops of chocolate ice cream in a dish." He raised his brow and glanced suspiciously at Lee. "You rarely come in."

Lee stayed calm, even after being identified as the driver for the bootlegger, the man who made deliveries and collected an envelope twice weekly. "Priscilla and I are cousins. We're just out for a drive today."

Billy Joe seemed satisfied. "Okay, two scoops, Priscilla?"

Lee pointed to a fancy soda with whipped cream and a cherry on top. "How about this one?"

Priscilla had a thoughtful expression on her face. Ordering a Brown Cow was something she could never do. It was too expensive. "Alright, a Brown Cow." Her tone held a hint of reluctance, as if she'd allowed him to talk her into it.

Lee nodded. "Two Brown Cows with everything."

Priscilla eagerly watched as the soda clerk made a delicious chocolate soda. As he presented it to her, she attempted to conceal her excitement. She dipped the long spoon into the tall glass, enjoying a few bites of chocolate ice cream before savoring the first sip of what she believed to be the most delicious drink she had ever tasted. She was so engrossed in her soda that she hardly noticed Lee had barely touched his drink.

He was more captivated by her. Taking in her features with his dark eyes, he seemed happy with what he saw. "It wasn't long ago that you were a little girl, and I saw you at my brother's wedding. Look at you now." He exaggerated his Southern drawl to sound enticing and charming. "You're as pretty as a Georgia peach."

A blush spread across her face. She tried to think of something clever to say, but her mind went blank. Finally, she found her voice. "Oh, I just remembered—you were with a girl. Didn't you get married?"

Lee shifted on the red stool, preferring to steer clear of his many romantic entanglements. "Oh, no, she was just a friend."

"But you married Mary Lou Davis. That's what my sister Amanda told me."

Lee shoved his soda away. "Mary Lou didn't wait. She ran off with another man after I left for the Army. My divorce was completed last week."

The look of abject sadness in his eyes tugged at Priscilla's heart, triggering deep empathy. She reached over and gently patted his arm, offering a slight comfort amid his pain. "I'm sorry," she murmured.

"Don't be," he replied, his gaze penetrating her as if trying to see what lay beneath her surface. "Are you seeing anyone?"

She gave a light laugh, feeling slightly embarrassed. "No, I'm only fourteen. I've never had a date."

"I saw you dancing with a boy at the square dance."

"Oh, that was just a friend," she quickly clarified. "He's our veterinarian's son. I've known him all my life."

His brows furrowed in confusion. A friend? He had just used those exact words minutes ago. *Was she playing him?* No, she was young and innocent, unlike other women he had been with - manipulative and scheming. Her beauty struck him again - porcelain white skin, clear blue eyes, and an air of innocence that he found refreshing in this jaded world. "I believe you are the sweetest girl I have ever known," he confessed, grateful she was his cousin. "We have so much in common already."

Priscilla secretly scoffed at his words, thinking them to be silly flattery. She barely knew him, and from what she could tell, they had little in common. In her mind, he was 'talking through his hat,' a phrase Amanda often used to describe men trying to win over women. As far as Priscilla was concerned, their brief meeting over soda was nothing more than an escape from the stifling heat and stench of death in her house. She would go back, dreading the return to her dismal reality but still holding onto hope that a letter from Amanda would be in the mailbox — a small glimmer of light in an otherwise dark and dreary existence.

A sharp gasp escaped from Priscilla's lips as Lee pulled out his wallet to pay. She couldn't believe her eyes as she saw the thick stack of twenties and hundreds. The sheer amount of money in one place made her dizzy. Amanda had a small coin purse filled with loose change to pay for her purchase, starkly contrasting Lee's lavish display.

"Do you need anything?" Lee asked.

"No," Priscilla lied. She needed everything now that Amanda had left her.

The drugstore owner, Mr. Wiggins, waited patiently behind the large metal cash register. "If you're feeling charitable, Fannie has a list of monthly items she buys," he said in a hushed voice. "And David has medications ready, but I can't release them until they pay the bill."

"Sure, not a problem," Lee said, handing Mr. Wiggins two twenties.

Priscilla felt her cheeks heat with embarrassment. With each resounding ding of the register, her anxiety increased. She couldn't help but wonder what was happening. Were they really in such dire financial straits that they couldn't even afford the necessities of life? As Mr. Wiggins rang up their items, Priscilla glanced at Lee's bulging wallet, feeling grateful yet guilty. They left the store with a large paper bag brimming with soaps, candles, David's medications, Fannie's beloved snuff, and a bottle of Snake Oil liniment for whatever ailed her.

Knowing her family was struggling to make ends meet, Priscilla couldn't shake off the feeling of shame. "Thank you. It wasn't your place to pay. I'm sure Mother was going to get to it. She's been busy with Daddy sick and has hardly left the house."

"I'm happy to help," he said, his voice filled with kindness. "That's what family is for - to care for each other in times of need, like you're helping me get through difficult times."

Priscilla couldn't help but feel a twinge of conflict within her. Despite her youth, she understood the unspoken expectation behind Lee's words. She was the repayment for his generosity, the one who would ease his burden in difficult times. But how could she refuse? Her family needed things, and as the only girl at home now, it fell on her shoulders to provide for them.

The tongues wagged that day.

Billy Joe went to Mr. Wiggins and voiced his concerns. "What is Priscilla Powell, an evangelist's daughter, doing with Lee Dodd, a bootlegger's son?"

"Don't know," Mr. Wiggins said. "But he is her cousin. Maybe he's trying to help because he knows her daddy is dying. The family is in deep financial trouble. Lee paid their outstanding bill and bought everything Fannie needed for this month. So, what's your gripe?"

Billy Joe looked leery. "All I know is... Lee Dodd is trouble with a capital 'T,' and so are his brothers. They're the biggest hell-raisers in Maury County. I saw Lee and his brothers going into the brothel across the street when I was closing up last night. And he hardly touched his soda. He drinks moonshine—not sodas. That man is up to no good."

"Go easy. Lee just got back from the war. He was a POW," Mr. Wiggins admonished. "Don't make a stink about it. I'm making good money from that moonshine, and I don't want to cause a rile with the big man. It's none of our business."

"What about Priscilla? There was something different about what was going on with her today. She wasn't carefree and laughing like she was with Amanda. It was as if she were uncomfortable and unsure of what to say or do. It was as if she were pretending to be someone she wasn't."

"Like I said...it's none of our business. You mind what I say and look the other way."

Billy Joe didn't like it one bit—no, sir, he didn't. He shuddered at the thought of what might happen to a young, innocent girl if she got mixed up with a man like Lee Dodd. Why, it could ruin her whole life.

He couldn't chance getting fired. But someone had to warn her.

Greed and Desire

When Belle set off for Nashville to pick up supplies, her girls took charge — greed driving them to make more money. Priscilla would be the star attraction.

"You'll never get to New York if you don't," they taunted, goading her forward with promises of money. With a deep breath, fueled by her drive and ambition, Priscilla left behind the safety of the kitchen and followed their lead. It was too tempting to resist.

The transformation was swift and startling. Belle's girls dressed Priscilla in a short, flashy red silk dress, spike heels, and net stockings, then adorned her with heavy makeup until she was almost unrecognizable. They applied mascara to her eyes, rouge to her cheeks, and heavy lipstick to her lips, each brush stroke erasing a little more of the girl Priscilla once was.

The air was thick with the scent of alcohol as glasses clinked and liquor flowed like a river. Loud music blared from the speakers while the girls danced on top of the bar, their movements wild and intoxicating. Priscilla found herself at the center of this chaotic scene. She had been dancing since she was five years old, and all she needed to do was follow their lead—and the money flowed like water.

One of Belle's girls acted as a lookout, stationed by a window to watch for any sign of trouble. Priscilla felt a twinge of unease when she saw her reflection in the mirror — a stranger, a painted doll with a painted smile. But the promise of money and escape from the drudgery of her life kept her there.

As the evening wore on, Priscilla waited tables, her heart pounding with each step she took. The saloon was alive with activity, laughter, and music filling the air. She brushed by Clint, the young millionaire, her hand lingering on his arm for a moment longer than necessary. He glanced up, their eyes meeting. Priscilla felt a flutter in her chest, a spark of something she couldn't quite name. Clint was handsome, with his easy smile and confident demeanor. However, there was something else about him, something that drew her to him like a moth to a flame.

As she served drinks to the card players, they slipped five-dollar bills into her bosom, their hands lingering on her skin. It made her uncomfortable, but she pushed aside her reservations, focusing instead on the money accumulating in her bosom.

It was more than she had ever imagined, a small fortune that promised a way out of the life she had known.

A romantic country song came on, its lilting melody filling the room with longing and desire. Clint rose and offered her his hand, a silent invitation to dance. Priscilla hesitated, her heart racing, before placing her hand in his and allowing him to lead her onto the dance floor.

"What's your name?" he whispered, his breath warm against her skin. "Why haven't I seen you before?"

His voice was low and intimate against her ear, making her feel like they were the only ones in the room. She was coy, her answers carefully crafted to conceal the truth. "My name is Sarah," she lied, her voice barely above a whisper. "And I'm visiting from Nashville. I normally work in the kitchen, but Belle needed extra help tonight."

"I'm Clint Wilder. Pleased to meet you. Tell me about yourself. I want to hear everything about you."

She spun a web of lies, weaving a story of a life she wished she had—a life with loving parents and a private school education. It was a fantasy, a dream of a world far removed from the harsh reality of her existence. But in Clint's arms, it felt real, a fleeting glimpse of something she could never have.

Clint was smitten, his eyes softening as he looked at her. "I've never met anyone as pretty as you," he said, his voice sincere. "You're different, Sarah. Special."

Before Priscilla could respond, the lookout came running; driven by fear. "Lee's coming," she gasped, her voice barely a whisper. "With his brothers."

Priscilla's heart stopped, fear coursing through her veins like ice. She dashed away, running up the back stairs and disappearing into the darkness.

The bouncer, an imposing figure, blocked Clint's efforts to follow. He watched helplessly as Priscilla vanished, a sense of loss gnawing at his heart.

Later that evening, while tallying her cash, Priscilla experienced an unusual feeling of self-satisfaction. With over two hundred dollars, she had more than enough money for a train ticket to New York and plenty to spare. As she considered the possibility of leaving and embarking on a new life in New York, doubt gripped her. The thought of being alone on the streets filled her with dread. She did not know where her sister Amanda lived.

After Belle returned to the saloon, she was shocked to discover that Priscilla had put herself in danger by mingling with customers and risking her safety. Belle revealed to Priscilla that she had been buying moonshine from Lee Dodd. If he found out she was there, all hell would break loose. Belle pondered her options, unsure of what to do next.

Worse, Priscilla had caused quite a stir, and Belle's patrons, the gamblers, lumberjacks, outlaws, and miners, their interest piqued, wanted her back. Lee was especially intrigued, his curiosity sparked by the mention of her name—Sarah. He wanted to meet the girl who had captured the attention of the saloon's patrons, and he was willing to do whatever it took to make that happen.

Belle, dressed in her finest apparel, a bright green satin dress with feathers in her hair, went from table to table, calming the patrons with free drinks. The girls were especially attentive to the men hanging all over them, trying to make them forget about Sarah, but nothing could silence them.

Lee pulled Belle aside. "Looks like I missed the big attraction tonight," he said with a sly grin. "They say your new girl is gorgeous. I want her upstairs in ten minutes." He pressed a hundred-dollar bill into Belle's hand.

Belle returned the money to him and said bluntly. "Sorry—she's off limits, Lee. Sarah is my niece and has returned to Nashville with my sister. My girls were playing a prank on me. That's all."

Lee's once lively dark eyes now bore a skeptical expression. "Really? That's not the rumor I've heard. Some guys are saying she can be had and was getting cozy with a guy named Clint."

Belle's red lips curled into a big smile. "In their dreams," she said, refilling his glass with her best whiskey, then secretly telling Lucy to keep him occupied. But it bothered her that Lee kept glancing at the kitchen door, and she had a bouncer keep an eye on him.

As the night drew to a close and the saloon emptied, Priscilla sat alone in the kitchen, drinking a cup of hot tea, her mind swirling with thoughts of what had transpired. She was shaken by the fear of being caught by Lee but was also exhilarated by the money she'd earned and the attention she'd received from Clint. She knew she had a choice between staying and risking her safety or leaving and facing an uncertain future. Her heart carried the weight of a decision that would reshape her life beyond imagination.

Priscilla ran her hand across her small breasts, her skin reddened by the rough hands of the miners and lumberjacks. The gambler's hands had been smooth, yet they still felt invasive. It was the first time she had truly noticed her sexuality. Unzipping her saloon costume, she allowed her saloon dress to drop to the wooden floor. She kicked it aside, approaching the small sink and cleansing herself with the rose-scented soap Belle had given her. She inhaled deeply, the scent reminding her of her mother's rose garden. Despite thoroughly washing every part of her body and enjoying the floral fragrance, the feeling of dirtiness around her bosom persisted.

Later, as she lay on her lumpy cot, unable to sleep, she wondered if she could ever do it again. Wouldn't that be better than being at a man's beck and call? Amanda had repeatedly told her how terrible it was, and she had overheard a few conversations between her married sisters and mother. One thing she remembered was their complaints about sex. Her mother had responded in a knowing voice, "Well, that's the only way you're going to have a baby, so you just have to lie there and take it." This had made a lasting impression on Priscilla, convincing her she never wanted to get married.

Yet she had felt something with Clint, something sweet she had never experienced before. However, her interactions with the other men had diminished those positive feelings. She felt foolish for her actions and sensed a change within herself. What would become of her? She was leading a secret life, cut off from her previous existence. Her thoughts raced, and she felt naïve for being so captivated by Clint. What would a man like him want with a kitchen maid? I might as well be dead, she said to herself. But then she realized that to the rest of the world, she was already dead — dead to everyone except to a few people inside the saloon.

Being a kitchen maid in a saloon wasn't the worst experience imaginable. The true struggle had been living under her mother's oppressive control and facing the incessant expectations she imposed on her. The porch swing had served as her refuge, a place to unwind and listen to the soothing sounds of the birds. As she reflected on those times, she realized she had felt like a caged animal, unable to break free from her mother's relentless pressure.

She tossed and turned on the small cot. As darkness enveloped her, she could hear the melodic call of the Whip-poor-will. Its repetitive cadence comforted her, making her feel as if she were back at home, reclining on the porch swing. Her sisters came to mind. Navigating new experiences without them was daunting.

Reflecting on her excursion with Lee, she felt like an idiot—singing the Jimmy Dickens song, though he had seemed genuinely impressed with her. Still, she questioned the authenticity of his reactions and struggled to discern the truth from illusion. She felt beguiled.

Fannie emerged and slumped onto the swing beside her, disturbing the rhythmic tranquility. The swing's once smooth motion now felt erratic and uneven.

"How is Daddy?" Priscilla inquired.

"He is feeling better now, thanks to receiving his medication. It was considerate of Lee to pick it up for us. Not many fellows would cover the cost from their pocket. You ought to be grateful that he is interested in you."

The tension in the air was thick.

"Well, I'm not grateful," Priscilla sniffed. "I have no desire to seek the affections of a man who surpasses me in age by ten years."

"You are such a sourpuss, Priscilla, questioning your cousin's intentions when he's done nothing but good for us. Your father was moaning and writhing in pain

before Lee brought the medicine. Besides, it's not unusual for girls in these parts to date older men. He is a good-looking man, and Vinnie says the family business has been thriving since Lee came home from the war."

Priscilla jerked her head as she danced through the shades of gray to find the heart of the matter. Bitterness tinged her normally calm voice. "Don't make me feel guilty, Mother, because I don't. Money's tight, and our financial resources are strained. It seems I have become 'the pawn' in this situation. All my sisters are gone, and you're looking at me to 'bring home the bacon' by luring a man with money into the family to pay our bills."

Fannie's mouth flew open in feigned surprise. "My word. I would never do such a thing. Is it not clear that divine providence is at work here? If I were in your place, I would pray and express gratitude for Lee's timely arrival during our crisis." She paused momentarily. "He also settled the telephone bill. They were on the brink of disconnecting our service, and without it, how would I possibly communicate with the doctor concerning your father's condition? We also expect to receive a call from Amanda at any moment—not that you should talk to her. She's done nothing but put wild ideas into your head."

The words rolled off her tongue before she could stop them. "I know I'm going to hell in a handbasket if I don't do things your way." It vexed her that her mother consistently portrayed Amanda as the culprit for what she deemed Priscilla's defiant streak. Although her mother toiled for endless hours advocating for women's suffrage, she loathed it when her daughters challenged her outdated evangelical convictions.

"You are so disrespectful, Priscilla. I've worked my fingers to the bone for you."

Priscilla was grateful for the darkness; it concealed her seething anger, comparable to a pot on the brink of boiling over. She had witnessed her sisters succumb to guilt, diminishing under their mother's sharp tongue. Priscilla and Amanda had invested hours dissecting their mother's penchant for manipulating them through religion. Given Fannie's status as the family matriarch, she ruled much like a queen, reigning over her subjects.

The swing had remained still for several minutes as they sat shrouded in darkness. Two women, at odds and in deep disagreement, each refused to give in. The silence was broken when her father's weak voice called out, "Fannie... Fannie... I need my

66

medication. The pain...it's flaring up again."

Her mother rose, setting the swing ajar. "Oh, before I forget. Lee is coming by tomorrow. I need Fels-Naptha soap to remove the stains from your father's clothes."

"Of course, Mother," Priscilla said, her tone bitter. "And tell Daddy I love him."

Later that night, Priscilla knelt beside her bed to pray. "God, please urge Amanda to call or write. If she doesn't reach out, I'm afraid I'll jump off the Sandy Hook Bridge because I cannot continue in this charade with Lee Dodd. Someone is going to get hurt." She embraced the framed photograph, pressing it close to her heart. With the radiant, joyful image of Amanda etched in her mind, she succumbed to slumber... and dreamed .... She and Amanda frolicked through an expansive field blooming with lavender, their laughter unfettered by worldly troubles. Suddenly, Amanda vanished. Stranded at a crossroads, an oppressive gloom and an impenetrable mist settled over her. Whichever path she chose led only to dead ends. Enveloped by a sense of foreboding, she felt the sensation of the earth spinning, as if being pulled into a cyclone.

With a sudden jolt, she opened her eyes, feeling dizzy and her skin covered in perspiration. She had an epiphany: Amanda was not coming back. A feeling of dread spread through her as she realized she was alone, with no one to save her.

The Fiddler

When morning came, she wearily trudged to the kitchen and proceeded with her tasks as if nothing had happened; chopping onions and vegetables with intensity and scrubbing the large pots as if she could remove the memory of what had happened the night before. Despite her efforts, she couldn't ignore the intense stare Jake gave her every time they crossed paths. She had disappointed him immensely.

By evening, Priscilla had convinced herself that the men had exploited her and that her life would never be the same. However, when a fiddler arrived at the saloon, the familiar tunes from his fiddle transformed the atmosphere and stirred her heart. He was playing the same songs her father had played. She dashed to the kitchen door and peered through the crack, only to find him encircled by a crowd. The fiddler played, inciting excitement in the crowd—toes tapped, hands clapped, and some danced to the music. She longed to join them — tormented that she couldn't see the fiddler.

Feeling an overwhelming desire to see her dying father with tears streaming down her face, she plopped down on a kitchen chair, laying her head on her folded arms on the table, lamenting life's cruelty. At that moment, life held no significance for her. It didn't matter if Lee found her; if he did, she would jump off Sandy Hook Bridge.

Priscilla started when Belle burst through the kitchen door. "The good Lord has answered my prayers," she said. "You have a benefactor, and he's waiting for you outside in the back alley."

"I don't understand. Are you firing me?"

"No, nothing like that. Someone saw you last night and wants to help.

That's all. You have a chance for a new beginning."

"I can't go," Priscilla protested. "The fiddle player reminds me of my father. He's been playing the same songs as my father used to play. I have to go home—back to see my dying father one last time."

A shadow crossed Belle's face. "I couldn't bring myself to tell you, but your father died two weeks ago. I'm so sorry."

Priscilla paled. "My father's dead?" she said in disbelief, the fiddle player's music ringing in her ears.

"That's not all. I also took it upon myself to find out what had happened to your mother since your father passed away. And your mother has remarried and put the house up for sale."

Priscilla felt an emptiness engulf her. "I loved that house. I would give anything to have just one more day there, sleeping in my room with the patchwork quilt and taking my boat out into the marshes and the swamps. It was my sanctuary. Oh, how I miss those days."

"Those days are gone, and you must be strong and move forward, Priscilla. Now, pack your things. He is waiting for you."

"My benefactor?"

"No. His brother."

"But I can't leave—the fiddler is still playing—I can't leave until he plays the last note," Priscilla said resolutely.

Suddenly, the music halted.

The silence struck Priscilla like a ton of bricks. "My father is dead," she declared as violent sobs racked her body. Belle caught her as she nearly fell off the chair, collapsing in a heap.

Belle hugged her close, comforting her. "I've never seen that fiddler in all my life, Priscilla. I believe it was your father—come back to say goodbye."

"Do you think so?" asked Priscilla with renewed strength as she forced herself to stand. With Belle's help, she staggered to the kitchen door and peered through the crack.

The fiddler was leaving, walking out the door, wearing his black hat and vest. Then he turned and looked over his shoulder. It was bittersweet to see his face again. He looked like a young man, happy, his body no longer racked with pain.

Priscilla swayed, feeling faint. "That's my father," she declared, so convinced that she attempted to muster the strength to run to him, but Belle held her back.

"Go now," Belle said firmly. "There's little time. There's been so much talk it's raised suspicion, and the sheriff wants to know about a girl named Sarah. If he finds out I've been harboring you, I could face a jail sentence and lose everything I have. And God only knows what Lee Dodd would do to me and my girls."

Priscilla threw her arms around Belle. "Oh, God, I couldn't bear it if anything happened to any of you — I'll miss you terribly, and I'll write, I promise. I'll never forget you, Belle. I love you. You've been like a mother to me."

"I would be proud to be your mother," Belle said, her eyes glistening. "I love you too. It's not goodbye, I promise."

After packing her few belongings, the girls hugged her, some weeping. "You've changed our lives," Belle said. "You've been a godsend, and now you must start your new life. Few of us get a chance like this, and you must make the most of it. Live for us, and do what we weren't able to do. Make your dreams come true for all of us."

Tears streamed down her cheeks as Belle shoved her into the passenger seat of the shiny Model T Ford. She waved goodbye and kept her eyes on Belle and the girls until they faded from sight. Only then did she turn to face the driver.

Becoming Priscilla

Priscilla watched as the town lights dimmed, leaving her bittersweet about the life she was leaving behind. Amid the uncertainty, the saloon, Belle, and the girls had offered her a sanctuary where she felt protected and accepted. She felt conflicted about trading that life for the unknown and giving up her dream of finding her sister, Amanda, in New York.

The road stretched before Priscilla like an endless ribbon of darkness, the Model T-Ford's headlights casting long, eerie shadows across the landscape. She sat in the passenger seat, her thoughts churning with excitement and doubt. Her eyes briefly met Blake Wilder's, his face intermittently bathed in the glow of the passing headlights as he concentrated on the road ahead.

Her curiosity got the better of her, and she turned to Blake with an inquisitive expression. "Blake, who is my benefactor? And why is he helping me?"

Blake's expression remained composed, but there was a hint of reluctance in his voice.

"It's my brother. He arranged everything."

"Your brother?" she repeated, her tone laced with curiosity. "Can I meet him?"

Blake shook his head, his tone firm but gentle. "It's impossible right now. He's out of the country on business."

As Priscilla leaned back in her seat, her mind racing with unanswered questions, the weight of uncertainty was heavy on her shoulders. She wanted to know more about the man who had taken such an interest in her future, but for now, she would have to be content with the mystery.

"My name is Priscilla, not Sarah," she said, feeling it was important to be honest.

"I know," he replied. "Belle told me everything."

An hour later, Blake turned down a long, winding driveway. Priscilla's eyes widened in awe at the grandeur of the surroundings. A grand Southern mansion stood before her, its white columns and sprawling verandas gleaming in the moonlight. The mansion exuded an air of elegance and history, with ivy climbing up its walls and the full moon casting a warm glow on the grounds.

Blake parked the car and extended his hand to help her — guiding her towards the front door where a woman stood, ready to welcome them. "Allow me to introduce my head housekeeper, Mrs. Ashton," Blake said, gesturing toward the poised and graceful woman standing before them. With her chestnut-colored hair styled to perfection, she exuded sophistication in her black dress. "You can trust her to take care of everything from this point forward."

Mrs. Ashton smiled warmly, her demeanor both welcoming and professional. "Welcome, Miss Priscilla. Please, follow me."

The opulence of the mansion overwhelmed Priscilla as they entered the grand foyer, which had towering ceilings, ornate chandeliers, and luxurious velvet drapes. Every little thing exuded wealth and sophistication as Mrs. Ashton guided her up the sweeping staircase and down the corridor. Enthralled by the portraits and ornate mirrors that lined the wall, Priscilla felt like she had entered a heavenly realm. In front of them stood a massive door, which Mrs. Ashton swung open to unveil a luxurious bedroom. Priscilla's eyes widened as she entered the room. She took in the elegant four-poster bed adorned with a plush pink comforter, the ornate vanity table and gold gilded mirror, and the stunning view of the manicured gardens outside the window.

The room boasted a large soaking tub in one corner, its glossy porcelain surface sparkling and beckoning for a relaxing soak. A surge of excitement washed over Priscilla as she imagined the warmth and relaxation of a hot bath. Mrs. Ashton patiently showed her how to operate the taps, ensuring she was comfortable before leaving her to settle in.

Priscilla treasured every moment in the bath, embracing the warmth of the water as it eased her worries. Memories of her daring escape from the saloon flooded her mind, contrasting with the unexpected luxury she now found herself surrounded by. Though filled with anticipation, a twinge of nostalgia for Belle and the girls clung to her thoughts. Leaving them behind was harder than she had expected; they had become her family, and their bond was strong.

After her bath, Priscilla slipped into a plush robe. Its luxurious fabric hugged her body as she sat by the window, captivated by the beauty of the night sky. Against the backdrop of the night, the stars sparkled with unparalleled brilliance, their light piercing through the velvety darkness. As she contemplated what lay ahead and whether she would ever reunite with her sister Amanda, the weight of uncertainty pressed heavily on her.

The next morning, Blake introduced Priscilla to his wife, Rosalee. Rosalee was a striking woman with pale blonde hair worn in a modern bob style. Her confident demeanor and brash personality surprised Priscilla, and she had a way of capturing everyone's attention with her presence alone.

"Well, aren't you a pretty little thing?" Rosalee declared as Priscilla followed Mrs. Ashton into the formal dining room. She rose and hugged Priscilla, then held her at arm's length. "You're perfect. I wouldn't change a thing about you, but Mrs. Ashton tells me you could use some new clothes, so we're going to Nashville today to buy you some new outfits. We don't want you to look like a country bumpkin."

Priscilla's head was spinning as she nodded. Even if she'd wanted to speak, she couldn't get a word in edgewise as Rosalee rambled on and on about what a lovely day they would have together and all the shops they were going to.

Priscilla's eyes widened as a servant set a plate of food before her, piled high with pancakes, scrambled eggs, bacon, and toast. When he placed a glass of milk before her, Rosalee said, "Make sure you drink your milk, dear.

You must have three glasses a day. It will give you great bones."

Priscilla took a large swallow, hoping to please her, and Mrs. Ashton quickly placed a white starched napkin across her lap. "Mustn't forget your napkin," she said, her tone as starched as the napkin. "Remember, we are ladies, and ladies always put their napkins across their laps before they touch their food."

"Of course," Priscilla said, though she'd never seen a starched napkin, only paper ones on special occasions. She dived into the food, savoring every bit. She'd never seen so many pancakes piled so high, and they were scrumptious.

While Priscilla ate, Rosalee drank tea out of a China cup, holding the handle delicately with her little finger out, and fed her fox terrier, Dandy, tiny pieces of scrambled egg. Though Priscilla pretended to concentrate on her food, she discreetly took in everything Rosalee did, making mental notes of the proper way to do things. She'd already been told in so many words that she looked like a country bumpkin.

"You're too quiet, Priscilla," Rosalee said. "You need to speak your mind. Do you hear?" She spoke with an exaggerated Southern accent, nothing like Priscilla had ever heard.

"Leave the girl alone," Mrs. Ashton reprimanded. "Can't you see she's famished?" Mrs. Ashton had been with Blake for years and didn't mind putting his wives in their places. To her, Rosalee was wife number three, and she didn't make any bones about it. She ran the household and kept the servants in their place, and Blake had turned Priscilla over to her to look after.

Priscilla pushed her plate away with a bright smile. "It was wonderful, thank you."

"No need to thank us, Priscilla," Mrs. Ashton said. "This is your home. We do not expect you to thank us for ordinary things that are part of everyday living."

Rosalee cleared her throat. "Can we get this show on the road now?" she said impatiently. "I have a hundred things to do in town, and I sure as hell hope Blake is here to drive us." She tapped the table with her French-manicured nails. "Do you realize you gave the driver the day off, Ash?"

"I am not making excuses to the likes of you," Mrs. Ashton sniffed, her tone laced with superiority. "He desperately needed a break, so I granted him a well-deserved day off." With a fierce expression, she directed an intense glare towards Rosalee. "It's his birthday... not that it matters to you."

Priscilla kept her head down and tried to make herself as small as possible. There was tension in the house, something she hadn't expected. She glanced at Blake, sitting in an easy chair across the room, heavily engrossed in the newspaper. He hadn't said a word.

Nashville

Nashville with Rosalee was an unparalleled experience. Priscilla had been to Nashville with her parents to pick up supplies, but it was nothing like this. The city was bustling with activity, and the air was alive with the sounds of music and people passing by high-end establishments. This part of town was for the affluent—people with money to spend.

While browsing the dress shops, Rosalee expertly led her through the latest fashions, encouraging her to try the newest trends.

"This is the bee's knees," Rosealee declared, holding up a flapper dress with intricate beadwork. "You need to look the part if you're going to make a splash in this town."

Priscilla hesitated as Rosealee suggested a new bob hairstyle, a popular trend many women adored. Just as she was about to agree, Blake intervened, his expression serious.

"Absolutely not. My brother wouldn't like it," he explained, his tone leaving no room for argument.

Rosalee rolled her eyes but relented, her playful nature returning as they continued their shopping spree. By the end of the day, they outfitted Priscilla in a new wardrobe that made her feel like a different person. The stylish dresses and accessories gave her a newfound confidence and a sense of belonging in this new world.

Priscilla and Rosalee quickly became fast friends. Rosealee's outspoken nature was refreshing, and Priscilla enjoyed their conversations and adventures together. They spent their days playing croquet on the expansive lawn, the clinking of mallets and laughter filling the air. They also went horseback riding, the wind whipping through their hair as they rode through the picturesque countryside.

One afternoon, as they lounged in the garden after a spirited game of croquet, Priscilla mustered the courage to ask Rosealee a question. Her time at the saloon had made her curious, but she had no one to talk to about such things. She was feeling comfortable with Rosalee, like she'd been with Amanda.

"Rosalee," she began tentatively, "can I ask you something? About men, I mean."

Rosalee laughed, her eyes sparkling with amusement. "Honey, you can ask me anything. What do you want to know?"

Priscilla hesitated, unsure how to phrase her question. "Well, I guess I'm just curious. How do you know when a man is interested in you? And what should you do if you like him?"

Rosealee's expression softened, a hint of nostalgia in her eyes. "Oh, sweetie, men are simple creatures. When a man is interested in you, he'll make it known. He'll find a way to be in your company, to make you laugh, and to show you he cares. And if you like him back, don't play too hard to get. Let him know you're interested, but make him work for it a little. Don't give him too much, too soon." She leaned in closer, her voice lowering conspiratorially. "But remember, not all men are worth your time. Some will charm you to get what they want and disappear from your life. Be smart, trust your instincts, and never settle for anything less than you deserve."

Priscilla listened intently, soaking in Rosalee's advice. She appreciated the older woman's candidness and the sense of camaraderie that had developed between them. Rosalee's wisdom and experience were invaluable, and Priscilla felt grateful to have her as a friend and mentor.

As the days turned into weeks, Priscilla grew more comfortable in her new life. She enjoyed her time with Rosealee and appreciated the stability and security that Blake provided. She even imagined a future for herself that didn't revolve around finding Amanda, though the thought of her sister was never far from her mind. One evening, as they sat on the veranda watching the sunset, Blake joined them, his presence a welcome addition to their little group. He had been busy with work at the law firm, but always made time to check on Priscilla.

"How are you settling in?" he asked, his eyes warm and kind.

"Very well," Priscilla replied with a smile. "Thank you for everything, Blake. I don't know how I can repay you and Rosalee for all you've done."

Blake waved off her gratitude, his expression earnest. "You don't need to repay us, Priscilla. Just focus on building a life you're proud of. That's all the thanks we need."

As the sun dipped below the horizon, casting a golden glow over the mansion and its grounds, Priscilla felt a deep sense of contentment. She was still adjusting to this new chapter of her life, but with the support of Blake and Rosealee, she felt ready to face whatever challenges lay ahead.

The journey to Nashville had been a turning point, a chance to leave behind the shadows of her past and embrace a future filled with promise. And though she missed Belle and the girls, she knew they would always hold a special place in her heart.

Priscilla was determined to seize this opportunity, to learn, grow, and become the person she was meant to be. With the guidance of her new friends and the strength she had found within herself, she felt ready to take on the world. Looking out over the vast landscape of her new home, she knew this was just the beginning of her journey—a journey that would lead her to places she had never dreamed possible.

Blue Moon

Four years later.

Four years had passed since Priscilla arrived in this bustling city, and the once shy girl had blossomed into a confident young woman. She was thriving and living her best life, surrounded by friends at Harpeth Hall, a prestigious college preparatory school on the tranquil Harpeth River.

But now, a new passion had taken hold of Priscilla's heart - Blue Moon, her beloved Tennessee Walking Horse. Under the tutelage of Blake, who had expanded his horse farm, Priscilla had become an accomplished horse-woman. She had excellent trainers and spent countless hours practicing jumps and routines with Blue Moon, their bond unbreakable.

Their performances were the talk of the town, as Priscilla's eccentric equestrian riding habits captured everyone's attention. But behind it all was Rosalee - Priscilla's trusted mentor, who had meticulously crafted her riding habit to perfection.

The day before Priscilla's first equestrian competition, Rosalee pulled her aside. With a mischievous glint in her eyes, she held up a pair of crisp white jodhpur trousers and a vibrant red riding jacket. "Horseracing is a man's sport, and if you want to stand out, you're going to have to look the part," she said firmly.

Priscilla's mouth fell open in surprise. "You want me to dress like a boy?"

"Exactly," Rosalee replied, nodding confidently. "And we have a male name picked out for you. From now on you are Jesse and Blue Moon."

Priscilla ran her fingers through her long, auburn hair, a question in her eyes. "What about my hair?"

Rosalee reached into her bag and produced a sleek riding cap. "We'll tuck it under the cap. You'll look just like a boy."

With this new image and persona, Priscilla's performance in competitions soared. The excitement of defying gender norms in the traditional world of horse competitions heightened the adrenaline rush. She finally felt like an equal. And she proved herself not only with Blue Moon but also with other thoroughbreds purchased by Blake. Her winnings skyrocketed, a testament to her skill and determination on the track.

Rosalee, Blake, and Mrs. Ashton were always there, their voices ringing out in joyful cheers and their faces beaming with pride, celebrating Priscilla's every win for days. The winds of change were blowing strong, bringing a newfound sense of freedom and equality for women. As society shifted towards more masculine fashion trends, Priscilla boldly led the way in her jodhpur trousers.

Winning gave Priscilla a new sense of liberation, but she was humble, never losing sight that she had once been a kitchen maid. Every time she won; she considered it nothing short of miraculous and would kiss the bible when she got home. The Bible was a gift from Mrs. Ashton. She had become Priscilla's biggest fan, always there alongside Rosalee and Blake for every competition. Mrs. Ashton compiled a scrapbook with newspaper clippings detailing Priscilla's success. Jesse and Blue Moon from Nashville were in all the newspapers. They had become famous—crowd pleasers—though her apparel often raised eyebrows in the polite equestrian society.

Priscilla was on a winning streak when she asked, "How much money do I have, Blake? Do I have enough to help Belle and the girls? And maybe buy my old house in Maury County?"

Blake's smile was wide and proud as he exclaimed, "You have more than enough!" His eyes sparkled with excitement as he continued, "I've invested every penny, and it's been growing steadily."

Rosalee's expression turned uneasy as she interjected, "It isn't safe to go back there." She gently touched Priscilla's hand; her voice filled with concern. "I know you've recently graduated from high school and are eager to spread your wings, but you have a multitude of scholarships waiting for you. I assumed you would stay in Nashville for college. Perhaps even attend Vanderbilt."

Priscilla bit her lip nervously. "I would hate myself if I didn't help Belle and her girls. Especially now that I have the means to do so. It just feels like the right thing to do."

Rosalee nodded in understanding before turning her gaze to Blake. "Perhaps it is time that you tell her about the murder."

"Murder?" Priscilla gasped in shock. "What has happened?"

Blake let out a sigh and ran a hand through his hair. "Lee Dodd's stepfather, James Marion Fautt, is dead." He hesitated before adding, "And I'm currently serving as the defense attorney for the accused: the Wallace brothers."

Priscilla's eyes widened in surprise and fear. "James Marion is dead? And you're defending the men who killed him? The Thomasons have been in a feud with the Wallace brothers for years."

"Yes, he's dead," Blake confirmed with a heavy heart. "It's become the biggest murder trial in Columbia. Unfortunately, Jim Fautt's death may not be the last casualty if the Thomason brothers seek vengeance." He paused before asking, "Do you know anything about this?"

Priscilla's heart was heavy with guilt as she sat across from Blake in the dimly lit room. She knew she had to speak the truth, even though it would betray her own family.

"The Thomasons are your cousins, aren't they?" Blake asked, leaning forward intently. "You must know that they've hurt many people with their long-standing feuds passed down from generation to generation. And Jim Fautt became a victim when he married Jerome's daughter, Winnie."

Feeling like a traitor, Priscilla took a deep breath and said, "Uncle Jerome was good to me and my family. He was generous when times were hard, and we needed a new roof. He paid for it. So, I can't talk bad about him."

"Isn't it true that Jerome's wealth came from being a bootlegger?" he asked with raised brows, sounding like an interrogator.

"Sure, many people make their living that way. The stills are all over Maury County. It was the family business. All of my cousins worked the stills, and Lee was the runner." Her voice faltered. "Lee was not Jerome's child; he was his grandchild, but Jerome raised him like a son. He was illegitimate, born from an affair between Jerome's daughter, Winnie, and a married neighbor named Dodd." She wrapped her arms around herself and rubbed them as if she were cold. "Jerome was a good man. He raised Lee like his own son and did many good deeds, such as bringing the homeless back to his property and providing them with jobs and food. That's how he came across Toby, his black farm worker. Toby loves Jerome and would do anything for him."

Blake closed his eyes and rubbed his temple. "What you are telling me is conflicting, Priscilla. I was told the Thomasons are bad people. Some say they're the meanest, most ruthless people in Maury County, Tennessee."

Priscilla swallowed hard. "Well, maybe Big Bill is, but not the rest. They all hang together—you know, all the brothers, so if one does something wrong, the others get blamed, too. Mama says the kids teased Big Bill when he was a child, and that's why he grew up mean." Priscilla sighed. "He was different—bigger than his peers. He's 6'8" and as strong as a horse."

"What about the killings?" Blake asked. "They say he killed six men."

"That's what happens when you're in a duel and you're the fastest draw in Maury County," Priscilla said, defending Big Bill's violent tendencies.

"Why isn't he in jail?" Blake asked.

"Mama says the law fears him. She says there's not a jail that can hold him; he can bend the bars."

Blake scribbled notes furiously on a sheet of white paper as Priscilla spoke. These stories would influence the jury in the upcoming trial for Jim Fautt's murder. But could they ignore the sixteen bullet holes found in his lifeless body?

Finally, Rosalee intervened. "That's enough for tonight, Blake," she said in a gentle but firm tone. "Priscilla needs her rest." Turning to Priscilla, she added, "Tomorrow, we'll do something fun. We can go to the movies, or I can buy you a new dress."

A small smile tugged at Priscilla's lips. "Thank you, Rosalee," she replied gratefully, though she knew she had more important matters to focus on. "But I have enough dresses. It's time for me to take responsibility and make things right."

"What do you want to do, Priscilla?" Rosalee asked, her eyes filled with concern.

"I told you. Helping Belle and the girls is important. It's time I went back to Maury County."

Going Home

Priscilla scrutinized her new appearance and neatly tucked an unruly strand of hair beneath her cap. The mirror showed a young boy, slender and fair, who seemed strangely familiar, concealing the girl she once was. Standing behind her, Rosalee wore an approving expression.

"Are you ready to go, Jesse?" Rosalee asked, using the designated name for Priscilla's disguise.

Priscilla nodded, her heart pounding in her chest.

Driving to Maury County was a nerve-wracking experience, as each bump and turn on the road stirred up memories of the past she had moved on from. In her vest pocket, she had an envelope that bulged with money, meant for Belle's girls to start anew.

Now, standing on the threshold of Belle's saloon, she felt a mix of nostalgia and trepidation. They slipped in through the back door, the one Priscilla had used countless times during her days in the kitchen. The familiar scent of simmering stew and stale beer hit her like a wave, bringing back a flood of memories. Glancing around, the bustling activity of the kitchen stirred a sense of comfort and unease in equal measure.

Rosalee gently nudged her. "Go on, they'll be glad to see you."

Priscilla bravely took a deep breath and moved forward; her light footsteps were barely audible on the worn wooden floor. She moved through the kitchen, unnoticed by the cooks and helpers engrossed in their work. As she reached the door that led to the saloon, she paused, peering through the crack. The saloon was just as lively as she remembered.

Though older and worn, the girls laughed and chatted with patrons. The years had added lines to their faces, a certain heaviness to their eyes, but their spirits remained unbroken. It was bittersweet, and Priscilla's heart ached—seeing them like this, knowing their hardships and all they had endured.

Priscilla hesitated to enter the saloon, knowing her disguise would draw attention to her. When a kitchen maid walked by with a tray of sandwiches, Priscilla said, "Please tell Belle her niece is here to see her."

Belle quickly made her way to the kitchen. "Priscilla?" she whispered, her voice trembling. "You're in disguise, but I would know you anywhere." She threw her arms around her.

One girl had overheard the kitchen maid, and the girls rushed through the door, enveloping Priscilla in a tight embrace. "We've been reading about you in the newspapers," Lucy said, wiping her tears with the back of her hand. "You're all grown up now, and a famous horsewoman." She bit her lip. "I'm proud to know you, Priscilla. You did it—you lived for all of us—just like I knew you would."

Priscilla's face lit up with a smile. "And you can do it, too. I've earned money from horse competitions, and I'm here to offer you an opportunity for a fresh start. You can do anything if you try. Someone helped me, and I'm going to help you." All traces of hope left her face at Lucy's unexpected reply.

"We would never leave Belle," Lucy said. "This is our family. And the guys in the saloon are like family, too." She raised her brows. "I've got my favorites."

Priscilla nodded, understanding their loyalty. "But you could start another business, all of you, Belle included, and still be together. Women can vote now. We can do anything a man can do."

Rosalee stepped forward. "Come on, don't you understand? Priscilla is offering you the chance of a lifetime. We'll help you get started—all you have to do is begin."

Belle stepped forward, placing a gentle hand on Priscilla's shoulder. "We appreciate it, dear, but the saloon is our life." She heaved a sigh. "When I was young, a man blindsided me—I let him use me. He left me penniless and destitute on the streets. I was sleeping in doorways, hungry and cold, when a wealthy woman found me and took me home to her big house. She had no family and treated me like her daughter. When she died, she left me everything, and I still live in her big house. I opened the saloon to help other girls." She strode over, hugging her girls to her. "All of my girls have a sad story. Men have left us with broken hearts, stranded, hungry, and with nothing. Some had to crawl back to feeling human again, but they made it."

"We'd never leave Belle," Lucy said.

"But the men are using you," Priscilla protested. "They're robbing you of your self-esteem."

Belle's eyes gleamed. "No. Can't you see? We are using them. My bank account is growing while theirs has dwindled. I'm very generous with my girls. It's like a sisterhood—we take care of each other."

"I understand," Priscilla said, her eyes glistening. She exchanged a look with Rosalee—it was time to leave. After a group hug, they slipped out the back door.

They sat for a while in the alley in the shiny Model T Ford as they digested everything that had transpired inside the saloon. Finally, the river of tears broke loose. "They're like broken china dolls," Priscilla said. "And they don't know it."

Rosalee patted her on the back. "Even broken china dolls are beautiful."

Tears streamed down Priscilla's cheeks. "They can't be fixed... can they?"

"It would take a miracle to restore all the damage that's been done to their bodies and minds. And you can't do it for them, Priscilla. They have to do it themselves." Suddenly, Rosalee began brushing her clothes, the look on her face filled with distaste. "Do you think we'll ever get the smell of smoke and stale beer off our clothes? Promise me you will never go back there again." She jerked her head and started the motor.

"Belle and the girls are my friends," Priscilla snapped. "Of course, I would go back."

"Let it go," Rosalee said in a firm voice. "You can't help them." She looked perturbed as she drove, rattling on about how a benefactor had saved Priscilla from life in a speakeasy, and she should be grateful. She had ended with,

"That part of your life is over."

But Priscilla wasn't so sure. Belle had saved her, went out on a limb, and staged her death. She'd lied to the sheriff and risked everything for her. As far as Priscilla was concerned, Belle Barker was a genuine, forever friend.

Rosalee broke the silence, exclaiming, "I'm starving. Where can we get something to eat in this one-horse town?"

"You've just left the best place in town to eat. People would come for miles around for Jake's chili and biscuits."

"I do not eat where there are cockroaches," Rosalee sniffed. "I'm sure I saw one crawling on the floor."

Rosalee was ecstatic when she saw a Five & Dime on the street corner. "We have to eat there. Five & Dimes are the "Bee's Knees." Rosalee loved food, and her attitude had improved. It seemed she had put their disagreement behind them as she perched on a stool at the lunch counter, savoring a plate of creamed chicken on toast and a cup of coffee for just fifteen cents.

The diner waitresses 'burned and turned' as the orders rose rapidly. Their coffee-stained aprons were a sign of their hard work. Priscilla eyed their tip jar full of shiny nickels, a pittance to Belle's girls, whose bosoms bulged with five bills. The waitresses had to hustle and barely noticed Priscilla, who kept her head down as she enjoyed a hamburger, fries, and a chocolate soda.

"Slavery," Rosalee whispered as they exited. "I swear, I would work in a speakeasy before I would be a waitress."

"You would do such a thing?" Priscilla gasped, thinking she sounded like a hypocrite.

"Both are jobs women take when life goes wrong — it is pure desperation — a life of misery and drudgery. Consider yourself fortunate that you have a benefactor. I thank my lucky stars that I'm married to Blake."

Priscilla thought it would be best not to answer. She was making good money in horse competitions and had thousands in her vest pocket, which she had earned. Rosalee was not a wage earner but worked hard for women's rights. Priscilla felt fortunate to afford a hearty meal, remembering what hunger felt like. Her eyes were alert for girls in doorways, still feeling the need to help unfortunate girls.

As Rosalee drove through the familiar streets, Priscilla's memories flooded back. The laughter, the sorrow, the dreams of a young girl who had once lived there. Once they were out of town, the wind in her hair felt freeing. The trees were a blur as Rosalee sped down the country road. Her face lit up as they approached the lane of the big brick house.

Her first thought was of the fiddler. "Daddy, I've come home," she whispered.

The Letters

The big brick house stood at the end of the lane, looking unoccupied and forlorn. Weeds had overtaken the garden, and the paint on the shutters was peeling. Priscilla felt a lump in her throat as she approached the front porch. She bent down and found the key under a flowerpot, just as it was four years ago.

Pushing open the door, a wave of nostalgia hit her. Everything was just as it had been when she left. Dust-covered furniture, framed family photos, and the faint scent of her mother's lavender perfume. She wandered through the rooms, each a time capsule of her past.

Entering her father's old bedroom, she paused. The room was untouched, his fiddle resting against the wall. She could almost hear him playing, the soft, mournful tunes filling the air. A tear slipped down her cheek as she knelt by the bed, lifting the loose floorboard where her mother used to hide valuables.

Her fingers brushed against the stack of letters hidden beneath. She pulled them out, her hands trembling as she opened the first one. They were from her sister, over a hundred letters covering two years. Priscilla's eyes widened in shock as she read, realizing her sister had been sending money for her to go to New York, money her mother had never given her. The envelopes were empty.

Betrayal and sorrow washed over her. She clutched the letters to her chest, feeling a deep sadness for the years lost and dreams unfulfilled.

Rosalee found her sitting on the floor with the letters scattered around her. She kneeled beside Priscilla, wrapping an arm around her shoulders.

"My mother kept Amanda's letters from me," Priscilla whispered. "All this time, my sister tried to help, and she never let me know."

Rosalee's eyes softened with understanding. "I'm so sorry, Priscilla. But you have the letters now, and you know she cared."

Priscilla nodded, wiping her tears. "I have to find her, Rosalee, and I have to know why my mother did this."

"We will," Rosalee promised. "But first, let's get some fresh air. Maybe a walk through the marshes will clear your mind."

The two of them made their way to the marshes, a place Priscilla had dearly missed. The air was thick with the scent of damp earth and wildflowers. Birds flitted about, their songs a sweet symphony that brought a sense of peace.

Priscilla took a deep breath, feeling the tension ease from her shoulders. "I've missed this place so much. It feels good to be home."

They walked along the edge of the water, watching the various birds skimming the surface. Priscilla's heart swelled with emotion, a mix of joy and sorrow as memories of her childhood flooded back.

"Look over there," Rosalee pointed to a Great Blue Heron spreading its wings and taking flight. "It's beautiful, isn't it?"

Priscilla smiled, nodding. "It is."

As they continued their walk, Priscilla noticed a movement in the trees. Her gaze sharpened, and she squinted, trying to make out the figure hidden in the shadows. Her heart skipped a beat when she realized a man was watching them intently.

"Rosalee," she whispered, her voice tight with fear. "There's someone there."

Rosalee followed her gaze, her eyes widening in alarm. "We need to go, now."

They turned and fled, their footsteps quick and light on the marshy ground. Priscilla's heart pounded in her chest, fear gripping her as they ran. The dark figure remained in her peripheral vision, a menacing presence that urged them to move faster.

They didn't stop until they were back at the house, breathless and shaken.

Priscilla leaned against the door, her mind racing. The peaceful marshes now seemed tainted with danger.

"Who do you think it was?" Rosalee asked, her voice trembling.

Priscilla shook her head. "I don't know, but we can't stay here. It's not safe."

Rosalee nodded, her face pale. "Gather your things and lock up the house. We must leave immediately."

The letters were of primary importance to Priscilla. She quickly gathered them together and stuffed them in a paper bag she found in the pantry, then carefully placed the floorboards back in place. Locking up the house, she returned the key under the flowerpot exactly as she had found it. Then they dashed to the car.

Priscilla's mind churned on the way back to Nashville with thoughts of the day. The joy of seeing her old friends, the heartbreak of her sister's letters, and the terror of the man in the marshes. The day had enlightened her, and now she was even more grateful for the haven that Rosalee and Blake provided. She was determined to find her sister and uncover the truth.

"Rosalee," she said in a soft voice. "I'm understanding what you said. Money is important in life. And a woman must have a safe place to live." She glanced at Rosalee. The moon cast a light on her beautiful face.

"Yes, a woman must have all those things to be happy," she said.

"I just want you to know that I feel safe with you and Blake. I thought I was ready to return home, but now I know I'm not. Thank you for teaching me about life, so I don't make so many mistakes."

"I can't teach you everything," Rosalee said. "You will make mistakes just like we all do. It's part of life, dear, but I want to be there for you during the good and the bad."

"Oh, Rosalee, I learned so much about myself today. And I thank God that you were there." She shook her head. "Here I am, back again, with the money I had set aside to give to Belle's girls. What do you think I should do with it?"

"Investing in yourself is always a good idea. Besides, I think there's a party coming up, and you'll need a new dress. We'll go shopping."

"A party!" Priscilla said excitedly. "I cannot wait!"

That night, she lay in bed, processing the day. With Rosalee by her side, she knew she could face whatever lay ahead. Together, they would unravel the mysteries of the past and forge a new path forward, one step at a time.

The Debutante Dance

The ballroom at the Nashville Country Club exuded Southern grandeur. Crystal chandeliers cast shimmering light on the marble floors, and the scent of magnolias, roses, and lilies filled the air. It was a lavish celebration—the debutante ball—marking Priscilla's official entry into society.

As Priscilla entered, the room fell silent, and all eyes turned to her as she descended the staircase. Her gown was a masterpiece of Southern elegance, composed of layers of ivory silk and tulle; it shimmered softly in the candlelight. The bodice, adorned with intricate beadwork and tiny pearls, accentuated her slender figure. The skirt flowed to the floor in gentle waves, a cascade of fabric that seemed to move with a life of its own. A hairdresser had arranged her hair in an elaborate chignon, with a few loose tendrils framing her face.

Earlier that day, Priscilla had stood before the gilded mirror in her room while Rosalee fastened the diamond necklace and earrings around her neck. "You will be the prettiest debutante there," Rosalee said, her eyes misting with pride. "The diamonds are a gift from your benefactor."

Priscilla gazed at the glittering jewels and drew in a sharp breath. "He is too generous," she said, while staring at the girl in the mirror. She had transformed from an awkward country girl to an accomplished, independent horsewoman, and didn't know how she could ever repay him.

Blake stood at the bottom of the grand staircase, his face beaming with pride. "Ladies and gentlemen," he announced, "may I present my niece, Miss Priscilla Powell?"

As the applause erupted, Priscilla's heart swelled with gratitude and joy, and she smiled. She made her way through the crowd, exchanging pleasantries and accepting compliments. The evening became a blur of faces and conversations, each guest eager to speak with her and offer their best wishes.

Priscilla felt a sense of déjà vu as she danced with countless suitors. The way men looked at her made her feel worthy. She felt like she had been preparing for this night her entire life. During a lull in the festivities, she felt a familiar presence beside her.

"May I have this dance?" a deep, familiar voice asked.

As Priscilla turned, she felt her breath catch in her throat. Clint, the man she had danced with at Belle's saloon, stood before her. Yet, he was hardly recognizable. The rough edges and casual attire were gone, replaced by a sleek black tuxedo that complemented his tall, athletic figure. And his piercing blue eyes hinted at mischief.

"Clint?" she whispered, hardly believing her eyes.

He smiled, a slow, charming grin that made her heart flutter. "It's good to see you again, Priscilla."

She accepted his outstretched hand, and he led her onto the dance floor. As they glided across the floor, Priscilla felt a sense of magic. The way he moved, the way he looked at her, was as if no time had passed since their first dance.

"I can't believe it's you," she said, her voice barely above a whisper. "You look so different."

"So do you," he replied, his eyes twinkling with admiration. "You're even more beautiful than I remembered."

Priscilla blushed, her heart racing. "I didn't think I'd ever see you again."

Clint's expression grew serious. "From the moment we met at the saloon, you have been constantly on my mind, every single day." He hesitated, then took a deep breath. "I'm the one who arranged for you to come to Nashville. I'm your benefactor, Priscilla."

Her eyes widened in shock. "But you didn't know me—we'd talked briefly," she said, her voice filled with bewilderment.

"It was long enough for me to see the strength and determination in you," he whispered. "I wanted to get you out of there and allow you to do something with your life."

"But I lied to you that night," she said. "I made up a story about how I wanted my life to be."

"And I wanted to make those lies come true," Clint said.

Speechless, tears filled Priscilla's eyes, and she blinked them away. Finally, she said, "I can never repay you for all you've done for me."

"No repayment is expected," Clint replied, his voice gentle. "Seeing the woman you've become is enough."

They continued to dance, the world around them fading into the background. Priscilla felt a sense of peace and belonging. She had come so far from the scared, uncertain girl who had fled from a life she didn't want. And now she was ready to embrace whatever the future held.

The dance ended, and Clint led her to a secluded corner of the ballroom. They sat down, and he took her hand in his, his touch warm and reassuring. "Tell me about your life, Priscilla. I want to know everything."

And so, under the soft glow of the chandeliers, Priscilla told him her story. She spoke of her time at Harpeth Hall, her adventures with Blue Moon, and her dreams of reclaiming her childhood home. Clint listened intently, his eyes never leaving her face.

When she finished, he squeezed her hand. "You've accomplished so much, Priscilla. I'm proud of you."

"Thank you," she said, her voice choked with emotion. "I couldn't have done it without you."

Clint smiled. "And I couldn't be happier to have been a part of your journey."

The rest of the evening flew by in a whirlwind of laughter, dancing, and celebration, as if she were living in a dream, surrounded by friends and loved ones. As the night drew to a close, they stood on the veranda, looking out over the moonlit gardens, with Clint a comforting presence at her side.

They brought the party back to the mansion and sat outside on the patio. Priscilla clung to Clint's arm, watching the star-studded sky, wishing the night would never end. It seemed a new chapter in her life was beginning, filled with promise and possibilities. But she couldn't have been more mistaken.

"You're all grown up now," Blake said, his tone serious. "And it's a bittersweet night for me because I have to be the bearer of bad news. Clint is here for more than one reason."

Priscilla looked confused. "I don't understand."

"Your pictures have been in newspapers lately, and the sheriff has figured it out. The Thomason brothers suspect you're alive. And they're causing a lot of trouble."

Priscilla tensed. "So, what's going to happen?"

"We have to go back and settle up with the sheriff," Blake said. "You need to tell your story that you ran away because you were afraid of Lee; he's dangerous, a gunslinger, and he'd beat his first wife."

"And then I'm going to pay the sheriff off to keep it quiet," Clint said. "He'll say it was a case of mistaken identity. It so happens there's more than one Priscilla Powell in Nashville."

"I'm not sure—they say the sheriff is in cahoots with the Thomasons," she said, her face pale. "And the Thomasons don't let things go. They hold grudges. The town couldn't save me before, and I don't think they can save me now. Lee and his brothers have every reason in the world to kill me."

Clint took her hand. "I'll be with you all the way. He won't touch you."

Priscilla's gaze was dubious. "I don't think you understand how dangerous the Thomason brothers are."

Clint's eyes turned steely. "I said I would take care of you, and I will. I have a gunslinger, Priscilla." He took her in his arms and held her tight.

Her heart thundered as she felt his warm breath next to her ear.

"We can do this, Priscilla," he said. "You're not alone."

Priscilla let out a sigh. She wanted to believe him, but deep down, she knew no one could protect her from the Thomasons wrath. She had crossed their boundaries, and they would hunt her down and maybe even kill her.

The Ambush

In a lighthearted mood, Rosalee, Blake, Priscilla, and Clint embraced the beautiful sunny summer day and drove to Maury County. Clint and Priscilla exchanged glances and subtle touches, their budding romance growing with each passing mile. The impending meeting with the sheriff held no weight on their disposition, as they felt invincible with Nashville's most renowned lawyer, Blake, by their side. And they had no worries about money either — Clint was a millionaire, his bulging wallet overflowing with cash that could easily bribe the sheriff if needed.

But just in case things took a turn for the worse and Lee and his brothers showed up to interfere, a hired gunslinger was waiting in town, prepared to protect them at all costs. Despite potential dangers, the group remained blissfully unaware as they continued their journey through the picturesque countryside.

As they rounded a bend, their carefully orchestrated plans came to an abrupt halt. Blake slammed on the brakes, causing the car to screech and skid to a stop as a herd of sheep slowly crossed the road. Oblivious to the danger, they fixated their eyes on the sheep and the herdsman, who guided them with a long stick. The air was filled with the gentle sounds of baaing and bleating, which seemed to amuse the group until Priscilla's memory was triggered. She recalled hearing stories about how the infamous Thomason brothers would use farm animals to block roads and lure unsuspecting travelers into their ambushes.

"Turn the car around," Priscilla shouted, her heart pounding. "It's an ambush!"

But it was too late. The screeching of tires and the sound of gunfire filled her ears as a tall, masked figure flung open the car door and dragged her out with brute force. She locked eyes with Lee Dodd, his dark gaze burning into her soul even through the black bandana covering his face. With terror coursing through her veins, Priscilla kicked and screamed as he carried her effortlessly to their waiting vehicle. Lee's menacing brothers held the others at gunpoint. Frozen in shock, they realized they had fallen right into an ambush. In minutes, this lightning-fast attack had turned their lives upside down.

Lee's hand tightened like a vise around her neck, causing sharp pain to radiate through her body. She winced and fought against his hold, but he was too strong. His face was inches away from hers, and the stench of his whiskey-laden breath made her stomach turn.

"Seen your picture in the paper with all those high-fluting people," he sneered. "I guess you figure you're better than us now."

Priscilla grimaced from both his grip and his words. "I don't think any such thing," she retorted. Her voice trembled slightly as she spoke, but she refused to let him see her fear. "Let me out of this car right now. All I've ever wanted is my freedom, and folks in this town are determined to make that impossible for me. I won't be a man's slave or let him control or belittle me."

A sly, almost smug grin played across Lee's face as he released his grip on her. Priscilla tried to maintain her composure, but she could feel her cheeks flushing with anger and embarrassment.

"There's no need to pitch a hissy fit, Priscilla," Lee taunted. "You've always been as stubborn as a mule. I think it's time you had a little manhandling." He tunneled his fingers through her hair and pulled hard.

She instinctively recoiled, feeling his hot breath against her neck. She looked down her nose at him, trying to maintain some sense of dignity despite the pain. It was stinging — the humiliation and degradation, but that's what mountain men did to women to control them and get their way. She'd heard her married sisters complain to her mother about their husbands; the worst thing was, her mother did nothing about it. She had no words to offer. Nothing.

A wry smile tugged at the corners of Lee's lips as he drawled in an exaggerated Southern accent. "Priscilla says she wants her freedom, boys. Should we let her go?"

Big Bill, a towering figure with broad shoulders and a rugged face, was in a foul mood. "Can't do it," he guffawed, his voice dripping with sarcasm. "The fun is just beginning." Despite his choirboy-like looks, his reputation as being the 'meanest man' in Tennessee preceded him. He turned and flung his long, giant arm across the seat, smacking Lee across the head. "Cut the horseshit. We've got her. What do you want to do with her?"

Lee's expression hardened, his dark eyes flashing with mild agitation. "She's mine," he stated firmly. "I'll do whatever I damn well please with her."

Priscilla's eyes widened in shock, and her body trembled with anger. How dare he try to claim ownership of her! She was not a mere object to be bought and sold. Her fury boiled inside her, threatening to burst like a raging wildfire.

But Lee's face remained stoic, his features hardening into a steely mask. His voice dripped with malice as he retorted, "Because I bought and paid for you four years ago, that's why." The words cut through the air like a sharp knife, causing Priscilla's heart to race and her mind to spin.

She realized then that she was merely a pawn in this twisted game. Lee had helped pay for her father's medications, and now he wanted repayment like her. Panic coursed through her veins as she remembered the rumors she had heard about Lee and the Thomason family's notorious tempers and violent tendencies. She knew she had to tread carefully to survive this encounter. She was facing one of the most dangerous men in Tennessee - a ruthless gunslinger who made his own rules.

The tension between them grew thicker, like a dense fog creeping in and enveloping them. Finally, the getaway driver, Gillie, spoke up, his voice hesitant and tinged with fear. "Can't we just let her go? She did nothing except run away because she didn't want to marry you, Lee." His hands trembled on the steering wheel as he spoke, and his eyes darted nervously between his older brothers. "Besides, she's kin. Pa always taught us to take care of our kin." Gillie was the youngest of the brothers, smaller in stature than the others, with curly red hair that set him apart. Whenever there was a fight, he would cower and run, earning him the nickname "Coward" from his eldest brother, Bill.

Priscilla was relieved to hear a friendly voice, but she knew he caused just as much trouble as the rest of the Thomason brothers. She dared speak, though she feared retribution. "Everything you said is true, Gilly. We're kin, and your mother will not take kindly to kidnapping me."

"Shut up," Lee growled. "This ain't no Sunday school picnic." He grabbed her; his dark eyes glittered as he examined every inch of her. He ran his hand across her breasts. "You're all grown up now—ripe for the pickin', and I aim to get my money's worth."

"Get your hands off me," Priscilla shrieked. A blood-curdling scream echoed through the valley as she struggled, fighting for her dignity, self-respect, and self-worth. A surge of adrenaline shot through her, turning her into something wild and untamed. Her teeth became her weapon, and she bit into his hand—sinking her teeth into his flesh and drawing blood. Then she spat in his face.

Lee backhanded her and wiped off his face with the bandana. A villainous smile showed gleaming, straight white teeth. "Looks like I have a wildcat on my hands." He cupped her face, taunting her. "I love a woman with a lot of fight in her." He grabbed her by the hair, but this time she didn't scream. She sat motionless, refusing to give him what he wanted—a fight.

Big Bill intervened, reaching over the seat and smacking Lee alongside the head. "Leave her alone," he commanded. "This wasn't part of the deal. You said you wanted to scare her, and then we'd let her go."

"Don't tell me what to do with my woman," Lee snapped, his dark, handsome face red with anger. Kidnapping Priscilla had seemed fair to Lee. He'd fought for everything he had. Fighting was part of his life, and Lee didn't enjoy losing. But now he was fighting both a bruised ego and passion for a girl he'd loved and lost.

Priscilla held her hand to her face, feeling the burn of his slap, but his words had been scalding. "I'll pay you back every cent," she said as she cradled her arms. She couldn't envision a way out, and no longer had the strength to fight. At that moment, she hated Lee, but she hated her mother more for arranging the marriage, taking his money, and using her as a pawn. Her intense, hot hate for both gave her the strength to keep going.

"I don't want your money," he snarled, his voice dripping with disdain. "I've got plenty of that. What I want is the old Priscilla." The words rolled off his tongue like a promise, laced with determination and desire. Nothing would come between him and his pursuit of her, no matter how she had changed over the years.

Escape was on her mind. The vast, mountainous terrain spread before her, a sea of verdant green stretching as far as the eye could see. She was lost in the rolling hills of Maury County, surrounded by nature's beauty but unable to appreciate it. Her heart raced as she tried to remember where she was and how she had ended up here.

She couldn't believe she had been so naïve, believing Clint's promises of a simple escape from Lee and his brothers by a visit to the sheriff. The reality was far more terrifying—the sheriff was in cahoots with Lee and the Thomason brothers, and she felt like a fool for trusting Clint. He'd promised to protect her. The betrayal stung deeper than any physical wound ever could.

Her mind was racing with thoughts and fears, but one idea stood out above all others - jumping off the mountain. She remembered Amanda's words about Big Bill's girlfriend taking this drastic measure to escape. She looked at the car door handle, feeling an overwhelming urge to hurl herself out of the vehicle and over the next cliff they passed.

But even in her desperate state, she couldn't do it. She closed her eyes and took a deep breath, trying to calm her racing heart and find a way out of this nightmare.

Falling

A sigh escaped Priscilla when she saw the Duck River winding through the countryside like a sinuous ribbon of life. The familiarity gave her hope that she might escape and find her way home by using the river to guide her. The sun was setting, casting a golden hue over the rugged terrain, and she found that in her favor. Even in the dark, she knew the river. The pain radiating from her blackened eye was a cruel reminder of her desperate situation. The verbal abuse he hurled at her stung nearly as much as the physical blows.

When the car came to an abrupt stop, Lee jerked her out of the car. She stumbled, then regained her footing and stood on the edge of Sandy Hook Bridge, peering down at the river. A dense forest of green surrounded them in a rugged and rocky terrain. The descent was treacherous, and no one who leaped survived. Death occurred instantly. It was disturbing that they had brought her to the very place where Big Bill's girlfriend had ended her life. It confirmed Big Bill's heartlessness.

Lee's 6'2" stature made her feel tiny and vulnerable. Afraid, she moved closer to the edge.

"You think you can just run away and leave your debts unpaid?" Lee snarled, his voice dripping with venom. "Your mother arranged this marriage, and you owe me, Priscilla. Your father's debts, your escape to Nashville—all of it costs money, money I provided." He kicked dirt at her with his boot. "You've caused me a lot of trouble."

The altercation grew more heated. In the ensuing struggle, Lee pushed her with a force greater than intended. She stumbled backward, her foot slipping on the loose gravel of Sandy Hook Bridge. With a gasp, she tumbled over the edge; her scream echoing through the hills.

Fate intervened as her dress caught on a thorny bush protruding from the cliff, breaking her fall. She dangled on a narrow ledge; the river raging below. Heart pounding, she clung to the bush, the rough branches digging into her skin. The ledge was barely wide enough to support her, and as she tried to steady herself, she felt a wave of despair.

In that moment of desperation, Priscilla thought she heard the soft strains of a fiddle. The melody was hauntingly familiar, bringing tears to her eyes. It was her father's song, the one he used to play on warm summer nights. She closed her eyes, allowing the music to wash over her, and for a moment, she wished for death, to join her father and escape the torment of her life.

Fate had other plans. From above, a deep, gruff voice broke through her reverie. "Hang on, missy. I'll get you out of there."

Priscilla gazed upwards and saw Big Bill, an enormous man, peering at her. He was a fearsome sight, notorious for his past crimes. At 6'8", his presence was imposing, but his eyes showed a flicker of concern.

His arm, long and powerful, reached down toward her. "Grab my hand," he commanded.

With trembling fingers, Priscilla reached up, her fear of the man momentarily overshadowed by her need for survival. Their hands met, and with a strength that seemed almost effortless, Big Bill pulled her to safety. She collapsed onto the ground, gasping for breath, her body shaking with relief and exhaustion.

Big Bill looked at her with a mixture of curiosity and pity. "You're lucky. This ridge has claimed many lives."

At that moment, she was so thankful to be alive that she could not pass judgment on him and his evil deeds. She could not say that he was a monster and that he had caused the death of a young girl right here, where she was hanging onto a thread of life. Her voice hoarse, she whispered, "Thank you for saving me."

Without another word, Big Bill helped her to her feet and led her to the car. The journey back to town was a blur for Priscilla. She closed her eyes and, despite the horrendous pain, tried to imagine herself in the marsh's safety while blocking out Lee's voice.

"I didn't push you, Priscilla. You fell, and I'm sorry. I love you and would never hurt you," he said, appearing sober and humbled. Empty words from a man with a mind twisted from moonshine who had let his obsession with her become a ruling force in his life.

"Shut up, Lee. You sound like a sick calf," Big Bill growled. "She'll never forgive you after what you did to her. Jesus, I wish I'd never agreed to this. My God, she's our kin, and once Mama gets wind of this, she's going to kill us all."

"That's right," Gillie said. "And remember, Priscilla, I had nothing to do with it. They made me drive, but I never wanted to do it. I'm sorry you're hurt."

Big Bill skewed his face. "You sniveling little son of a bitch, you were in it just as much as Lee and me. Why do you always try to weasel out of everything?"

"Because I don't want to get beat," Gillie spat.

Priscilla remained stone-like and silent, ignoring him, her mind reeling. No number of apologies could undo the harm they had caused her. When they finally came to a screeching stop across from the drugstore, her eyes glistened at the sight of the small, familiar town. Thankful to be alive, she whispered, "Thank you, Jesus."

They let her out of the car and roared away. Priscilla stumbled towards the sheriff's office, her appearance drawing gasps from the townsfolk. They froze at the sight of her hair matted with blood, her dress torn and stained, and her face streaked with dirt, bearing the marks of her ordeal.

The sheriff looked up from his desk as she entered, his expression turning to shock. "My God. What has happened to you? Was it a cougar?"

"Worse," she said, crumbling to the floor. "It was Lee Dodd and the Thomason brothers. I'm Priscilla Powell." A deputy picked her up and laid her on a cot in a jail cell. Then went to fetch the doctor. She recounted her tale, her voice trembling with emotion.

The sheriff listened, his expression growing grimmer with each word. When she finished, he let out a sigh. "My deputies tried to track down

Lee and the Thomason brothers, but they disappeared. Later, my deputies safely escorted Clint, Blake, and Rosalee out of town. It isn't over, Priscilla. Everyone is afraid that Lee and the Thomason brothers will retaliate. They want revenge."

Priscilla's heart sank at the news, and she felt alone and abandoned. The sheriff handed her a letter, and she recognized Clint's handwriting.

With shaking hands, she opened the letter and read:

Dearest Priscilla,

If you are reading this letter, you made it out alive. And I thank God for keeping you safe because we couldn't do anything except pray after the attack. The sheriff kept us at the jail and then forced us to return to Nashville. Through a banker who was kind enough to come to the jail, I arranged for you to return to your ancestral home. It's yours now. I know how much you love the marshes at Big Duck River, and I believe you'll find peace there until we can be together again.

The gunslinger I hired has agreed to protect you until justice is done. He's trustworthy. Blake and I will work from Nashville to do everything possible to ensure your safety. I have set up an account for you at the bank. I wish I could do more, but my hands are tied.

Stay strong, and keep a candle burning in the window for me.

Yours always,

Clint

Tears welled up in her eyes as she read the letter. She had longed to return to her ancestral home, a place filled with memories of happier times. Coming back filled her with conflicting emotions, with danger casting a shadow.

The doctor confirmed she had no broken bones, and Priscilla stayed at the hotel that night. The next day, Belle helped her find a housekeeper. Together with the gunslinger Clint had hired, they made their way to her ancestral home, riding in a wagon with a team of mules. She was bruised and battered, and the journey was arduous on the bumpy road. The sight of the familiar house, nestled by the marshes of Big Duck River, lifted her spirits. It was the best medicine she could have.

The gunslinger lifted Priscilla out of the wagon. "Thank you," she said, appraising the tall, silent man. "What's your name?"

"Wyatt," he said with a steely gaze. "I won't be any trouble. I'll bunk in the barn."

"No. I won't hear of it. You'll stay in the house with us. You can have my father's bedroom."

"Much obliged," he said. "You don't have to worry. I'll keep you safe."

The housekeeper, Martha, a stern woman, nudged Wyatt. "If we're going to have supper tonight at a decent hour, you must help me carry these supplies."

Wyatt grinned as he carried the boxes of supplies into the house.

Priscilla stood surveying the property overgrown with weeds, feeling overwhelmed but strangely contented. She was grateful to Clint for everything. He and Blake had underestimated Lee and the Thomason brothers, but everyone did.

And that's how it began. Wyatt chopped wood for the wood stove, and soon the house was filled with the aroma of freshly baked cornbread and fried chicken. Martha's coffee was strong, just like her—a hefty woman who worked from sunrise to sunset to restore the house to its former glory.

These weeks were healing for Priscilla. The soothing sounds of the river and the marshes brought solace to her soul. As she ventured through the familiar landscapes, the vigilant gunslinger quietly protected her, a continual presence that reassured her she wasn't alone. Despite the lurking dangers, Priscilla found a renewed sense of purpose. It felt like she'd come home.

Stones Cast

The town was bustling with activity when Priscilla, Wyatt, and Martha drove the mule team into town to pick up supplies. The smell of mules hung heavy in the dusty air, and the mules brayed loudly, greeting each other.

Wyatt adjusted the brim of his hat, the sun casting a shadow over his rugged, blonde-haired features. The scar from his left temple to the edge of his jawline gave him an air of dangerous allure, a mark of battles fought and won.

While Priscilla was concerned about being well-received by the town, her expression remained pleasant. The sheriff's words were still vivid in her memory. *Some townspeople tirelessly searched for you during the four years you were missing.* Their reactions ranged from recognition and nods to disbelief and disapproving looks, leaving her with a hint of guilt. She nervously wrung her hands, aware of what they were thinking: *Priscilla Powell had traded one gunslinger for another.*

Martha's powerful presence lent support. They were best friends, and Priscilla depended on her. She had worked relentlessly, washing windows and quilts, scrubbing floors, and cooking wonderful home-cooked meals. Everything she'd done had helped restore Priscilla to a healthy, vibrant woman. Her cheeks were pink, and her shiny hair was tied back with a yellow ribbon.

There were cars parked beside horses. It was a rural area, a mule town, and many country folks were reluctant to give up their mules and horses for cars. Wyatt tied the team to a hitching post near some stables beside the telegraph office where her father once worked. Priscilla bit her lip, remembering the countless times they'd come to town as a family, tying the horses to the same hitching post. She had once been a person of excellent reputation, but things had changed. The locals' judgmental looks alone made her feel inferior.

Priscilla walked down the street beside Wyatt with a determined stride, her heart heavy with the knowledge of the town's divided sentiments. Martha strode confidently next to them.

"We should go to the General Store and buy some material," Martha said cheerfully. "You could use a new dress."

Priscilla smiled. "We'll get enough for both of us."

As they walked onto the bustling main street, Priscilla's eyes flicked nervously toward the women gathered near the church. Their whispers grew louder, and venomous words carried on the summer breeze.

"Come back from the dead, a devil—living with a man under your mother's roof," one woman sneered.

"Ignore them," Wyatt said. "We don't need trouble."

Priscilla kept her head down, her cheeks burning with shame and anger.

Martha, however, had no such reservations. She whirled on the woman, hands on her hips and fire in her eyes. "Priscilla is doing no such thing," Martha retorted. "It's not her mother's house—it's hers. She's a good girl, better than any of you."

In response, the church women began hurling stones at Priscilla. Wyatt positioned himself in front of her, but a blow landed on her shoulder, causing her to flinch.

Martha retaliated, picked up the stones, and launched them back with unexpected precision. Her aim was true, and the women scattered, shrieking as they fled.

"Well, I guess we took care of them," Martha said with a wicked grin. "Witches, that's what they are—bad to the bone. They're lucky I let them get away."

Priscilla raised her brows in surprise. "I didn't know you were capable of such malice."

Wyatt put his arm around Priscilla in a friendly gesture and hugged her, his hand rubbing her shoulder. "Are you okay?"

"I'm fine," Priscilla said. "It's only my pride that's wounded."

At the general store, the atmosphere was noticeably different. The shopkeeper greeted them, and the other patrons offered polite nods. Priscilla couldn't help but notice the contrast; the town was divided. Not everyone in town was vindictive. It was mainly the women from her mother's church. After gathering their supplies and buying fabric for dresses, the trio made their way to Belle's Saloon.

The sounds of music, laughter, and the clink of poker chips filled the lively establishment. Belle eyed them immediately and rushed over. "You are like a breath of fresh air," Belle said, throwing her arms around Priscilla and hugging her. "You look wonderful."

"I owe it all to them," Priscilla said, gesturing to Martha and Wyatt.

Belle ushered them to seats at a corner table and sat down, leaning forward confidentially as if she had something of great importance to say. "There's a lot of talk about the big trial coming up," Belle whispered. "As usual, the town has taken sides. I don't know how Blake could lose. The Wallace brothers shot James Marian Fautt and killed him, and they admit it. And the story is that James Marian made the mistake of marrying a Thomason. That's why he's dead."

Priscilla's brows wrinkled. "I don't understand?"

"Winnie Fautt is Lee's mother, and Big Bill's sister. The Wallace brothers have been in a feud with the Thomasons for decades. Fautt was on their land, near their stills, and when they got a chance to kill him, they did." Belle looked around to make sure she was out of earshot of nosy patrons and continued. "Trouble's brewing. The Thomasons get crazy when something happens to kin, so keep a lookout."

"Don't worry," Wyatt replied, "I'll take care of her."

Belle heaved a sigh. "That's what I needed to hear. Now, I'm going to have Jake dish up three plates of our finest."

They dined on fried chicken and dumplings, fresh peas, and cornbread served with Jake's strong coffee. Priscilla chatted with Belle and the saloon girls, finding comfort in their company. However, the lighthearted atmosphere was shattered when a group of poker players at a nearby table began to whisper and snicker.

Martha closed her fist, ready to defend Priscilla at a moment's notice.

"That's her, livin' in sin with a gunslinger," one of them muttered, just loud enough for Priscilla to hear.

Wyatt's jaw tightened, and he stood, his chair scraping loudly against the wooden floor. He walked over to the table, towering over the men.

"Got somethin' to say?" Wyatt's voice was low and dangerous.

The poker players sneered but didn't back down. "Just callin' it like we see it. She's a disgrace."

Lightning fast, Wyatt grabbed the nearest man by the collar, dragging him outside. The other two followed — a fight breaking out in the dusty street. Wyatt moved with lethal efficiency, his fists meeting their mark as he took down all three men. The commotion drew a crowd, and soon the sheriff arrived, breaking up the fight.

"Enough!" the sheriff barked, stepping between Wyatt and the fallen men. "You're gonna bring the whole town down on you. Get outta here before there's more trouble."

Wyatt nodded, wiping the blood from his knuckles. He rejoined Priscilla and Martha, and they made their way back home.

Once inside, Priscilla tended to Wyatt's wounds, her hands trembling slightly as she cleaned the cuts and bruises. "I'm so sorry, Wyatt," she whispered. "This is all my fault."

Wyatt cupped her face in his hands, his eyes fierce and unwavering. "Don't be sorry, Priscilla. If I have to whip the whole town to keep you safe, I will. You're worth it."

Priscilla gazed at him, confusion mingling with gratitude. "Why would you do that for me?"

Wyatt took her hand, his grip strong and reassuring. "Because I care about you, Priscilla. More than you know. I'd take a bullet for you."

The intensity of his words left Priscilla speechless, her heart pounding in her chest. Her loyalty was to Clint, but Wyatt held a dangerous attraction—something she could not deny.

She dared to put her cheek next to his. "You scare me the way you talk," she murmured.

With his hot breath on her neck, he replied, "I didn't plan on falling in love with you, Priscilla. It just happened. And what we do about it is up to you."

"Martha must not know. We'll go to the marshes tomorrow afternoon. I know of a place. There's a clearing deep in the marshes. We can be alone."

"Are you sure?" Wyatt asked, his voice husky.

"Yes. I'm sure, but no one must know."

The Sins of the Fathers

The following morning, a sharp knock on the door interrupted their peaceful breakfast. Priscilla's heart plummeted when she saw her mother, Fannie, standing on the porch with her husband. The atmosphere was tense and charged as Priscilla stood firm in the doorway, determined that they would not cross the threshold.

After four years, Fannie had not offered so much as a 'good morning.' Her piercing blue eyes scanned Priscilla. "You've ruined yourself, Priscilla," she said with an icy voice. "You're a Jezebel, and no decent man in these parts would have you."

Priscilla stepped onto the porch. She jutted her chin. "Do you think I care what you think? You've got a lot of nerve showing up here. I know about the letters my sister wrote. I know you hid them and stole the money she sent me."

Fannie's face twisted with rage, her voice rising as she quoted biblical passages. "Honor thy mother and father! You're living in sin, and you will burn for it!"

Her husband, emboldened by Fannie's ranting, shoved Priscilla. Before she could react, Martha stepped in, brandishing a frying pan. She struck him on the head with a swift and decisive swing, sending him sprawling to the ground.

Wyatt appeared in the doorway, his presence commanding. He helped Priscilla to her feet, his eyes locked on Fannie. "Leave now, before I lose my temper," he warned.

Fannie, undeterred, put her hands on her hips. "I'm not leaving until I've had my say. You've ruined my daughter, and you're going straight to hell for fornication!"

Wyatt's expression darkened, his voice a dangerous whisper. "I haven't touched your daughter. I'm her bodyguard." He glared at her. "You don't know who I am, do you?"

"Who are you?" Fannie demanded.

"Look me over good," Wyatt said in a taunting voice. "Do I look familiar—like anyone you used to know?"

The words hung in the air, heavy with implication. Fannie hesitated, uncertainty flickering in her eyes. "No, you don't look familiar," she stammered, backing away.

"Well, I know who you are, Fannie. And if you try hard, you might remember Hank Adams—he was a fiddler, someone you knew well—someone from your past that you chose to forget."

Fannie paled. Her slumped shoulders showed she knew exactly what he was talking about, though she remained silent.

Priscilla strode up, her eyes hard. "I don't know what's in your past that you're hiding, Mother, but I want to know why you took the letters and money Amanda sent. You knew how I missed her—you knew how I looked for her letters every day. How could you have made me suffer?"

"I needed the money. And I'm not apologizing," Fannie said in a belligerent tone. "I knew if I gave you the money and letters, you would have been on the next train to New York, leaving me with a dying husband and no money." She pointed her finger at Priscilla. "You were the last daughter. All of my others were married off. And you were the prettiest. And I had a match for you. A match that would have left us sitting pretty if you had just married him."

"Mother! Lee Dodd is a gunslinger and a bootlegger. You would have me marry someone like that? I was only fourteen."

Fannie's face turned dark. "He's my kin, your Aunt Vinnie's son. A handsome man. He was treating you well, Priscilla, but you didn't appreciate it and ran off. Do you know the pain your father went through when he thought you were dead? The whole town thought you'd jumped off Sandy

Hook Bridge."

"I'm sorry if I hurt Pa, but I'm not sorry I left," Priscilla said in a firm voice. "Marrying Lee would have been the worst thing in the world. He showed his true colors after he kidnapped me. He pushed me off a ridge near Sandy Hook, and I'm lucky I'm alive. If it weren't for Big Bill, I'd be dead."

"Lies," Fannie spat. "Lee wouldn't do such a thing. I don't know why you hate him so much. He saved me after you left, bought your pa's medicine, and paid my bills."

"And now he wants repayment. Do you understand what I'm saying? He tried to rape me."

Fannie shook her head, her anger smoldering. "What a lost soul you are— I've never heard such lies. The devil's got a hold on you, and you need to apologize to Lee and his family."

"I'll do no such thing, and I never want to see you again," Priscilla hissed. "You threw me to the wolves. You're not fit to be a mother."

"Everything I've ever done has been for you," Fannie glared, and this is my repayment. "You come back from the dead, take my house, and cavort around town with a gunslinger. You've turned into a brazen hussy."

"I've heard enough," Wyatt said, stepping between them. His tall form towered over Fannie. "Tell me, Fannie, do you remember Hank Wilder?"

Fannie's mouth gaped.

"He's my father and wants to know how his little girl is—the daughter you kept from him."

Priscilla's face paled. This was the first time she had heard of this; it was more than she could absorb. She just wanted Fannie to leave, but she looked like a beaten woman, and she was looking at Wyatt as if he were a ghost from her past. It was as if she were reliving everything.

"Get off my land, Mother," she said sternly.

Fannie swayed, then turned to her husband, who was lying on the ground looking dazed. "Get up, you old fool," she said.

He scrambled to his feet, and they retreated to their car.

"Good riddance," Martha called after them.

As they drove away, Wyatt turned to Priscilla and took her hand. "They

114

won't bother you again," he said quietly.

Priscilla nodded, tears of relief and frustration welling in her eyes. "Thank you, Wyatt." She gazed at him. "I have a lot of questions. I need to know about Hank Adams. I need to know everything."

He squeezed her hand gently. "I was going to tell you everything, Priscilla. I didn't plan on telling you like this. The sins of our fathers have come back to haunt us. But don't worry; we'll get through this."

She grabbed his arm, holding it tight. "I don't understand. Are you my brother?"

He pulled her close. "I'm not your brother."

She rested her head on his chest. "Thank God."

Dragonflies

The morning sun cast a warm, golden glow over the horizon as Priscilla sat on the porch swing, her mind racing with thoughts from the previous day. The altercation with her mother had left her shaken, and Wyatt's cryptic words echoed in her mind like a never-ending refrain. *"You don't know who I am, do you? But I know who you are, Fannie."* What had he meant by that? She needed answers.

Wyatt emerged from the house, his blonde hair tousled and his scar standing out against his tanned skin. He looked at Priscilla, sensing her turmoil with the sharpness of his gaze. His monotone was gentle yet firm. "Morning, Priscilla."

"Morning, Wyatt. Can we talk?" Her voice was tinged with uncertainty.

He sat down next to her on the porch swing. The wooden boards creaked beneath their weight as they settled in. "What's on your mind?" he asked, his eyes softening before returning to their usual intensity.

She took a deep breath, steadying herself for the conversation ahead. "If I'm not your sister, what's the connection?"

Wyatt's expression darkened, and he glanced toward the back door as if he feared Martha would overhear their conversation. As he spoke, each word was heavy with emotion. "Your mother has secrets. Big ones that involve me. If you want to hear about it, I suggest we go somewhere private."

Priscilla searched his steel-blue eyes, feeling uneasy. "Tell me... was your showing up in town an accident?"

"It wasn't an accident."

A shiver of premonition ran down her spine. She had always suspected something different about him—an air of mystery that intrigued her. His admission that he was in town for a reason confirmed her suspicions about him. The truth was—she wasn't sure what side of the law he was on. He seemed too refined to be a gunslinger. But that scar had come from a fight—she was sure of it.

"We'll go to the marshes," she said. "The marshes already know all my secrets, hopes, and dreams and won't tell."

Priscilla packed a bag with a quilt and a picnic lunch, eager to escape the confines of the house and find solace in the wild beauty of the marshes. They bypassed her motorboat and took the well-trodden path, a winding trail through tall, lush greenery and wildflowers. "I know a place with a clearing where the water is crystal clear; my sister, Amanda, and I used to swim there."

They walked shoulder to shoulder, surrounded by the sounds of nature—the birds singing, katydids chirping, and the soft rustling of leaves in the gentle breeze.

As they entered the clearing, Priscilla felt a wave of tension release from her body. The marshes were a sanctuary of serenity and beauty, calming her worries and fears. Her heart fluttered with excitement as she walked, knowing she was about to uncover the truth behind her inexplicable connection to Wyatt. They reached a secluded spot by the water's edge, where Priscilla spread a quilt on the soft, verdant grass. As they settled down, she breathed, inhaling the sweet fragrance of blooming water lilies that filled her senses. In the distance, the gentle croak of frogs added to the symphony of nature around them. "What do you think?" Priscilla asked. "Is it me, or is this the most beautiful place in the world?"

A contented smile graced Wyatt's face as he leaned back on his elbows, taking in the breathtaking view. The vast expanse of marshes stretched out as far as the eye could see, with tall reeds swaying in the cool breeze. The crystal-clear blue water shimmered in the sunlight. "It's beautiful," Wyatt murmured, his gaze lingering on the picturesque landscape. "I can understand why you love it here."

"Look," she said as delicate dragonflies flitted about, their shimmering wings catching the light in iridescent flashes. Tiny jewels of emerald and sapphire danced in the air, weaving intricate patterns against the backdrop of a clear blue sky. "Dragonflies are magical — omens of good luck. It means change is coming."

Wyatt's touch was gentle, and his lips brushed against her cheek in a tender kiss. "Change is already upon us, Priscilla, and I don't believe a dragonfly is magical. We make our magic."

Priscilla's heart raced with nervous anticipation. She couldn't bear another moment of waiting. "What is it you're trying to tell me?"

With a steady tone, Wyatt delivered the shocking truth. "Your mother is not the saint she portrays herself to be. She had an affair with my father while your father was away fighting in the war."

Priscilla's eyes widened in shock, her mouth falling open slightly. A million questions flooded her mind as she stared at the man before her. How could this be possible? "What? I can't believe it. You said his name was Hank Adams, and your name is Wilder."

A flicker of emotion passed over Wyatt's rugged features as he spoke, his voice calm as he explained. "My father was a fiddler when he was younger, and he used the name Hank Adams as his stage name. Your sister, Amanda, is my half-sister. I came to Maury County looking for her. Belle at the saloon told me she'd left town and gone to New York." He paused, taking a deep breath before continuing. "Around that time, Clint needed me to protect you. And fate brought us all together."

She couldn't help but feel a sense of awe at the unlikely chain of events that had led them to this moment in time. As she gazed into Wyatt's piercing blue eyes, she couldn't deny the growing connection between them that seemed to transcend his shared bloodline with her favorite sister, Amanda. She loved the subtle twang in Wyatt's accent, evidence of his southern roots, and how he used his words told her he was a man of good breeding.

Wyatt's expression mirrored her shock and disbelief; his eyes filled with sympathy for Priscilla.

"My father told me he met your mother at a dance. She stood out among the crowd like a rare and beautiful gem. She mesmerized him, and they fell in love for a moment, an hour, a lifetime—I don't pretend to know. Despite the circumstances, Amanda resulted from their affair."

"I've seen pictures of my mother when she was a young girl. She was beautiful, and I suppose lonely. She used to say that music cured loneliness, especially the fiddle. I always thought she was talking about my father, but now I realize he wasn't the only man in her life. She found someone else."

He reached out, brushing a stray strand of hair from her face. "I'm sure it was an accident. In searching for my sister, I didn't know I would find someone like you."

He had a way with words—a sweetness like honey that made everything seem right even when it wasn't. Flummoxed, she dropped her eyes, not wanting him to see the growing conflict within her as she questioned which side of the law he was on. He could be dangerous, but even the danger seemed sweet, and she didn't want to spoil their moment by asking too many questions.

A look of curiosity flickered in Wyatt's eyes. "What's Amanda like?"

Priscilla's face gave way to a fond smile as she thought of her sister. "She's always differed from my other sisters — headstrong and determined to forge her path in life. But she's also the most wonderful person I've ever known. I can see the similarities between the two of you — both strong and daring. She was the one I shared my secrets with, and I trusted her more than anyone." Priscilla's voice grew resolute as she added, "We must find her."

"We will," Wyatt promised, his words resolute. They lay side by side on the cool grass, their whispers carried away by the gentle breeze of the surrounding marshlands.

Priscilla felt contented. Their connection went beyond physical desire; it was a bond forged from mutual understanding and shared experiences. As the symphony of crickets filled the air, the sun set behind the horizon, painting the landscape in a shimmering golden light. A tranquil sense of peace settled over them.

Their lips met in a tender kiss. The kiss deepened, fueled by unspoken desires and repressed emotions, but they both knew there was a line they wouldn't cross. Their touches were tantalizing, hinting at a deeper intimacy, but they held back. Someone stood between them: Clint. Neither had mentioned him, but he was on their minds.

There was someone else who hadn't been reckoned with—Lee Dodd. Unbeknownst to them, they were being watched. Drunk on moonshine, his obsession with Priscilla had led Lee to hide amongst the reeds to see if he could glimpse her. It was unexpected to see her there with Wyatt. Fury blazed through him as he watched the intimate moment unfold before his eyes.

Priscilla's voice echoed across the calm water, teasing him. *Amanda and I used to skinny-dip here. It's hot; let's cool off.* She sounded innocent, but this act was not innocent, and Lee felt a fierce rage ignite within him.

He watched with a nagging sense of unease as Priscilla and Wyatt frolicked in the cool, crystal-clear water. His finger hovered over the trigger, ready to take his rival out once and for all. Lee's fingers moved to the gun at his side.

"Cut the horseplay," Lee growled under his breath. The timing had to be right. He couldn't risk killing his beloved Priscilla.

Suddenly, the tranquility was shattered by a rustling in the nearby bushes. As he was about to fire, a wild pig burst forth from the brush, grunting and barging into Lee's legs. Startled and disoriented, Lee stumbled backward and almost fell into the water. As he regained his footing, the reality of what he had done hit him like a ton of bricks. His heart raced with fear and adrenaline as he turned and ran away from the scene.

Oblivious, Priscilla and Wyatt's laughter and playful splashing mingled with the sounds of nature, unaware of the danger lurking nearby. After a while, they emerged from the water and laid back on the grassy bank, soaking up the warm rays of the evening sun. As the sun dipped below the horizon, the sky painted in shades of pink and orange shrouded them.

Priscilla felt safe with Wyatt—too safe. Suddenly, she felt chilled and pulled away from his embrace, her head spinning. "We should go. I don't want to be sorry like my mother," she whispered, coming to her senses. "Martha will be worried."

"We were only kissing," Wyatt said. "Babies aren't made by kissing."

"I know," she murmured. "But I've never kissed anyone like this before." She wrapped her arms around herself, her eyes sweeping over him, her expression pensive. "You're a lot of man for a young girl like me."

Wyatt chuckled. "I'm not sure how to take that—is it good?"

In a surprising turn of events, she threw her arms around him, kissing him passionately. "It's not just good, it's amazing."

Wyatt's jaw twitched. "Slow down. You've got a wild side that comes out when you're in the marshes."

She laughed, but it was true. There was more. How could he tell her there was more—it wasn't just about finding Amanda? He hadn't meant things to go so far between them, but now there was no going back.

They gathered their things and headed back, the sounds of the night wrapping around them like a comforting blanket. Unlike anything she had ever known, Priscilla felt a bond with Wyatt, a deep connection forged by his being Amanda's half-brother. Still, she thought he had secrets, things he didn't want her to know.

As the darkness deepened, a sense of foreboding lingered in the air. Lee's anger and jealousy simmered, a threat that would soon come to a head. Lee Dodd and the Thomason brothers aimed to settle the score. They were in a feud with their kin — the worst kind.

Bees and Honey

The air was brisk, and there was a slight chill as Priscilla and Martha picked apples in the large orchard behind the house. Priscilla climbed higher on the ladder and admired the changing colors of the leaves in the distance: reds, oranges, and yellows. She threw a few apples in the basket and said, "I feel a change coming, Martha."

Martha held the ends of her apple-filled apron. "It's only the weather. October is bittersweet: the leaves fall right before the miseries of winter." She then dumped the apples in the basket and swatted at a honey bee buzzing around her.

Priscilla's expression was mischievous. "They say a bee sting is good for arthritis."

Laughter escaped Martha. "A heart sting hurts much worse than a bee. I've noticed you've grown closer to Wyatt. Is it about him?"

Priscilla gazed up into the clear blue sky. "Oh, it isn't Wyatt. I feel something in my bones—as if something life-changing will happen today. Mama never liked it when I told her something was getting ready to happen. She said it was the devil talking."

A smile tugged at Martha's lips. "I think your mother gave the devil too much credit. I call it a gut feeling. They're real. So, we'd better get these apples picked to be ready, girl."

Priscilla's ears perked at the sound of a Tin Lizzy coming up the lane, and Martha dropped the apple she was holding into the basket and grabbed the rifle leaning against the tree.

Priscilla panicked, the hair-raising on her arm. "Where's Wyatt?"

"He's in the drawing room," Martha said. "He said he had some phone calls to make."

The two hurried up the hill and peered around the house cautiously. The tires crunched softly on the gravel as the Tin Lizzy stopped in front of the house.

"It's Amanda," Priscilla whispered, scarcely believing her eyes. "She's come home. God has answered my prayers."

Amanda eased out of the car, her wealth and prestige reflected in the clothes she was wearing and her sleek bobbed hair. Her hand went to her heart when she saw Priscilla running toward her. "Sister," she said in a weak voice. "I thought you were dead." She swayed, feeling lightheaded.

Wyatt came out of nowhere and caught her in his arms. "Are you okay?" he asked, steadying her, his face reflecting concern.

Priscilla was there in an instant, her cheeks wet with tears. "I always knew you would come back." She hovered over Amanda, sobbing, until Martha ushered them all into the house.

After Amanda freshened up and calmed down, Martha made hot spiced tea, and they sat in the drawing room, catching up.

"Everything happened quickly once we arrived in New York," Amanda recounted. "John had contacts and immediately began sewing and designing dresses for the governor's wife. Soon after, the business flourished. I wrote to you weekly and sent money, but received no response. Finally, Mama wrote to inform me you were missing, and the search party found the dress I made for you on a rock in Duck River. Everyone thought you were dead."

Priscilla reached over and squeezed her hand.

"It depressed me for months," Amanda continued. "Eventually, our sister, Ada, wrote and said there was a rumor that you were alive and had run away. And I prayed that was the case."

Priscilla filled Amanda in and told her about the letters she'd found under the boards in her father's room.

Amanda looked around; doubts lingered in her mind like shadows. "How could Mama have done something so cruel? It's as if she turned into a monster after Daddy got sick. She did everything she could to keep us apart.

She thought I was a bad influence on you. Lee Dodd was making good money from moonshine and was supporting her while Daddy was sick and couldn't work. She knew that if you left, the money would stop."

Wyatt cleared his throat. "Do you know that for a fact? About the moon shining?" he asked. "I'd heard rumors."

"Everyone in town knows about it. It isn't a secret. Lee's grandfather, Jerome Milton Thomason, started the stills decades ago, and Lee's the runner."

Wyatt nodded. "So, the whole family is involved, the Thomason brothers, as well?"

"Well, I've been gone for four years, but that's how it used to be," Amanda said. "The Thomason brothers and Lee are 'thick as thieves.' They're all in it. They raised Lee, and for years, he believed his grandparents, Jerome Milton and Vinnie, were his parents."

"Let's not dwell on it," Priscilla said. "We have so much to be thankful for. You're here now, and we're together."

"Yes," Amanda said. "And we never have to be separated again. You've changed, and I'm wondering—do you still want to be a telephone operator?"

Priscilla laughed. "My dreams have changed over the past four years. I had a benefactor, lived with his brother and wife, and attended a girls' school. I did well and plan to go to college this fall."

Amanda's face registered surprise. "Oh my, you're all grown up now—so different from when I left."

"And I'm a horsewoman," Priscilla beamed. "I've won several competitions and have my horse in Nashville."

"Oh, my. Well, I must meet the wonderful people who helped you."

"You can meet them after the trial," Priscilla said. "The trial's next week."

Wyatt's jaw twitched at the mention of the trial.

"And there's something else," Priscilla stammered. "I'm not sure how to tell you, but Wyatt is not just a hired gunslinger. It's like fate, and I believe all of this happened for a reason."

Amanda looked puzzled. "Gunslinger?"

"Yes, my benefactor hired Clint to protect me from Lee Dodd and the

Thomason brothers, but there's more to it...you see...Wyatt is your half-brother. Do you see the resemblance?"

Amanda paled. "What are you saying? Our mother may be many things, but she would never cheat on Daddy."

"Don't you remember Mother talking about how poor we were when Daddy worked in the coal mines? She used to say that music was the only thing that lifted her spirits. So, while Daddy was away at war, Mama went to a dance with her sisters and met Wyatt's father. He played the fiddle."

Amanda's dubious expression told Priscilla she doubted it was true. She glared at Wyatt. "That's quite a story, but it's a lie. You've been filling my sister's head with rubbish."

Wyatt spoke up. "I can understand your feelings. Your mother is an evangelist, but she's also human. I'm sure she was very lonely when your father was away. My father saw you once when you were an infant. He told me you have a strawberry birthmark on your right thigh."

Amanda flushed. "Well, that's true, but...it still isn't proof..."

"Your middle name is Ellen, after my grandmother," Wyatt said firmly, pulling a letter from his shirt pocket. "Your mother wrote to my father when you were an infant and ill with pneumonia. She was afraid you would not make it, and in the letter, she professes her love for him."

Amanda took the letter, her eyes moving quickly over the yellowed paper, written in her mother's handwriting. Finally, the letter dropped to her lap, and her understanding of her family history was shaken. "Thank God our father is dead, so he doesn't have to know of this," she said, gazing at Wyatt with hard eyes. "David Powell raised me and is my father. And as far as you're concerned, I don't exactly relish having a gunslinger for a brother."

Priscilla looked pained. "I thought you'd be happy. Wyatt is very nice and has done so much for me."

"I can see you're quite taken with him," Amanda said, as her thoughts churned with an undercurrent of hostility. "Maybe he is my half-brother, but he's also an imposter. It's written all over his face. And the letter proves it. The man who raised Wyatt was refined; I can tell by how Mama speaks of him. He read her poetry, something a gunslinger's father would never do."

Amanda's eyes narrowed. "Who are you, Wyatt?"

"I'm Amanda's bodyguard. You're right, I'm not a gunslinger," Wyatt confessed. "But I'm more than qualified to protect Priscilla, and I'm here for a reason. I'll tell you everything after the trial."

"I'm not a patient woman," Amanda sniffed.

"Well, it looks like we have something in common," Wyatt said with a wry smile.

Deception

Later that evening, while Wyatt took his shower in the secluded outdoor stall, Amanda seized the opportunity to search his room. Her fingers trembled slightly as she rifled through his belongings, uncovering the hidden compartment where his federal badge and identification card lay concealed. The realization had hit her like a thunderclap—Wyatt wasn't just her stepbrother; he was deeply enmeshed in a dangerous game of deception.

Among the papers and notes scattered on Wyatt's desk, Amanda found damning evidence linking him to a covert operation aimed at bringing down Lee Dodd, described as a notorious bootlegger known to operate through Belle Barker's saloon. After the trial, three federal agents, including Wyatt, were planning to use Priscilla as a decoy to lure Lee Dodd out into the open, away from his protective brothers. The plan hinged on Lee's moonshine deliveries to Belle's Saloon, intending to ensure Belle received a substantial fine for her involvement.

The weight of these revelations hung heavy on Amanda's shoulders as she navigated the dark corridors of her ancestral home. She couldn't reconcile the image of the affable Wyatt with that of an undercover agent, risking his life in pursuit of justice. Her skepticism gnawed at her, driving her to take drastic action that evening.

Priscilla's heart plummeted, a wave of disbelief washing over her as Amanda shared the troubling news. The room felt heavy with unspoken emotions as Priscilla murmured, "I believed he cared for me, but now I see I was just a pawn in his game," she said in disbelief. "We have to warn Belle."

It was pitch dark when they slipped out of the house after they were sure Wyatt and Martha were asleep. Dressed in Amanda's finest creations, they drove into town, parking discreetly behind the saloon to avoid unwanted attention. They moved with purpose, their heels clicking softly on the cobblestones as they made their way to Belle's Saloon, now viewed as a notorious den of vice and intrigue that held the key to unraveling Wyatt's secrets.

They stepped into the dimly lit interior. The air was thick with the mingling scents of tobacco smoke and whiskey—a familiar haze that enveloped the room like a shroud. Priscilla stayed in the kitchen, fearing Lee Dodd or his brothers might be in the saloon. Amanda wasted no time. She approached Belle with a steely resolve, her voice pitched low to avoid attracting undue attention. "Belle," she began, her tone measured yet urgent, "we need to talk about Wyatt. We searched his room and found some papers. He's a federal agent, and they're planning a 'sting'—going to use Priscilla as bait to arrest Lee Dodd."

Belle Barker stood behind the bar, her gaze flickering over the patrons with practiced scrutiny. "I suspected something was going on—those two guys in the corner have been asking questions." Her expression remained inscrutable, but Amanda could sense the tension coiling beneath the surface. "Where's Wyatt?" Belle asked, her eyes narrowing slightly.

"He's at home asleep. Priscilla and I snuck out after he went to sleep. We had to warn you."

Belle's facade cracked a flicker of disdain crossing her face. "Jesus, cougars are roaming those dark country roads at night, and you girls are out," she said, scanning the saloon with a practiced eye. "Where is Priscilla?"

"She's in the kitchen—afraid Lee Dodd and his brothers might be around."

"I appreciate the information, but you need to stay out of this," Belle said. "I can handle it."

"We came all this way, Belle," Amanda pleaded. "Let us help."

"Go home," Belle commanded. "You shouldn't be meddling."

Amanda shrunk back, aware of Belle's expression changing as the man in the corner, whom Belle had pointed out as a federal agent, sidled beside her.

"Can I buy you a drink?" he asked in a friendly voice.

Before she could answer, Belle poured a shot of whiskey and shoved it in front of her.

"Well, I..." she stammered, uncertain of Belle's motive, but figured she was trying to keep things normal, and men thought a woman alone at a bar to be easy.

"Are you from around here?" he queried.

"No. I'm from New York," she lied. It was a half-lie.

"I believe Sally Sue was just about to leave," Belle pressed, intentionally giving her a fake name to throw the undercover agent off.

"I'm just getting started," Amanda said, throwing back her head and downing the jigger of whiskey. She intended to turn the tables and play her part, engaging in casual conversation with the undercover agent—whose every word she parsed for hidden meaning.

"Are you from around here?" Amanda asked casually, her gaze steady. "What do you do for a living?"

The man hesitated, caught off guard by Amanda's directness. "No. I'm not from around here. I'm in shipping, just passing through," he replied vaguely, his eyes flickering nervously.

"And how long do you plan to stay in town?" Amanda asked, her voice soft but insistent.

Before the man could answer, a commotion erupted nearby. Amanda, inadvertently drawn into the spotlight by a persistent poker player, was pulled onto the dance floor against her will. She resisted half-heartedly, her discomfort palpable as the man attempted to assert his unwelcome advances.

Across the room, Lee Dodd and his brothers entered—a formidable trio whose mere presence sent a ripple of unease through the saloon. Amanda struggled to extricate herself from the poker player's grasp, her eyes darting nervously toward Belle for help.

"He won't take no for an answer," Amanda muttered under her breath, her voice tinged with frustration.

Lee Dodd, ever the imposing figure, intervened swiftly. With a single, decisive gesture, he grabbed the offending man by the collar and hurled him bodily through the swinging doors. The saloon fell silent in the wake of his display of authority, but Amanda remained acutely aware of the danger lurking beneath the surface.

In a darkened corner of the saloon, Amanda huddled with one of Belle's girls, her voice barely above a whisper. "I need to get out of here," she murmured urgently. "Lee Dodd is my cousin. I think he recognized me. Tell Belle to call me... but it's a party line, so we must be careful of what we say." She paused, her eyes searching for the federal agent, finally landing on him. He was talking to his partner covertly with their heads together, his eyes shifting and darting about. She had no doubts they were undercover agents.

"Go before Lee comes back inside looking for you," the girl warned.

A fight erupted nearby before Amanda could even respond, with fists flying and curses being exchanged, completely disrupting the usual atmosphere of the saloon. The sheriff, drawn by the commotion, entered the saloon just as chaos threatened to consume the room. Sensing an opportunity, Amanda and Priscilla seized their chance and slipped away through the kitchen, the sounds of the brawl fading behind them as they raced toward the safety of the back exit.

Outside, the cool night air enveloped them like a cloak of relief. Amanda leaned against the rough-hewn wall of the saloon, her heart still racing from the adrenaline-fueled escape. Priscilla stood beside her, her breath coming in ragged gasps as they caught their breath.

"We made it," Priscilla murmured, her voice tinged with relief.

"For now," Amanda replied softly, her gaze fixed on the distant glow of streetlights. "But this isn't over. Not by a long shot. Lee Dodd recognized me and took on a fight for me. He didn't have to do it, and I'm grateful."

Priscilla's tone was accusing. "You stirred up trouble for Belle. Why didn't you leave after you warned her? If you had left, none of this would have happened. Besides, Belle doesn't like it when people meddle in her business."

"I was drawing him out—making sure he was a federal agent. Someone has to take charge," Amanda said as they jumped into the Tin Lizzy.

As they disappeared into the night, Amanda knew that the shadows of their past would continue to haunt them, shaping their destinies in ways they could scarcely imagine.

Priscilla's mind was on Wyatt. Despite who he was, she cared for him. She'd made a mistake—and her heart would pay for it.

Regret

As the trial loomed just days away, Amanda felt a knot of anxiety tightening in her stomach, nagging at her thoughts. She couldn't shake the uneasy feeling that Lee might scheme something sinister against Priscilla, who sat unaware. Shadows of doubt hovered over them as they sipped steaming cups of tea in the drawing room.

"Every day brings a sense of uneasy anticipation—wondering if they are hiding in the shadows, watching and waiting," Amanda said, her voice laced with a hint of dark irony. "What is Lee's motive? Why does he want you to testify at the trial?"

"Blake Wilder is the criminal defense attorney for the Wallace brothers," Priscilla said. "I lived with Blake and his family for four years after I ran away. Lee wants me to testify on Jim Fautt's behalf and sit with his family in the courtroom at the trial to show support. It's all about throwing Blake off during the trial. But I will not do it. I didn't even know Jim Fautt."

"You could go to jail for perjury if you testified," Amanda said. "Why did the Wallace brothers kill Jim Fautt?"

"According to Belle, the Thomason brothers claim that Jim Fautt was trapping and hunting that night, but the Wallace brothers insist he was on their property to destroy their still. Jack, Rufus, Otey, Ollie, John, and Willis were charged with Jim Fautt's murder and also charged with making moonshine. Jim Fautt was alone. He had a gun and holster around his waist when he was found, but an investigation proved it wasn't his."

"Everyone knows there has always been bad blood between the Wallaces and Jim Fautt," Martha said. "The feud grew worse when Jim married Winnie

Thomason because the Wallaces hated her father and brothers even more than Jim Fautt."

They didn't notice Wyatt standing in the doorway. "Cowardly, shooting a man in the back of his head four times," Wyatt said. "Once would have been enough—but four times is pure hate."

"Have you ever shot a man?" Amanda asked as she bit into a piece of banana nut bread.

"Yes, I have," Wyatt admitted, his voice tinged with regret. "I'm not proud of it," he added, his eyes filled with a haunting intensity.

Amanda fixed her gaze on Wyatt. "It's time to cut the games. You're an undercover agent, and two more agents are hanging out at Belle's Saloon."

Wyatt's face turned red with anger. "If this information is leaked, it could ruin everything."

Priscilla jutted her chin. "The jig is up. I'm not your decoy. The nerve of you—swimming naked with me in the marshes while all the while you were planning to use me as a decoy to draw Lee Dodd out without his brothers."

Amanda gasped. "Naked! If you swam naked with my little sister, you will damned well marry her."

Wyatt gestured to lower his hands and reassured, "Calm down. Nothing happened. She invited me to swim with her. I didn't ask her." As the realization hit him like a ton of bricks, Wyatt felt a lump in his throat. Taking a deep breath, he said, "I can't marry her. I'm Clint and Blake's younger brother. I swear, I never meant for this to happen."

Priscilla's mouth fell open in shock. "Oh my God, you tricked me. You said you had feelings for me."

"I have feelings for you—but I can't act on them," Wyatt said. "You asked me to go skinny-dipping with you—and I did, but nothing happened. You're wild and uninhibited in the marshes, but I remained a gentleman." He grimaced. "Nothing happened—as I recall—we fell asleep."

Priscilla pressed her hands to her head, her frustration clear. "Nothing happened?" she exclaimed, her voice dripping with venom. "My God, everything happened!" Her eyes flashed with hurt and disbelief as she took a step back. "I thought you cared for me." With that, her emotions erupted, and she let out a piercing scream before storming out of the room, her footsteps echoing in the silence that followed.

Amanda's voice was low and mean. "You've about pushed me to the limit, Wyatt. First, you tell me you're my half-brother, and then I find out you're an undercover agent, and to top it off, you went skinny-dipping with my little sister." She tapped her foot. "I'm going to go take care of Priscilla's broken heart, and tonight we are going to sit down with a glass of whiskey, and you're going to tell me everything."

Martha had been sitting, taking in everything and keeping her thoughts to herself. "Stings like a bee," she said, crossing her arms. "I hope she's okay."

Tension hung heavy as Amanda turned on her heel and hurried away, ascending the stairs to Priscilla's room. The days leading up to the trial had taken their toll, each moment fraught with apprehension and uncertainty. She hesitated before knocking on the door, steeling herself for the conversation ahead.

"Priscilla?" Amanda's voice was gentle, tinged with concern.

Inside, Priscilla's tear-streaked face turned towards the door. "Go away, Amanda," she said, her voice muffled by the pillow.

Ignoring the plea, Amanda pushed open the door and entered. Priscilla was curled on the bed, her posture one of defeat. Amanda sat beside her, enveloping her in a comforting embrace. She patted her back. "I know you're hurting, dear. But you're not alone in this."

"He made a fool of me," Priscilla sniffed, sitting up and wiping her tears. "How could I have been so blind?"

"Men can be deceptive," Amanda said., "They promise the world and leave us with shattered dreams. It's not your fault." She paused. "I didn't understand what he said about being unable to act on his feelings."

"Wyatt's brother, Clint, is my benefactor. He's been wonderful, but I felt abandoned when he left after the ambush. He said he was sending Wyatt to protect me." Priscilla gazed off into the distance, a pensive look on her face. "What's a girl to think?" Her voice held a hint of uncertainty. She shook her head, her expression a mix of sadness and bewilderment. "And then I thought Wyatt cared about me. I believed his every word." She squinted as if trying to make sense of her feelings.

Amanda's heart ached for her sister. "Sometimes, people hide their true intentions. Wyatt... he's caught up in something bigger than us. But that doesn't excuse his actions."

Priscilla's eyes filled with fresh tears. "I feel so ashamed." She heaved a sigh. "How can I face either Clint or Wyatt again?"

Amanda hugged her sister, enveloping her in a warm embrace. "Don't be ashamed," she whispered. "I remember feeling just as confused when I was your age. It's normal for your emotions to be all over the place." Amanda paused, looking into Priscilla's eyes with compassion. "Trust your instincts and listen to your heart. Sometimes, it's best not to overthink it. Just follow what feels right."

They sat in silence, the weight of the moment hanging heavy between them.

Amanda stood up, her resolve firm. "Rest now. We'll face tomorrow together."

Later that evening, Amanda found herself in the drawing room with Wyatt. The flickering firelight casts haunting shadows across the room. She poured him a glass of whiskey and handed it to him, her expression guarded.

Wyatt took a sip, meeting her gaze. "Thank you."

Amanda sat opposite him, her eyes searching his face. "Tell me, Wyatt. Are you my brother?"

He sighed, setting down the glass. "Yes, Amanda. I am."

The revelation hit her like a thunderbolt. "Why didn't you tell me sooner?"

Wyatt looked pained. "Your mother forbids it. She thought she was protecting you. Our father... he's a powerful man in Nashville—wanted to provide support and take care of you, but she didn't want him in her life."

Amanda's mind raced. "Our father... it has a strange ring to it. After all this time—you turn up..."

"He wants to see you," Wyatt said, cutting her off.

Amanda's anger simmered. "And Priscilla? What about her? You led her on, made her believe..."

Wyatt shook his head. "I swear, Amanda, nothing happened between us. There's something about those marshes... they bring out a wild side of her. But I never took advantage of her. I care about her."

Amanda studied him, torn between anger and understanding. She took a long swallow of whiskey and said, "You've caused us all so much pain, Wyatt. Do you even realize? And now what's going to happen? Are you going to tell Clint?"

"I have to tell him, but don't worry, he'll blame me, not Priscilla. I'm trying to make things right. Our father... can help bring us all together. He's a great man. But we have to trust each other."

Amanda's shoulders sagged. "Trust is earned, Wyatt. It's not something you can demand."

Wyatt's expression turned solemn as he nodded, showing his unwavering determination. "I'll do whatever it takes," he said with conviction.

Sensing his resolve, Amanda placed her hand over his, her eyes filled with urgency as she spoke. "If you mean what you're saying, please don't divulge what happened in the marshes to Clint. It would only cause him pain."

Wyatt, caught between loyalty and concern, struggled to respond. "You're very persuasive, Amanda, but Clint is my brother, and we've never kept secrets."

With determination in her eyes, Amanda leaned in closer, her voice low and intense. "Priscilla is my sister, and you must safeguard her reputation just as fiercely as you protect your own."

Wyatt's brows wrinkled, feeling conflicted.

"Shall we raise our glasses to this?" she asked as she filled their tumblers.

A searing sensation lingered in Wyatt's throat as he swallowed, reflecting the turmoil within. It burned.

The Trial

It was the morning of the trial, and a heavy blanket of gray hung over the sky, casting a sad shadow on the day. The cool March air nipped at Priscilla's skin, awakening her senses as she trudged toward the courthouse alongside her steadfast companions—Martha, Amanda, and Wyatt. A shiver raced down her spine, a visceral reaction to the moment's weight as if the elements mirrored the tension and uncertainty ahead.

As Priscilla approached the Maury County courthouse in Columbia, Tennessee, she couldn't help but marvel at its imposing grandeur. The sturdy brick structure stood tall, a testament to resilience, adorned with intricate architectural details that whispered stories of the past. Despite its beauty, the courthouse had been a silent witness to countless somber events. It had seen the harrowing specter of controversial hangings and the fierce, often contentious battles for civil rights, which frequently led to unjust and biased rulings. This building was more than just stone and mortar; it was a powerful symbol of history and conflict. The lingering impact of the Civil War was palpable in Maury County, where the echoes of past injustices reverberated through the community. The locals harbored deep scars from the devastation wreaked by the Yankees, the violation of plantation owners, and the suffering of the enslaved population. Even though more than half a century had passed since the end of the Civil War, the wounds remained fresh, and the struggle for justice and reconciliation persisted in Maury County, Tennessee.

The steps of the courthouse were alive with a vibrant tapestry of life, a diverse crowd bustling in every direction. Horses trotted alongside buggies, while the distinctive hum of Tin Lizzies added a modern note to the age-old scene. It was a vivid reminder that, despite the seriousness of the situation, life continued. The sound of horses neighing and donkeys braying and snorting. There was an earthy, dusty smell mixed with Madagascar periwinkle blooming nearby. It was bittersweet—that day when the whole town came together to decide the fate of Rufus Wallace, a moonshiner who had shot James Marion Fautt down in cold blood.

Wyatt weaved through the bustling crowd, a sea of eager faces and hushed whispers, with Priscilla, Amanda, and Martha trailing closely behind him. As they ascended to the balcony, the tension in the air was palpable. Wyatt claimed a spot in the front row, where they could gaze at the scene unfolding in the courtroom below. The balcony still held an unspoken division. Before the Civil War, the law designated it for black individuals. Whites and blacks could not sit together. Mingling between races was social suicide unless the black person was an employee of the white person. Everyone knew the balcony was the best seat in the house, and it was filled primarily with black folk.

It goaded on the blacks as they peered over the worn railing at the jury, with not one black amongst them. It was a somber assembly of all white jurors with furrowed brows and thoughtful expressions, who occupied the right side of the courtroom, each member lost in contemplation of the case before them. At the center of attention, the Wallace brothers sat at their tables, their faces revealing an intricate blend of anxiety and determination as they awaited the proceedings. Beside them, Blake exuded an air of confidence in his tailored dark blue suit and crisp tie, meticulously reviewing his notes with focused intensity.

The polished wooden railing that separated the spectators from the courtroom served as a physical barrier and enhanced the charged atmosphere. It underscored the gravity of the moment as the trial officially began, promising twists and revelations to unfold.

Priscilla nervously scanned the courtroom, filled with anticipation and uncertainty. When her eyes met Clint's, she let out a surprised gasp. It felt like no time had passed, and Clint's expression exuded warmth and reassurance, offering Priscilla a much-needed sense of comfort amid the tense atmosphere of the trial. Rosalee sat elegantly beside him, adorned in a stunning black fur coat and hat. With a subtle wink and wave, she exchanged a quiet greeting with Priscilla, both exhibiting discretion in acknowledgment of the solemnity of the proceedings.

Despite the serious nature of the trial, some in attendance treated it like a spectacle, openly pointing and whispering at the accused, who was seated at a long table with Blake and several other individuals connected to the case.

The accused, Rufus Wallace, appeared ashen and fearful as his restless fingers tapped the tabletop. After weeks of anticipation, the moment of reckoning finally arrived. Despite the town's awareness of the complicit Wallace brothers, Rufus stood alone to answer for the crime. It was a cold, overcast day in the fall when Rufus aimed his shots at James Marion Fautt. Instead of a single shot to the head, which would have been fatal, Rufus unleashed a volley of four shots.

Priscilla jerked involuntarily when Lee and the Thomason brothers entered, their presence casting a shadow over the proceedings. They sat amongst kin, and as Priscilla's eyes roved over the familiar faces, she noticed her mother sitting in a row with Vinnie, and Fautt's wife, Winnie.

William Stuart Fleming Jr., the special prosecutor, articulated his words with a rich, resonant Southern accent that wrapped around each syllable like a warm embrace. His voice, deep and commanding, carried a blend of warmth and authority that captivated those who listened, drawing them into his presence with an air of confidence and assurance. He was a man of notable distinction, his demeanor polished and poised, reflecting the strong values instilled in him by his father. Standing in the exact spot where his father had once stood, he felt the weight of tradition and legacy pressing upon him, a reminder of the unyielding beliefs passed down through generations. He presented the theory that the killing occurred when Fautt, out setting steel traps, surprised the defendants at the moonshine still. The Wallaces followed him for a considerable distance up the hill, and Rufus Wallace, son of Jack Wallace, fired four shots which took effect in the back of Fautt's head, ending his life.

There were groans in the courtroom at the words, 'back of the head.'

Winnie looked pale and withdrawn, but when she was called to the stand, her voice was steady as she recounted the events surrounding her husband's death. She faced scrutiny, not for what had happened to her husband, James Marian Fautt, but for who she was: the sister of "Big Bill Thomason," a notorious gunslinger and moonshiner. Still, she held her ground.

Dressed entirely in black, she exuded an air of mystery, her coal-black hair elegantly pulled up in a chic style that accentuated her features. However, the fierce intensity of her gaze and the unyielding lines of her face gave her an almost impenetrable demeanor, overshadowing the beauty beneath.

"Jim was out trapping. He was unarmed and strayed onto the Wallaces land, and they shot him in the back of the head," she said in a harsh voice. Suddenly, her composure shattered, and she pointed an accusing finger at Rufus Wallace, her voice rising to a shrill pitch. "You murdered my husband. Eight children are now without a father because of you. You're despicable." Her venom voice echoed through the courtroom until a deputy gently guided her back to her seat.

As the courtroom proceedings progressed, a heavy silence fell over the room when Judge S. E. Stephan called Priscilla to the stand to testify on behalf of the state. Two deputies, their uniforms crisp and imposing, approached her and gently but firmly guided her toward the witness stand. With each step, she could feel the weight of the atmosphere pressing down upon her. Wyatt, her ever-watchful protector, trailed close behind, his presence a silent reassurance amid her growing anxiety. Even with him nearby, Priscilla couldn't shake the overwhelming sense of vulnerability that enveloped her like a thick fog.

"What do you know about James Fautt?" Blake asked, his voice direct.

Her voice was steady. "I didn't know Jim Fautt, and cannot vouch for his character."

Blake countered, "You were engaged to be married to your cousin, Lee Dodd, and surely you would know his family—they are your kin." He stared at her hard. "James Fautt was Lee Dodd's stepfather. Surely you knew him," he prodded.

"I was never engaged to Lee Dodd," she said in a firm voice. "My mother is a matchmaker and arranged dates with him, against my will. I have never met James Fautt." She heaved a sigh, then continued. "I am indeed kin, and it was common knowledge in the family that the Thomason brothers were always in a feud with someone—that's all I can tell you."

Blake's forcefulness had been unexpected, and she felt jolted when she left the stand. He had stirred up old woes and indiscretions she had tried to put behind her: the whole town knew she was alive and had never jumped off Sandy Hook Bridge. She could not help but glance into the crowded courtroom, her eyes locking with Lee's, exuding pure hatred as he mouthed, "*Liar.*"

As her eyes scanned the entire clan, their expressions filled with hatred and loathing for her—her mother, Aunt Vinnie, Jerome, Milton, Big Bill, and all her cousins—it was all she could do to remain calm. She stumbled on the stairs, and Wyatt quickly righted her.

As she returned to her seat on the balcony with Wyatt, nods of encouragement greeted her. A kind older gentleman she knew from the General Store leaned in and asked, "Are you okay, Miss Powell?" "I'm going to be," she whispered with a faint smile, feeling grateful for the support. A well-dressed Black lady patted her on the shoulder and said, "You're a free woman—you have a right to marry whomever you choose." Her supporters filled the balcony. Below, the courtroom buzzed with whispers, the revelation reshaping perceptions as they recalled Priscilla running away four years ago and being thought dead. She had spoken what everyone knew — that the Thomasons were always feuding with their neighbors.

When Big Bill testified, everyone felt nervous as he took the stand. His size was intimidating, and he had a reputation as a known killer. His testimony aligned with that of his sister, Winnie, but it had little impact on the case. However, his notorious background ultimately harmed their defense more than it helped. No one realized that the trial would mark the beginning of Big Bill's troubles, which would lead to his death just a few months later, at forty-four.

When a local man, Solon Wooley, testified for the Wallaces' defense, he didn't know he would die for his testimony. Big Bill's choirboy expression concealed his hidden anger and thoughts that Solon Wooley had become his worst enemy. No one could predict that this trial would lead to Solon Wooley's death. Big Bill kept a count of the number of bullets Rufus had fired into James Fautt's head — four bullets. He would not forget.

Blake's closing statement asserted that James Fautt bore a grudge against Jack Wallace and had gone there to destroy the still. As the trial ended, Priscilla felt a potent mix of weariness and determination. The tension intensified as the jury deliberated, ultimately returning with a guilty verdict, but the jury exonerated the Wallace brothers due to compelling mitigating circumstances.

Priscilla stood frozen in disbelief as she processed the shocking news. Rufus Wallace had callously murdered James Marion Fautt, firing four shots at his head, yet would walk away a free man.

There was a low growl of discontent on one side of the courtroom. There was no mistake. The town was out to bring down the Thomason brothers and anyone connected to them. Her kin's surly, accusing stares bore into her, each gaze heavy with blame as if she alone ruled. Despite the weight in her heart, she defiantly jutted her chin, refusing to accept the unwarranted guilt they sought to place upon her.

She hadn't brought this turmoil upon herself; rather, their own defiant and aggressive behavior led to the tumult they faced. It all began the day they were born, as their father, Jerome Milton Thomason, instilled in them a deep-seated hatred. This upbringing perpetuated ongoing conflicts among his children. The war had ended fifty-seven years ago, but it felt like it had never truly ended in Maury County.

In the charged atmosphere of the courtroom, the tension was palpable, as if it could explode into chaos at any moment. Priscilla's apprehensive gaze scanned the room while Wyatt urgently escorted her out, his grip firm on her arm. Amanda and Martha hurried along behind them. Their footsteps echoed down the corridor as they escaped in the vintage Tin Lizzy, leaving Priscilla relieved as she closed her eyes. However, beneath the surface, she knew it was far from over. The threat of Lee and the Thomason brothers' looming retaliation lingered in the air.

The White Lie

Once they returned to the house, there was a bustle of activity as they packed up and prepared to leave the trial's aftermath.

Priscilla spoke in a voice that quivered, reflecting her despair. "When will this unjust treatment end? The town is punishing the Thomasons and the dead man, James Marion Fautt, while the Wallaces go free. I've stirred things up and made myself a target for Lee Dodd and the Thomason brothers."

Wyatt's voice rang with urgency. "That's why you must leave immediately."

Priscilla refused to be intimidated. "I'm staying," she said with unwavering determination. "I'm tired of running. I'm standing my ground."

Amanda, concerned for Priscilla's safety, sought to reason with her. "Don't be reckless," she cautioned. "You don't have any other option."

"What will happen to me?" Martha lamented, her anxiety evident in her voice.

"You're coming with us," Wyatt said firmly. "We're not leaving anyone behind."

Martha began cleaning out the icebox, and Wyatt tended to the livestock.

After packing, Priscilla looked longingly out the window, and movement caught her eye on the path to the river. She ran out the door, believing it was Wyatt going to check the boat. She was thinking of a stolen moment at the river, a quiet place where she would thank him for his support at the trial. Relieved to have the trial over, she felt giddy and intoxicated as she ran toward the marshes.

Priscilla's happiness was short-lived, and a scream stuck in her throat when a hand reached out and pulled her into the tall grass. Her eyes widened in fear, and she grimaced at Lee's whiskey-laden breath as he lashed out at her.

"How could you have testified against your kin?" he barked. "You're going to pay for this, Priscilla." A huge buzzing noise drowned out his voice.

She braced herself for the blow as he drew back his fist. Before he could strike, nature intervened to save her. Bees, intoxicated by the sweet scent of whiskey, swarmed around Lee, inflicting relentless stings upon him.

With a supple twist, Priscilla slipped out of his grasp. A scream stuck in her throat, and her heart pounded as she fled toward the river, seeking safety in the protective embrace of the marshes. She fell in her hurry to escape, allowing the enemy to regain his footing.

Fear surged through her as a powerful hand closed around her throat, squeezing tightly and cutting off her air. Panic set in, but then the enchanting melody of a fiddle drifted through the air, calming her senses. She instinctively stopped fighting, momentarily believing that her father was near to rescue her. Just as suddenly as the threat had come, she felt Lee's weight lift from her, granting her the sweet relief of breath. In the haze of confusion, she sensed that someone had intervened. Yet, she couldn't see the figure who had come to her aid.

A familiar voice called out to her, urgent and insistent, "Run, Priscilla, run. Go to the marshes." As she struggled to regain her footing, the sounds of a fierce struggle echoed from the dense underbrush, blending with the rustle of leaves and snapping twigs.

The small boat, tethered to the landing, seemed almost like a lifeline to Priscilla. With skilled movements, she quickly untied the rope and stepped onto the boat just as Lee's hand futilely reached out to grab the rope. As she seized an oar, the adrenaline-fueled swing sent Lee sprawling on the river bank, the impact echoing across the still water.

Priscilla held her breath as the motor sputtered and then started. Overcome with fear, she disregarded Lee's desperate pleas for help, believing them to be trickery. The treacherous, muddy bank had ensnared him, pulling him further into darkness—his grave.

She hesitated for a moment, then glanced back over her shoulder. In the dim light, she spotted a figure with enthusiastically raised arms. His steady but urgent voice slicked through the stillness. "Find your safe place," he urged, the intensity of his voice sending a shiver down her spine.

She heaved a deep breath as she motored deep into the marsh. It stretched out like a living, breathing entity, the still waters reflecting a thousand stories told by the reeds that swayed gently in the breeze. Eventually, she found serenity in the afternoon light as she breathed in the cooling mist like a tender embrace, creating a realm where time seemed to stand still. Each ripple in the water felt like a whispered secret, shared only among the egrets and frogs that called this place home.

Memories of her and Wyatt lying naked shrouded her as she found their special place and lay down. The earthy scent of damp soil and decaying leaves filled the air, intertwining with the sweet fragrance of wildflowers that bloomed at the edges. Here, she felt a discovery and a reunion with nature's quiet symphony. In its quiet grandeur, the marsh formed a sanctuary of reflection and connection where every element resonated with the rhythms of a wild and tender world.

She was not sorry, nor would she ever be for her stolen moments with Wyatt. It was her safe place, and the memory was special. Priscilla rested there contented and did not venture out until she heard Wyatt's voice calling. She motored back to the landing.

Wyatt's expression of concern unsettled her as he assisted her out of the boat. His arms enveloped her firmly as though reluctant to release her. He then gestured towards the skid marks on the bank. A black hat lay nearby, showing where Lee had presumably met his fate.

"I wasn't sure what had happened," he admitted. "I feared he might have dragged you under with him, but with the boat gone, I maintained hope that you were still alive."

Priscilla narrowed her eyes as she surveyed the surroundings. "Do you think he's dead?"

"I have to believe it. All signs suggest he's drowned."

Priscilla stared at Lee's black hat lying on the bank. Neither made a move to pick it up. It was a haunting scene that Priscilla would remember for the rest of her life.

Only when Wyatt fetched her suitcase from her room and they were alone did she dare ask, "What's going to happen?"

"I don't know," he said solemnly. "You'll have to talk to the sheriff once we get into town. And tell him what happened."

A brooding darkness enveloped her countenance as a profound hostility towards Lee Dodd compelled her to fabricate a bold untruth. "I am innocent and have no secrets to hide. Lee assaulted me and forcefully pulled me into the dense undergrowth. A throng of bees set upon him, allowing me to flee. That was the last time I saw him. I motored far into the marshlands, hoping that he would leave."

Wyatt studied her, his eyes dubious. "Okay, if that's your story, I'll back you on it, but stick with it. Don't change it. Do you understand?"

Priscilla nodded. "But what about us?" she pressed. "Is it over between us?"

Wyatt paled. "Look, I didn't mean for this to happen. My brother is my best friend and I would never take his woman."

Priscilla looked hurt.

Leaving her childhood home once again was a bittersweet experience for her. Despite the sense of closure she felt after resolving issues with her mother, she knew deep down that it wasn't truly over. The best part was that Amanda had finally returned home, bringing a sense of joy and comfort during this emotional transition.

Once in town, they went straight to the sheriff, and Priscilla repeated her story to the sheriff.

The sheriff's intense gaze locked onto her. "So, you're saying that Lee attacked you, and you escaped after bees stung him? You were scared and took your motorboat into the marshes to hide, and you didn't come out until you heard Wyatt calling for you," he asked, his voice grave. "Then Lee's hat was found on the riverbank, but there's no sign of Lee anywhere."

"That's right," Priscilla affirmed, her demeanor remaining composed. "Everyone knows Lee is never without his hat, and I intentionally left it there, assuming that he might return to retrieve it."

The sheriff's focused gaze fixed on her as he spoke in a low, serious tone. "I highly doubt that Lee will return for his hat, Priscilla. There's likely been foul play, and I suspect he may be lying at the bottom of Duck River just behind your house."

His accusatory tone jolted Priscilla. His words seemed to insinuate that she was involved in Lee's death. "I had nothing to do with it," she declared emphatically. "There was no foul play."

Wyatt's voice was filled with disbelief as he spoke up. "How can you talk about foul play when we don't even have a body?"

As Martha stepped forward, her heart raced with determination as she addressed the sheriff. Her voice was steady, echoing in the tense air. "I assure you, Sheriff, there was no foul play. I witnessed everything unfold from the upstairs window of our home. It was exactly as Priscilla described—when she boarded the boat and motored away, Lee was standing on the bank. I dashed to the barn to fetch Wyatt, but by the time we arrived, Lee had disappeared without a trace."

The sheriff fixed a stern gaze on Martha. "Martha, you wouldn't lie to me, would you? Lying is a serious offense."

"I swear on my mother's grave that it's all true." Her expression was sincere.

Amanda stepped forward. "I believe our business is finished here," she sniffed. "We have people waiting for us at the hotel."

The sheriff appeared disgruntled. "Are you leaving town?"

"Yes, the trial is finally over. We are heading back to Nashville."

"Why are *you* leaving Priscilla? It looks like the threat is over. If Lee's hat was on the riverbank, it looks like he drowned."

"There's bound to be a backlash from the Thomason brothers, being that he disappeared behind my house," Priscilla said. "Besides, I have to get ready for a horse competition."

The sheriff gazed at her with narrow eyes. "I think there's more to the story, but only two people know the truth: you and Lee Dodd. And Lee's not here to tell his side of the story."

Amanda stepped forward. "My sister had nothing to do with Lee Dodd's disappearance. I saw you at the trial talking to the Thomason brothers, so I guess we all know which side you're on," she said with a smirk.

"I don't take sides," the sheriff countered. "I'll tell you what — if me and my men fish Lee Dodd out of the marsh behind Priscilla's house—the Thomason brothers will go on a rampage. And I sure as hell don't need more trouble."

"We best be going," Wyatt said, ushering the women out the door.

Priscilla, trembling with a mix of fear and excitement, grasped Amanda's arm tightly as they rushed towards the hotel. Blake, Clint, and Rosalee stood waiting inside the grand lobby, their expectant faces mirroring the palpable anticipation hanging in the air.

At that moment, she realized how much she had missed them. A brief, awkward pause ensued as Clint embraced her and softly murmured, "I have missed you so much, Priscilla."

A faint blush crept across her cheeks as she noticed Wyatt's observant gaze. It was undeniable; her affections were strong for both men. And now that they were going off to Nashville, she pondered how to make it work.

Amanda made it easier when she approached Wyatt and put her arm through his. "You will ride with me in my car, won't you? I'm not familiar with the roads. Martha and I would appreciate it greatly."

"Of course," he said, though his eyes lingered on Priscilla.

Clint noticed. "I'll take it from here, brother," he said with an affectionate slap on the back.

Once they were on the road, Priscilla nestled against Clint's shoulder, feeling a sense of contentment in the cozy back seat. Rosalee chattered aimlessly about their upcoming activities in Nashville.

As they left Maury County behind, Priscilla found herself swept up in the excitement. And when Clint's warm lips met hers, she felt a profound sense of belonging.

Back in Nashville

Priscilla breathed a sigh of relief as she stepped back into Nashville, the familiar city that wrapped around her like a warm embrace, offering a much-needed sense of safety. Clint, with his genuine charm and gentle demeanor, always left her feeling cherished and valued. However, a surprising twist caught her off guard: Wyatt's newfound interest in Amanda. As she witnessed his attention shift toward her sister, Priscilla felt an unsettling knot form in her stomach. To shield herself from the sting of jealousy, she cloaked herself in a thin veneer of indifference, masking the turmoil within. Deep down, though, she wrestled with bitterness as the realization settled in.

Priscilla found Wyatt's approach to their recent romantic encounter in the marshes maddening. Their undeniable attraction had flourished; however, he ignored the chemistry crackling between them, leaving her uncomfortable as he remained silent and shunned her. Despite her growing affection for Wyatt, she reminded herself of her obligation to remain faithful to Clint. He was, after all, her benefactor; without his support, Lee Dodd would have found her and murdered her.

During a social gathering hosted by Rosalee, Priscilla experienced a moment of jealousy as she observed Wyatt and Amanda sharing a dance and laughter. She bit her lip, yearning to be in his arms, even as she reminded herself that he was dancing with his sister, offering no cause for concern. Clint, who may have noticed her discomfort, remained silent, adhering to his principles of honor and integrity.

As the group stood together, flutes of champagne in hand, the atmosphere shifted with the arrival of a distinguished gentleman. His entrance sparked a wave of excitement among the attendees. It soon became clear that Andrew Wilder was the father of Blake, Clint, and Wyatt, a man of significant stature. The gathering erupted in cheerful exchanges, embraces, and handshakes.

Upon Clint introducing her, he remarked, "Why have I not had the pleasure of meeting this enchanting lady before? How have you kept her hidden from me for so long?"

Priscilla blushed, captivated by his inherent charm and undeniable charisma. She would become an enthusiastic admirer of Andrew Wilder. Little did she know the significant role he would assume in her life and that of her sister. He was, after all, Amanda's father.

Andrew's presence commanded the room, and he possessed an almost irresistible magnetism. Throughout the evening, he cut in on Clint during their dance, mentioning his horses and stables. He looked her square in the eye and said, "Clint has spoken of your horsemanship, and I have an Arabian horse that would be perfect for you. An Equestrian Competition with a substantial prize of eighty thousand dollars is coming soon. I propose we train for it together and share the winnings." He paused, then added, "You are the most beautiful woman in this room, and I do not doubt you can win the competition."

Priscilla's thoughts were a whirlwind. The immense trust placed in her by a man of his stature was overwhelming. However, her composure faltered when he convened the family later that evening and declared that Priscilla would move to his mansion. He explained that the training regimen would be strenuous, beginning at 5:30 a.m. every weekday.

The color ebbed from her cheeks as he announced, "Wyatt will also live there. He will be your primary trainer, as he is well-acquainted with the horse." An unmistakable tension permeated the atmosphere when her gaze locked with Wyatt's. Although she was ready to proceed, she harbored doubts about Wyatt's willingness, given his apparent desire to maintain a distance between them.

With a stern expression, Wyatt remarked, "Priscilla, are you aware of the immense challenge this endeavor entails? To secure victory in this competition, your efforts must exceed anything you've ever done. It will be demanding. And I'll have to be hard on you."

Priscilla flinched, perceiving Wyatt as both arrogant and condescending. However, she reminded herself that the dynamics had shifted. He was no longer her bodyguard; now, he was her trainer. Reunited with his esteemed brothers, she saw him in a different light: wealthy, admired, and respected.

She set aside her inner turmoil. This was the greatest opportunity she had ever encountered. "I will work hard, win the competition, and make the family proud," she declared with a bright smile, overwhelmed at their generous offer.

"You will emerge victorious, my dear; you will claim the most prestigious trophy presented in Nashville in quite some time," Clint declared. He lifted her and spun her around. The prospect of this significant opportunity invigorated her, fueling her determination to succeed and establish herself as the premier equestrienne in Nashville.

Throughout the evening, she was aware of Wyatt's persistent gaze, yet she restrained her burgeoning attraction to the assertive and rugged Wilder brother, whom she had deemed the most untamed of the trio. To her astonishment, he grasped her arm, guided her to the dance floor, and held her as he led her in a commanding dance.

"I am almost looking forward to this," he remarked, gazing into her eyes. She maintained her gaze without hesitation and allowed herself to be captivated; her lips parted, and her eyes softened.

"Why are you doing this?" she asked. "You know it will lead to complications."

"It's only complicated if you want it to be," Wyatt replied in a measured voice. "We're both adults, and we must contain our feelings for each other regardless of what they are. I aim to see you win and am eager to see your true potential."

"My true potential?" she repeated, puzzled. "I thought we knew each other."

"You have many layers, Priscilla," he continued. "And I intend to peel them away until you're as naked as you were in the marshes."

Priscilla's brow furrowed. "Nothing happened. You're toying with me. I've put that day in the marshes behind me, and I would ask that you do the same."

Wyatt's dark eyes burned in hers. "You've got it all turned around. You're toying with me. It was all a game for you. You lay with me and kissed me as if I were your long-lost lover. I was a perfect gentleman despite your brazenness. Once we returned to the house, it was as if it had never happened." He tightened his hold on her. "You want me, Priscilla. You're not a schoolgirl anymore, and I think it's time we did something about it."

"Don't be a fool," Priscilla whispered. "Clint is my benefactor, and I owe everything to him. You need to remember that he is your brother." It was as if he'd turned a deaf ear as he glided her across the room and out to the patio.

"What on earth are you doing?" she asked as he pulled her down a walkway behind the bushes. He kissed her, and she knew in her heart it was a battle she could never win. Wyatt evoked wondrous, warm, dangerous feelings within her, and even though her mind objected, her heart betrayed her.

She pulled away. "That must never happen again," she murmured, her voice trembling. "I have to go," she said, smoothing her hair as she composed herself. With a furtive glance over her shoulder, she hurried back to the gathering.

Clint met her at the open French door, looking puzzled.

"I needed a breath of fresh air," she lied.

"Are you okay? Your face is flushed."

"I'm fine. It's too warm. I need a glass of water."

As she crossed the room on Clint's arm, she made eye contact with Andrew, who appeared perplexed. A flush spread across her neck. *Had he seen her leave with Wyatt?* The uncertainty was overwhelming. She felt an urgent need to talk to Martha, who always provided her with a sense of stability. She had entangled herself in a complex situation and wasn't sure how to extricate herself.

Clint summoned a server to request some water just as Martha approached, her expression inscrutable. "Are you okay?" she inquired with a look of concern.

"Yes, I just felt too warm."

Leaning closer, Martha whispered, "Would it have anything to do with Wyatt?"

Priscilla inhaled, almost suffocating on her water, and wondered if her *secret rendezvous with Wyatt had been revealed.*

Clint grasped Priscilla's arm. "I don't believe it's water you require," he remarked as he guided her away. "Perhaps some time alone would be more beneficial."

Her guilt and repressed passion for Wyatt were stifling. As she walked alongside Clint, the fresh breeze soothed her tumultuous emotions.

"Wouldn't you agree that it's a beautiful evening?" Clint remarked as they passed the precise location where Wyatt had kissed her thirty minutes prior. *Was he aware of her indiscretion and testing her?* The uncertainty was excruciating.

"It is," she responded, trying to compose herself. Clint's calm and reassuring presence prompted her to dispel the doubts and fears concerning any potential discord between them.

He led her to a rose-adorned gazebo, cradling her face before kissing her.

She felt an unexpected spark at his tender kiss. It was nice, but she wanted more, so she kissed him again. At that moment, she realized the passion had always been there, but he was too much of a gentleman to reveal his true feelings. She found herself falling in love with him all over again.

"This is nice," he murmured, embracing her and caressing her arms. "For some time, I feared your interest had waned. But kisses don't lie, do they?"

"No, they do not," she answered, her heart surging with relief. Her affection for him remained steadfast. Despite her moonlight tryst with Wyatt, she loved Clint. Her kiss had proven her love. Hadn't it?

Blaze

The unique aroma of hay, straw, and manure and the inherent scent of horses evoked a sense of nostalgia and comfort. Priscilla once more felt deeply content in her familiar environment and profoundly proud that Andrew Wilder had selected her to ride Blaze in the forthcoming competition.

Blaze pinned back his ears and swished his tail, showing his wariness toward her as she brushed him. His persona changed, and he became more tolerant of her once Wyatt and António, a professional trainer, joined her.

"There are twenty-two award-winning horses in the stable, but Blaze is regarded as the epitome of elegance and is our most prized possession," Antonio bragged. "The black stallion carries himself with an attitude that shows his winning spirit."

A smile of pure pleasure played on Priscilla's lips as she methodically made long, sweeping strokes with the brush across the stallion's gleaming black coat. Wyatt placed his hand over hers and advised, "Apply a gentle touch. Blaze can sense your nervousness. So whatever hostility you feel for me—set it aside."

Priscilla drew in a sharp breath. "This isn't the first time I've groomed a horse, but last night is the first time I've encountered such arrogance from a man."

"The problem is you have more experience and expertise with horses than you do with men," he said casually as he tossed the brush aside. He gave a cocky wink as he lifted the saddle and goaded her on. "Let's get you saddled up and see how you do with a horse with spirit. He's not like the English horses you're used to."

Priscilla raised her brows at the innuendo—a veiled reflection of something much deeper. Was he trying to break the horse or her? A smile tugged at her lip. She saw right through him—he'd had the audacity to compare their relationship with horsemanship. But she had to admit—she lacked experience with unpredictable men like him who challenged her. Self-doubt crept in, and she gritted her teeth as Antonio offered his clasped hands to hoist her into the saddle.

True to the Arabian's unique personality, Blaze snorted when she mounted him. However, she dismissed her apprehension, asserting dominance by pulling back on the reins and digging in with her boots to signal her command. Blaze, however, resisted, showing his displeasure by bucking—hell-bent on throwing her off his back. She remained composed, drawing a deep breath, and attempted to lift his head. Despite his repeated bucking, she steadfastly maintained her patience.

Wyatt rested against the pristine white fence, a knowing smile on his lips. "Antonio, bring out Blaze's favored filly," he instructed.

In a realm of refined equestrian elegance, Priscilla and Wyatt navigated the opulent estate. The sun shone brightly, and the air was invigorating, creating an idyllic atmosphere as Wyatt and Priscilla trotted side by side. Blaze was no longer focused on bucking her off and was on his best behavior with the filly nearby. She and Wyatt rode around the expansive land for an hour, stopping at a creek to let the horses drink.

"The Arabian horse is renowned for its intelligence," Wyatt remarked. "It perceives everything about you—your scent, demeanor, and whether you possess strength or frailty." He scrutinized her, his eyes sweeping her from head to toe. "This task isn't suited for a mere girl; it demands a strong woman to manage such a high-spirited horse."

Priscilla could not hide her disdain. His implication was clear: he doubted her capability to handle Blaze. "I've got this," Priscilla said with determination. She crinkled her nose to show her displeasure. Did Wyatt think she would let a powerful nine-hundred-pound horse stand between her and eighty thousand dollars? It was a lot of money, and she wouldn't let it slip through her fingers. Besides, she had something to prove—to herself and the Wilder family.

When she and Antonio arrived back at the stables, Wyatt dismounted and helped her off the horse. "What happens when we take the filly away?" he asked.

Wyatt's attitude in treating her like a schoolgirl left her speechless. "Blaze will not like it," she stammered.

"That's an understatement," Wyatt said. "Blaze could throw you—break your neck and leave you paralyzed. Worse yet, he could kill you."

Antonio intervened. "Give her time, Wyatt. Blaze will calm down."

Guileless, Priscilla clung to his words, needing Antonio's support and expertise. He was one of the most acclaimed horse trainers in the arena. She was an accomplished horsewoman, feeling inadequate by Wyatt's critical remarks. She felt something was going on, some underlying reason for him to bring her down and cause her to lose her self-esteem.

"He will not calm down until she does," Wyatt stated, fixing his gaze intently on Priscilla. "You are tense. I can sense it, and Blaze can sense it as well."

Priscilla lowered her head during the strained exchange. The atmosphere between them was so thick that time stretched, becoming more painful by the minute. At last, she murmured, "I will do better tomorrow. I promise."

"You are afraid of Blaze, Priscilla. And until you conquer your fears, this will not work. I'll have to find another rider."

Overwhelmed with distress, Priscilla hurried to Martha's room and knocked hard. When the door opened, it surprised her to find Martha's suitcase on the bed, filled with clothes.

"What on earth are you doing?" Priscilla's voice betrayed her anxiety. "You cannot leave. I need you here. I have just experienced the most dreadful day of my life."

Martha didn't look up but went back to her packing. "It gets worse. Maury County is in utter chaos. — Belle called and said Big Bill has a list of trial witnesses, and Solon Wooley's dead. They say Big Bill's on a killing spree and is going to kill all the witnesses."

Priscilla's expression held a look of disbelief. "What!"

"Big Bill and Solon Wooley had a confrontation, and Big Bill shot Wooley five times, and then his gun jammed. He said he was going home and get another gun and shoot the rest, but after the sheriff pursued him, he fled to the woods."

Overcome with fear, Priscilla's mouth gaped. "I'm next," she whispered.

"The good news is—you're last on the list. He's targeting the Cummins brothers next, and they're a tough bunch. They might, very well, take him out before he gets to you."

Martha's brow furrowed. "I can do more for you there than I can here." She heaved a sigh. "This is a lovely place, Priscilla, but it isn't where I belong. I miss my sister and all my friends. I plan to meet with Big Bill's family to persuade them to speak with him and remove your name from the list. You didn't know Fautt. If you had testified, you would have committed perjury."

"That's true, but Big Bill has more than one reason to hate me. Lee Dodd drowned behind my house. I'm sure he holds a grudge against me and means to settle it." Priscilla strode to the window and gazed at the distant stable, considering the immense challenge of handling Blaze and doubting her capability without the filly. Her mind was spinning out of control. Should I leave with Martha? Abandon everything and return to the safety of the marshes? What did it matter if I won the horse competition? Big Bill will kill me—it's only a matter of time. Suddenly, it was all too much—the inner conflict of loving both Wyatt and Clint—leaving might be the kinder option to avoid hurting either of them. Wyatt had hurt her today, so why should she care?

Clint Knows

Priscilla was on the verge of packing her suitcase when the door swung open, and Amanda entered. She took one look at Priscilla and perceived the uncertainty etched on her face. "What is happening here? You aren't leaving, are you? You cannot afford to let an opportunity of this magnitude slip through your fingers."

"Blaze is skittish and won't follow my commands. If I can't gain control soon, I won't be able to enter the competition."

"You have the capability, Priscilla," Amanda assured. "I have every confidence in you. You've already proven yourself in competitions with Blue Moon." She paused. "But that's not why I'm here. I have good news. Big Bill's reign of terror will cease; it is only a matter of time. Belle called and informed me that the Cummins brothers had devised a strategy to eliminate him. It's the talk of the town."

Priscilla raised a hand to her forehead and said, "There are always rumors circulating about the Thomason brothers. It is common knowledge that Big Bill is the quickest draw in the county." She let out a weary sigh. "Every bone in my body aches from Blaze's bucking. I cannot concern myself with Big Bill at the moment."

"Assert your authority," Amanda advised in a hushed tone. "Show him who's in charge."

"But the horse weighs nine hundred pounds. He's powerful."

Amanda held Priscilla at arm's length. "Do you remember those nights when we were younger, and you were frightened?"

"Yes," Priscilla replied, her voice wavering.

"Back then, I encouraged you to be strong, and you were. Look at the results—it all worked out. You've achieved so much—and won trophies, and awards, and earned money and recognition."

Priscilla looked wistful. "That was when I was riding Blue Moon—my Tennessee Walking Horse. The audience fell in love with the girl in Jodhpurs. Rosalee brought a touch of fashion to the show, and people couldn't get enough. But this competition is different. This time, I'm the girl in black who must prove I can handle a high-spirited Arabian horse. Blaze is like a bolt of lightning from a cannon."

Martha had a look of concern. "There's a saying that if one is to master a living creature, they must first master oneself."

Priscilla looked weary. "You don't understand. I can't break him. He's unruly with me, but he has perfect behavior with Wyatt and Antonio. He senses something about me isn't right."

"Which is out of control? The horse or the man?" Martha questioned. "I saw how Wyatt danced with you last night—not much left to the imagination. And then he whisked you away, and you were gone for a long time."

Priscilla looked weary. "There's been bad juju between us. He brings it up when we're training for the competition, and I think Blaze senses it."

"My word," Amanda exclaimed. "What in the world has happened between the two of you?"

"It's about what happened in the marshes," Priscilla said. "When I persuaded him to go skinny-dipping with me."

"Why can't he get past it?" Amanda asked. "He said nothing happened, and it was a mistake. He knows you're promised to Clint."

"It isn't his fault," Priscilla said. "I encouraged him."

Overwhelmed, Amanda covered her eyes with her hand. "I must be blunt, Priscilla. What did those women at Belle's Saloon teach you? Engaging in such intimate behavior with a man who is not your husband is something a shameless hussy would do."

"They taught me not to take any wooden nickels," remarked Priscilla. "And that there was no need to bind my chest because I'm small-breasted." She tossed her head. "The five-dollar bills fit well in the low neckline of my dress. As for some of their other suggestions, they are better left unsaid. Regardless, Belle's girls' intentions were good and aimed to steer me in the right direction." She straightened her back. "It was better than peeling potatoes in the kitchen."

Amanda flushed with embarrassment. "How scandalous! You were so sweet and innocent when I left. Now, it appears these women of ill repute have corrupted your mind. Have you lost your sense of morality, Priscilla?"

"Isn't that the pot calling the kettle black?" Priscilla retorted. "You and John were living in sin."

"That's different. John and I intended to marry. Wyatt was your bodyguard," Amanda huffed. "It is improper for an unmarried girl to skinny dip with a man when she is not promised to him."

Priscilla lifted her chin in defiance. "Then I suppose I'm a shameless hussy. I felt no remorse. Enjoying the sun on a beautiful day with an attractive man beside me was quite pleasant." She hesitated. "I had never seen a naked man before, except once when I intruded on one of Belle's girls when she was turning a trick." She wrinkled her nose in distaste. "It was rather awkward."

Amanda's complexion paled, and she pressed a hand to her forehead, appearing on the verge of fainting. "Please...do not say another word."

"And what of John? You have not mentioned him since you arrived."

Amanda sighed; her frustration was apparent. "I dedicated myself to my work, and the business was flourishing. But he left me for another woman. He gave me half of our savings, and I returned home intending to establish another business."

Priscilla, tactless and critical, remarked, "It seems the tables have turned, just as Mother predicted." She blinked while scrutinizing Amanda. "You're in a precarious position. I might as well say it: You're ruined."

Amanda's intense stare didn't waver. "I am not ruined, Priscilla. I learned a great deal from John. He taught me the intricacies of running a business. I have worked hard to get where I am today."

Priscilla shrugged. "You're no better than the girls at Belle's. You slept with John without being married. In comparison, sunbathing naked seems trivial." She pointed her finger at Amanda. "Mother is responsible for our predicament—she relied on the hard work of a coal miner during the early years, all while engaging in brief episodes of infidelity, of which you are the result. Don't you understand? It was about survival—and matters of the heart." Her expression turned blasé. "As if—Mother had a heart."

"Of course, she has a heart," Amanda said in a rueful tone. "Every woman has a heart."

Priscilla's gaze was steadfast. "Like the girls at Belle's say, a roll in the hay is a roll in the hay. There's not much difference once the lights are out."

Amanda's patience had worn thin. She tugged at her hair, her expression contorted with distress. "How can you be so callous? I loved John and worked just as hard as he did."

Priscilla folded her arms. "It might surprise you that the women at Belle's share a deep affection for their men. They also labor from dawn until dusk, and, contrary to some opinions, they are human beings with genuine emotions."

Martha, assuming control of the situation, interjected. "That's enough of your mutual insults. It is disgraceful for sisters to treat each other in this manner." She grasped Priscilla's arm. "I'm taking you back to Maury County, Priscilla. Perhaps some time away from your suitors will help you gain perspective."

True to form, Amanda felt compelled to have the final say. "While you are away, I will ensure I set everything right. There can only be one man, Priscilla."

The resilience within Priscilla had waned. Not only had she endured the physical battering from the horse, but her sister's cutting remarks and allegations had deeply wounded her. She departed on the train with Martha within the hour.

Amanda was forthright as she pulled Wyatt aside and said, "Priscilla's gone. Martha has taken her back to Maury County."

"Why?" he asked, astonished.

"She's upset because she can't control Blaze, and she suspects the horse senses a certain tension between you two. What is this about—why are you angry?"

"I'm not angry. She's afraid of the horse. And he perceives her fear."

"She has every reason to fear both the horse and men—especially you," she retorted, straightening her posture. "You have shared intimate moments with my sister, and it is my responsibility to protect her reputation. You will marry her, Wyatt."

Wyatt's expression darkened with indignation. "I did not lay a hand on her. Your sister possesses a spirited and adventurous nature, and I indulged a fantasy—hers, yet I conducted myself as a perfect gentleman."

"A true gentleman does not find himself naked with a young woman they entrust him to protect," she said.

"I have feelings for Priscilla," he confessed.

"Feelings for my sister?" Amanda exclaimed in disbelief. "What sort of man are you? Your brother is courting Priscilla."

A chill laced Wyatt's voice. "He is aware. I disclosed every single detail."

"What!" Amanda exclaimed. "Clint knows you've lain naked with Priscilla?"

"Yes. It's caused conflict, but it's not beyond repair. He loves her and is unwilling to let her go. And I can't give her up either."

Dumbfounded, Amanda's mouth fell open. "Are you implying that Priscilla is in a love triangle?"

"Yes, but no one intended for this to happen. I believe her feelings for my brother stem from gratitude rather than love; after all, he is her benefactor. However, she cannot differentiate between the two."

Amanda crossed her arms. "One can experience both gratitude and love," she countered. "Love encompasses a multitude of emotions."

"What do you know of love, sister?" he asked. "It is my impression that love has not treated you well."

Amanda blushed crimson. "What I believed was love was an illusion. It served as an escape from the constraints of my circumstances, into which I had been born. It was my path to freedom, though I was unaware of it. The crucial truth that I desired a career over companionship only came to me after John fell in love with another woman.

"I'm sorry for you," Wyatt said.

"Don't be," Amanda said. "I achieved my goal. I have become an accomplished dressmaker. I'm independent now, and I don't need John."

"What of your feelings for him? Do you feel any affection at all?"

"No. But I care about my sister, and I swear, if you break her heart, you will face serious consequences."

The Coin Toss

Andrew Wilder had resolved conflicts between his sons in the past, but never ones involving matters of the heart. Clint and Wyatt had always shared a close bond, but now a barbed edge between them threatened their family unity. After much reflection and careful consideration of the circumstances, Andrew decided it was time to address and resolve the love triangle.

As they sat together in the formal dining room, the three looked relaxed, all dressed in plaid shirts and blue jeans. Rosalee and Amanda were attending a women's suffrage meeting, providing him with the freedom to express his thoughts without the concern of disapproval from Rosalee. She was a caring and protective mother who abhorred family conflict. Her method of giving the boys 'their way' meant they had grown up somewhat spoiled, but they had become responsible young men and outstanding citizens.

Andrew sat at the head of the table, a commanding presence. He held a piece of steak with his fork and said, "I believe this is the finest steak I've ever had. What do you think, boys?"

"Daddy, how can you possibly consider food at a time like this?" Clint drawled; his Southern accent pronounced. "Wyatt has committed an atrocity—frolicking with Priscilla, stark naked, in the marshes. His actions are irreparable."

Wyatt shrugged. "I did nothing she didn't ask me to do."

Andrew seemed to savor the steak as he chewed, then washed it down with a long swallow of Western Reserve. "Son, everything can be fixed. Forgiveness is a choice. We must think beyond a whimsical day when a young girl forgot herself and acted like what she is—an eighteen-year-old with raging hormones." He took another drink and set his glass down hard. "She's a beautiful girl and, unfortunately, enticed your brother. It was a single day wiped away by the winds of time, never to be repeated. But this expensive whiskey and Angus beef is something we can enjoy forever—as a family, under our loving roof."

The atmosphere in the room was tense as Clint struggled to come to terms with his emotions. Despite his brother's obvious distress, Wyatt seemed completely absorbed in the pleasure of his meal and his third tumbler of whiskey. He lifted his fork and pointed it at Andrew. "Damn straight. This is the best steak I've had in a long time," he exclaimed before devouring it.

A smile tugged at Andrew's lips. While he had never admitted his preferences, he was drawn to Wyatt's unwavering positivity and his remarkable ability to find silver linings in even the most challenging circumstances. While Clint often came across as a complainer in Andrew's eyes, he couldn't deny the sense of adventure that fueled Clint's pursuits. It was through mining that Clint had amassed a fortune beyond Andrew's financial standing.

Anger overtook sorrow as Clint gripped his knife and stabbed the steak, watching the blood pool on the plate. He looked repulsed when his potato turned bloody red on the edge. He pushed the potato to the side.

Wyatt was aware of his brother's idiosyncrasies and held a basket of biscuits out to him. "Sop it up," he said in an off-handed, careless way.

It was a disparaging remark, and Clint did not take it lightly. "My ass," he shot back. "My potato is ruined! It's bloody ruined."

Wyatt shrugged. "Still tastes good."

Clint stared at the potato and the server standing at the side of the table near his father, as if deciding whether to ask for another. This was not new; he was a finicky eater.

"If you don't want it—I'll eat it," Wyatt chimed. When he reached over with his fork to stab the potato, Clint shoved his hand away.

"I want it," Clint spat. "Do you have to be so quick on the draw? Can't you just wait for me to decide?"

Andrew gave Wyatt a stern look. "You know your brother doesn't like a messy plate."

Clint's eyes blazed with defiance as he eagerly cut into his steak, devouring each bite as if he were ravenous. He drained a tumbler of whiskey, emphatically placing it on the table before raising it for the server to refill. His mind raced with tumultuous thoughts. *How could things ever be the same between him and Wyatt? And did Priscilla favor Wyatt over him? The mere notion threatened to consume him from the inside out.* He pushed his plate away with a disgruntled sigh, then glared across the table, accusingly stating, "You have no consideration — you would take the food right off my plate."

"Calm down," Andrew mused. "He thought you didn't want it, and everyone knows your brother is an opportunist."

"Nah, I'm just hungry," Wyatt said casually. "What's the big deal?"

Clint could not contain his anger as he directed his frustration at Wyatt. "You're downplaying the situation, but you overstepped your boundaries. And I hired you as her bodyguard."

Wyatt spoke with firm conviction. "I did my job," he asserted. "I didn't mean for it to happen, and I can't change it. What's done is done. I don't think you can forget and move on with her, any more than you could handle that bloody potato."

"I ate it," Clint said through clenched teeth.

"But you didn't like it," Wyatt said. "And I don't mind."

Andrew spoke up. "Fact is, son,—you have to swallow what happened between Wyatt and Priscilla or let her go."

"Daddy, there's a big difference between a messy plate and a girl," Clint declared.

"The question is—can you forget and forgive?" Andrew asked. "It isn't as if your brother defiled her, he just..."

"I gave in to temptation," Wyatt said, cutting him off. "The reality is—I believe I'm in love with her."

Clint's hand curled into a fist. "Get over it. I'm not giving her up."

The air was thick with tension and male angst.

"Let's let Daddy decide what to do," Wyatt said, as Clint's eyes bore into him accusingly.

Andrew grappled with the weight of the decision he had to make. He knew that the choice he made at that moment would have a profound impact on their lives. Closing his eyes, he deliberated on which man was the best fit for Priscilla and their family, considering the complexities of love and the tainted past. His fingers found the half-dollar coin in his pocket, a token from his father, and he fiddled with it, feeling the gravity of the decision weighing on him.

Andrew spoke in a sympathetic tone, acknowledging the challenging nature of the situation. "The only solution I can think of is to settle this by flipping a coin," he suggested.

"Flip a coin!" Clint said, his voice full of opposition. "My God. This is my life."

"Sounds fair," nodded Wyatt.

As they stepped into the drawing room, a palpable sense of apprehension filled the air. Andrew reached into his pocket and produced a gleaming half-dollar. "Heads is the winner," he announced, his voice cutting through the tension in the room.

"No," Clint said stubbornly. "Tails is the winner."

Andrew wiped away the beads of sweat and turned to Wyatt. "Is that okay, Wyatt?"

Wyatt shrugged. "Dad should pick. It's only fair."

"Well, Lady Liberty is on the front of the coin, and I think it should be heads," Andrew said.

"Fine. I'll pick tails," Clint said, his tone sounding like an unruly child.

As Andrew made the high toss, it was as if time stood still. Their eyes were on the shiny coin, and Clint and Andrew gasped as it landed, showing Lady Liberty.

"Heads," Andrew said firmly.

Wyatt's dark eyes flashed with excitement.

"I will not let a coin toss determine my future with Priscilla," Clint argued. "She must choose."

As the metallic clink of the coin echoed in the air, Andrew deftly slipped the uniquely crafted two-headed coin into his pocket, a wry smile creeping onto his face. The unexpected twist of fate during the coin toss left him grappling with mixed emotions as he reassured himself that it wasn't his decision, but an act of destiny that favored Wyatt.

"I'm leaving first thing in the morning to claim my woman," Wyatt declared, dismissing Clint's comment.

"Your woman—my ass," Clint hissed. "I will not give her up without a fight."

Tension crackled in the room. "Bring it on," Wyatt said.

"Stop it right now," Andrew said to halt the escalating argument. But it was too late - fists started flying. Before Andrew could separate them, Clint had a cut upper lip, and Wyatt sported a blackened eye. A chair had been knocked over, and a lamp had fallen precariously onto the carpet without breaking. Minutes later, a maid arrived to clean blood off the thick gray carpet, and another restored order to the drawing room.

"It's a good thing your mother didn't see this," Andrew scolded.

As the dust settled, neither Clint nor Wyatt emerged as the victor. Both had traded fierce blows, but no one suffered serious injuries. Clint and Wyatt departed to tend to their wounds, leaving Andrew to contemplate the outcome with a stiff drink. Retrieving a silver dollar from his pocket, he examined it closely. Never in his wildest dreams had he imagined that a bitter conflict would erupt between his sons over a woman. But she wasn't just any woman—she was the most gorgeous, well-spoken girl he'd ever known, and he was determined to have her in the family.

Priscilla's Plight

Priscilla felt a wave of nostalgia as she sat at a table with Martha, Belle, and Lucy. The lingering scent of stale cigarette smoke and whiskey evoked memories of the arduous days she had spent in the kitchen, laboring over scrubbing pans and peeling potatoes. She coughed as Belle took a long drag from her cigarette and exhaled. Despite the irritating smoke, she found the food to be exquisite. After wiping the barbecue sauce from her fingers with a napkin, she pushed aside a plate of ribs, now cleaned to the bone.

Lucy, elegantly attired in an emerald green, low-cut gown that accentuated her figure, leaned forward and spoke confidentially, "You were only fourteen when Clint took you away from this saloon. I remember it vividly, and now look at you—all grown up, dressed in the finest attire, and driving your own Model T Ford." She smiled, revealing teeth stained with lipstick and marked by a slight overbite. "Are you going to get hitched?"

Priscilla flushed. "No. He is a close friend, but we've never spoken of marriage."

"It seems you owe him something. He's given you everything a girl would want." She batted her heavily mascaraed eyes. "If it were me, I'd show my gratitude in a more personal way."

Belle interrupted Lucy with a sharp tone. "That's enough, Lucy. Priscilla is a refined woman; she received a formal education and is known for her skill as a horsewoman."

"That's because she had a 'sugar daddy,'" Lucy replied, adjusting her posture by placing her hands under her wired bra, a habit aimed at accentuating her bust.

"A benefactor," Belle corrected.

Lucy shrugged. "It's the same thing—a wealthy older man supporting a young woman is a benefactor or a sugar daddy." A hint of jealousy flickered in her amber eyes.

The truth hurt. "I'm grateful to Belle and all of you for your help and support," she said in a small voice, feeling humbled.

"You escaped a life of misery with Lee," Lucy said. "Even a woman as striking as yourself cannot change a man's bad temper or his penchant for brothels and wayward women—like me."

Priscilla's face flushed deeply. "You have been with him, haven't you?"

Lucy responded with her characteristic bluntness, "All the girls in the saloon have slept with him."

Priscilla felt a mixture of pity and irritation toward Lucy. The sense of camaraderie they once shared had noticeably diminished. It had been four years, and nothing about Lucy's demeanor had changed, but she now appeared much older than her thirty years. Her overly red lips and heavily rouged cheeks starkly contrasted with her pale, wrinkled skin, aged by smoke and alcohol. Whether it was because of jealousy or simply a bad mood, she couldn't quite tell. Priscilla felt a strong desire to alter the negative atmosphere between them.

"Are you still as naïve as you once were?" Lucy asked.

Priscilla hesitated to divulge details. "Probably not," she answered, reflecting on the day in the marshes with Wyatt. Although it felt inappropriate to seek relationship advice from a prostitute, their suggestions were valuable. It seemed worth attempting once again. "I'm entangled in a complex romantic situation," Priscilla confided. "I have feelings for Clint's brother Wyatt as well." She exhaled, her expression becoming pensive. "If you must know, Wyatt is handsome and an exceptional kisser. I swam naked with him."

Belle's face reflected her surprise at Priscilla's candor. "Are you in love with Wyatt? I suspected he might be a temptation. From the moment I saw you two together, I could see the sparks fly."

"I don't know what love is," Priscilla stammered. "I've never been with a man before. Besides, nothing happened. I'm still a virgin."

"It could be lust," Lucy said with a wry smile.

Belle looked over her shoulder. "Well, in this town, societal expectations dictate that if you swim naked with a man, you will marry him or become an outcast. Does anyone know?"

"They may not know she swam naked with him, but they know they're entangled romantically," Martha responded in a measured tone. "Gossip is rampant in Nashville, and Priscilla has not been discreet. We were at a ball last week, and she was dancing with Wyatt, but abruptly vanished for an extended time."

"He swept me away to the garden," Priscilla confessed. "And I found him irresistible—I cannot say no to the man."

"I never would have taken you for a hot pants," Lucy said, her voice derisively mocking. "You appear prim and proper, like sugar wouldn't melt in your mouth."

Priscilla's eyes flashed in anger. "It wasn't like that — I'm not like you."

"Well, you were one night," Lucy said in a smug voice. "You made a ton of money that night and were proud of it. You were shameless, taking their money, shoving drinks in their hand."

"It was one night," Priscilla said. "I needed money. It seemed like the right thing to do."

"Stop it, you two," Belle scolded. "There's a little whore in all of us. Wouldn't you agree, Martha?"

Martha sniffed at the baited question. "What about you, Belle? You have owned a successful brothel for years—surely you must possess some insights into men and circumstances such as this. What does a woman do when she's in a triangle?"

Belle chuckled. "I am a madam, and the brothel is a business for me. I was once married, but my husband left me for another woman, rendering me penniless. That experience left me embittered, and I had no desire to pursue another relationship. My widowed aunt took me in, and I worked as a housekeeper in a hotel. Over time, I saved enough money to start my business. Perhaps you should ask Lucy what she thinks."

"In the dark, men are all the same," Lucy said. "They don't come to me to be nice; they come to me to be bad—to indulge in acts their wives refuse to engage in. Sometimes, they don't even take off their boots, and once the door slams behind them, they're so drunk they don't even know my name. Then I get that sinking feeling. I feel alone and used. But some treat me better than others. I would go with the one that is the kindest."

"What about love?" Priscilla asked. "Have you ever been in love?"

A shadow crossed her face. "Love? I know nothing about love. To me, it is merely a job." Her tone softened, and a warm smile spread across her face. "Belle and the girls are my family. I have a sense of belonging here. My money has enabled me to send my niece to college. She's a schoolteacher now."

Although Lucy claimed she was happy, a deadness in her eyes suggested otherwise. Priscilla suspected she might be a bit psychologically damaged from being used and subjected to acts of degradation. Lucy rarely held eye contact for long and sometimes stared into space, appearing emotionless. Tears welled up in Priscilla's eyes. *They were selfless people who had taken her in and loved her when she had nowhere else to go. By the grace of God, that could have been me,* Priscilla thought to herself.

Suddenly, the cacophony she had been striving to ignore grew prominent: the metallic clinking of coins at the poker table, the distinct ting of beer glasses, and the laughter of Belle's girls. Yet, amid these noises, one sound made her ears sharpen—the melancholic strains of a fiddle. It broke her composure, causing tears to cascade down her cheeks like a river. God, how she missed her father.

A familiar voice abruptly drew her attention. "Would you care to dance?" Clint inquired, standing over her, exuding confidence and charm.

"Speak of the devil," Martha remarked wryly.

"What a surprise," Priscilla responded, a smile forming on her lips as she wiped away her tears while Clint led her to the dance floor. "How did you know I was here?

"I figured you'd gone back home. When we went through town, I saw your car," he said. "But did not expect to find you and Martha in the company of a madam and a prostitute, crying in your beer."

"Tonight I had an epiphany," Priscilla confessed. "I simply realized what good people they are and how fortunate I am that Belle took me in. If not, they could have forced me into an arranged marriage with a man I could never love. And if you hadn't come into my life, I may have become a 'woman of the night' like Lucy."

Clint's blue eyes danced in glee. "I remember you in that red dress, and all that makeup covering your beautiful face. I fell in love with you that night."

Priscilla's heart raced as the familiar emotions from their first encounter surged back. He was the man who had transformed her life, and she loved him dearly. Yet, there was something crucial he needed to know.

"There is something you're unaware of," Priscilla began. "I wish I could go back and alter things—but I cannot."

"I know about you and Wyatt. You went for a swim together, and that's all it was. If you can move past it, then so can I."

"But he has become a significant part of my life, and I'm feeling uncertain," she confessed.

Suddenly, Wyatt interceded, his tone filled with urgency. "We need to leave immediately."

"What's happening?" Clint asked, a hint of irritation in his voice.

"A sheriff's deputy at the bar alerted me that Big Bill was spotted at Watt's Hill, driving recklessly. They say he's intoxicated on moonshine, shouting threats and obscenities at everyone he encounters. He has a hit list, and Priscilla is on it. We have to get the hell out of Maury County."

"I can't leave until I get my father's violin," declared Priscilla. "I continually forget about it, and if anything were to happen to it, I could never forgive myself." Caught in a whirlwind as Wyatt hurried her out the door, Clint went to fetch Martha, whose protests that she had not seen her sister or friends echoed throughout the saloon.

Wyatt's voice was earnest. "We cannot afford to return to your house. Big Bill is a madman."

"I understand, but if he's at Watt's Hill, he's likely searching for men he's been feuding with for years. I am his cousin; he saved my life once, and I cannot fathom that he would harm me."

"Believe it," Wyatt replied. "The deputy said that Big Bill thinks you had something to do with Lee's death. He wants you dead, Priscilla."

Priscilla stood motionless, her heart racing and her mind struggling to comprehend the weight of his words—so damning, so utterly unforeseen. The air around her felt tense as she finally summoned the courage to speak.

"That's utterly preposterous," she declared, her voice trembling with disbelief and exasperation. "I had nothing to do with Lee's death. Whatever happened, he brought upon himself." The shadows in the room seemed to deepen, as if echoing the gravity of the situation.

The Attack

With every mile Priscilla covered in the Tin Lizzy, her awareness grew that she was fighting an enemy lurking in the shadows. Clint and Wyatt had stayed right behind them in the first few miles, but their headlights vanished from sight several miles back. Mules running loose along the country roadside often blocked traffic. And she figured that's what had delayed them.

The porch light wasn't on when she pulled into the drive. They always turned on the porch light when they knew they would be home late.

"I'll leave the car running with the lights on while you unlock the door—then I think I'm going to run down to check the boat's moorings."

"Okay, but don't tarry," Martha warned. "Clint said we have to leave at once."

The headlights shone over the worn path to the marshes. But the light was dim, and she had to feel her way to the boat as she checked the knotted rope.

Out of the inky night, with no warning, someone grabbed her from behind, and a massive hand covered her mouth. Overwhelmed by the struggle to breathe, she watched in anguish as her dreams slipped away, leaving her with a sense of hopelessness.

"Don't scream," Big Bill's gruff voice warned. "I will not hurt you. We need to talk. Why didn't you stand with your family at the trial?"

Priscilla didn't believe a word. Everyone knew the Thomason brothers were liars. Her voice trembled as she spoke. "I didn't know James Fautt and couldn't commit perjury."

Gripping her with his muscular arm, he snarled, "Is that all you can say in your defense? This isn't just about the trial, and you know it. What happened to Lee? It was right here where he died. You caused him to drown, didn't you?"

The sound of fear was unmistakable in Priscilla's voice. "I swear I did nothing. He was standing there when I motored away in my boat. That's the last time I saw him."

"You're lying," accused Big Bill, his voice filled with suspicion. "I examined his corpse, and there was a long, straight mark across his forehead like someone had hit him with a blunt object. I've been here many times to check out the scene, and I'd say you hit him with the oar, and he lost his balance and fell into the water. It's muddy, and he couldn't get out. Did you leave a drowning man stuck in the mud in the water—a man who couldn't swim?"

Priscilla's voice quivered as she spoke. "I swear. Lee was fine. He was angry and cussing at me when I motored away."

Big Bill tightened his grip. "You were the last person who saw him alive, and you had to have hit him with the oar," he raged. "I noticed you weren't at his funeral. If you were innocent, kin would want to be at their cousin's funeral. But you took off with the high-fluting city men. You always thought you were better than we were."

When he jerked her around to face him, the dim glow of the moon showed the battle waging behind his dark eyes. Her voice choked with fear. She replied, "I never thought I was better than anyone else. I was young and scared. I didn't want to marry anyone at all."

A sense of eeriness hung in the air as oppressive silence enveloped her surroundings. A profound sense of dread coursed through her as his large hand gripped her neck. Convinced he was about to snap her neck or strangle her, she gave up. She closed her eyes, and as darkness enveloped her, a vivid montage of memories emerged, chronicling her life: her father playing the fiddle and the cherished moments spent with her sister, Amanda, as they picked flowers in the rose garden.

She started at the sound of his raspy voice in her ear, his whiskey-laden breath causing her stomach to churn. "Do you have anything to say before you die?"

177

Priscilla mustered up all the courage she possessed, her voice strong and convincing. "I'm innocent. I swear I had nothing to do with Lee's death. My father would turn over in his grave if he knew you were threatening me. He liked you."

"Uncle David was a good man—but that doesn't excuse you for treating your kin like they're dirt and killing my brother."

Priscilla knew well that attempting to reason with him was futile. He exuded an aura of heartlessness and callousness. However, she couldn't shake the memory of how, in his younger years, he would sing and dance to her father's captivating fiddle tunes.

"Sometimes, in the night's stillness, I can hear my father's fiddle echoing through the house," Priscilla whispered, her voice filled with a sense of foreboding. "It feels as if he never left."

Big Bill's eyes turned glassy. "Are you trying to spook me?" His sole fear in life was ghosts.

"Everyone knows there are ghosts in these parts," Priscilla said. "And the blood of a Confederate soldier is right there in my foyer. It will always be there."

"Are you shitting me? You've got the blood of a Confederate soldier right there in your house?"

"I swear it's true. People claim they've seen him in the marsh, but I've never encountered him. Still, he could very well be here. A ghost can appear anywhere."

The hair stood up on Big Bill's arm. A nightbird screeched, making him jump. Priscilla felt his grip loosen, and she slipped out of his arms.

Her heart thundered as she ran towards the house, screaming. "Help! Help!"

The gunshot was loud, and the sound echoed in her ears as she stumbled and fell to the ground, the booming noise resounding in her ears, and then everything went black. She awoke to the sound of Wyatt's name echoing throughout the hills. Through a slit in her eyes, she could see Wyatt hovering over her. There were others, but it was dark, and they looked like shadowy figures.

"Are you okay?" Wyatt asked with grave concern.

Priscilla's voice was faint. "I'm not sure. Did Big Bill shoot me?"

"No. That was me shooting into the air. When you didn't come back. Martha called the sheriff. Then we crept down and hid in the bushes. We've been holding a shotgun on him, but could never see our way clear to shoot until you ran."

The sheriff crouched down. "Did Big Bill hurt you?"

"He threatened to kill me and manhandled me," Priscilla said. "When I heard the gunshot, I thought he had shot me."

"If he wanted to shoot you," he would have, the sheriff said. "The deputies handcuffed him and took him to jail. He didn't put up a fight."

"The Sheriff and his deputies arrived just in the nick of time," Wyatt said.

Her tone was cautious. "Where's Clint?"

A voice came out of the darkness. "I'm here, Priscilla."

Priscilla thought his voice sounded strained, as if something were wrong, and then he asked something that stunned her. "Did you kill, Lee?"

The silence was deafening until Martha spoke up. "My Lord, I cannot believe we're having this conversation. Priscilla would hurt no one. And she's lying here in the grass. Doesn't anyone have any decency? The poor girl is in shock."

Wyatt swept Priscilla up in his arms and carried her into the drawing room. Martha brought her a blanket and made a pot of tea.

Priscilla sipped her tea, relieved that Big Bill was behind bars, but uncomfortable with all eyes upon her. The sheriff stood in the doorway while Clint paced the floor. Wyatt sat beside her.

The sheriff cleared his throat and said, "I'm going to ask you again, Priscilla. Did you kill Lee Dodd?"

"No. I did not," Priscilla said. "My God. That happened months ago. And you investigated. It was an accident." Her voice grew haughty. "Don't you remember? I was the victim then, and I'm the victim now. Both men want me dead."

"Calm down," the sheriff said. "I just have to ask. Because Big Bill is making a stink about this, he's convinced that you killed Lee by striking him with the oar and pushing him into the water. Did you know he couldn't swim?"

"No, I did not," Priscilla replied in a level voice. "And I did not hit him with the oar. Why are you treating me like I'm a criminal?"

"I'm just doing my job, Priscilla," the sheriff said.

Clint strode over to the sheriff. "I don't like the way this is going. Do I need to get an attorney?"

"No need to get your hackles up," the sheriff said. "I have a report to make, and when I go back to that jail, I know what Big Bill is going to say—and I'm giving Priscilla a chance to clear her name."

"Clear my name?" Priscilla countered. "A madman attacked me. He had his hand around my throat and could have snapped it. He threatened to kill me."

"We were there and heard it all," Wyatt confirmed. "Everything she said is true."

But the sheriff had had enough. His dark eyes were piercing. "I told you to stay gone, didn't I? Why did you come back to stir up trouble?"

Priscilla rose and straightened her spine. "This is my house. I have a right to be here."

"Well, I can't keep you safe, and I'm advising you again to leave." He appeared flustered when he muttered. "I can't keep Big Bill in jail for long—he'll break out and I can't be responsible."

"What about the other people who are on his list?" Priscilla asked. "Aren't you going to protect them?"

The sheriff let out a heavy sigh. "There's nothing I can do. We're dealing with Big Bill Thomason. He's never lost a gunfight, and I can't take the risk of putting my deputies' lives in danger. You have two hours to leave town. After that, I'll have to let him go."

Priscilla inhaled. "But he threatened to kill me."

"He's threatened to kill many people. And there's nothing I can do to stop him."

Priscilla felt a sinking sensation. She realized that justice would never prevail in this town because Big Bill intimidated the sheriff, and he feared his retaliation. Big Bill's reign of terror could last a lifetime.

The Nightmare

In her dimly lit bedroom in Nashville, Priscilla struggled with an overwhelming sense of failure. Big Bill again triumphed, and the sheriff ran her out of town. Not only had Big Bill branded her a murderer, but he also planted a seed of doubt in the sheriff's mind regarding her involvement in Lee Dodd's death.

A profound sense of despair and shame enveloped her—how could she have been so naïve to fall into Big Bill's trap? He had been the actual perpetrator, yet he had ingeniously turned the tables, making her appear guilty. She shuddered as the grave realization set in that this accusation would subject her to public scorn and provide his hoodlum friends a reason to despise her.

Recollections of Big Bill and his menacing stare consumed her thoughts, and it exacerbated the trauma when she stood at the very spot where Lee had perished. Memories she had desperately attempted to suppress resurfaced with a vengeance. She knew that those harrowing experiences had irrevocably altered her. Where she once felt secure, she found herself constantly vigilant, startled by even the slightest sound.

Priscilla vividly recalled the chilling image of Lee's sinister, shadowed face—angry and drunk. Then the man had pulled him off her. Narrowly escaping, her youthful agility proved to be her saving grace as she gracefully vaulted aboard the boat. Her recollection became hazy as Lee reached out for the boat's bow, and in a frantic attempt to escape, she pushed off with the oar. With Lee dangerously close, there was no time to start the motor. She had to paddle away in haste before starting the motor to make her escape.

She tensed, recalling the vile words he had hurled at her. "Bitch, bitch. I'm going to kill you when I catch you."

Seeking refuge, she ventured deeper into the marshes, her sanctuary. A heron glided effortlessly ahead of her boat, leading her away from the looming peril. The symphony of sounds in the marshlands—the gentle rustling of grass and the harmonious chorus of katydids, crickets, and cicadas—masked Lee's desperate cries for help. Whether her mind shut him out or she deliberately ignored him, it didn't matter—she spoke the truth: she neither heard nor saw his demise because she had mentally retreated, and no earthly force could compel her to return and confront the monster.

The sheriff's initial investigation concluded that in his struggle, the mud had swallowed Lee up—and he had dug his own watery grave.

Priscilla grappled with the decision to release the memory, knowing that holding onto it could lead to madness. Her thoughts approached each scenario methodically, attempting to untangle the web of emotions that consumed her. The accusations made by the sheriff had left her in a state of disbelief. Clint had always been her unwavering support, fiercely defending her honor. The hostility she encountered was entirely unprecedented, and the sheriff's allegation of murder, directed at her, the victim, was beyond her wildest nightmares.

Wyatt remained silent, but his comforting presence spoke volumes. She vividly remembered calling out for him as she slowly regained consciousness; he was the first person she saw. Her emotions tugged at her heart like a pendulum, leaving her torn about whether to let him go.

Strength triumphed over a yearning heart. She knew that if she were to survive, she needed a powerful man who believed in her. Clint had already proven himself. He had been her benefactor, paid for her education, and encouraged her to become a horsewoman. Why was she struggling so? Why was she so drawn to Wyatt?

Priscilla closed her eyes and swiftly descended into a dream. A dark cloud loomed overhead, and suddenly, a torrential downpour began. She stood at the riverbank where Lee had perished, the very spot where Big Bill had once held her captive. A flash of lightning, followed by a resounding clap of thunder, punctuated the sky. Despite being drenched, she felt no fear. The serene sound of a fiddle then permeated the atmosphere. She laughed and tilted her head upwards; the rain stinging her face, yet she remained unfazed. She danced, inadvertently stumbling into the water. A hand extended toward her and pulled her from the river.

As she slowly awoke, she found herself enveloped in Clint's muscular arms. "Oh, God," she murmured, desperately clutching onto him. "I had a dream that I was drowning."

"It must have been terrifying because you were screaming—loudly," he comforted her, softly running his fingers through her hair.

"I've been overthinking things," she confessed softly, savoring his clean, rain-like scent. Their intimacy sent a tingling sensation through her from head to toe. Never had she felt such a sense of security and completeness. A moment so pivotal that she needed to be sure.

As they gazed into each other's eyes, she asked with a hint of uncertainty, "Did you truly mean it when you said you wanted to marry me?"

In a soothing voice, he responded, "I've always wanted to marry you. You're the woman of my dreams. From the first moment I saw you, I knew you were the one."

Concern etched her face as she spoke again, "You want to marry me even though Big Bill has branded me a murderer? Do you realize if this gets out, it could ruin you?"

"I know you're innocent, my darling," he reassured her. "You're my angel, the sweetest woman in the world. There's not a mean bone in your body."

Priscilla locked eyes with him, her expression unwavering. "But what if I did it? Would you still love me?"

Clint furrowed his brow. "Stop playing around, Priscilla. We both know you're not a murderer." He drew back. "Are you trying to tell me something?"

"Only that Lee Dodd got what he deserved. And I know it's wrong to feel this way—but I wish the same for Big Bill. I don't think it's wrong to want someone dead who is terrorizing the entire county."

"Are you afraid?" Clint asked. "Do you doubt I can keep you safe?"

"You weren't there when Lee was trying to kill me. I was alone, fighting for my life."

Clint looked hurt. "Are you blaming me? It's not my fault that we got separated during the trial."

"I'm not blaming you. I'm blaming society for allowing this to happen. The Thomason brothers have always been a wild bunch."

"I know you're upset, Priscilla," Clint murmured, his voice breaking the stillness of the night. He pulled the comforter up to her chin, sensing her distress and feeling a pang of guilt for his tiredness. "But it's 2:00 a.m., and I need to get some sleep. I have a busy day tomorrow."

"I'm sorry I woke you," Priscilla whispered, her voice carrying a note of regret.

Clint couldn't hold back a yawn. "Goodnight, Priscilla."

"Night," she replied quietly, watching him retreat as she lay in the dimly lit room, her thoughts still swirling.

The Accusation

The following day, Wyatt appeared distant in his mannerisms, causing Priscilla to suspect that he may have overheard Clint's visit to her room the previous night and mistakenly assumed something had happened. With her heart heavy and her mind unsettled from the nightmare, she opted to avoid talking to him about it, worried it would only make things worse.

Wyatt eventually approached her at the barn, where she was grooming her horse. He was agitated. Placing his hands firmly on her shoulders, he asserted, "Priscilla, you are acting out of fear. Marrying my brother will not resolve the conflict with Big Bill. He will not simply disappear. I heard everything he said to you; maybe if you were honest with him, he'd take you off his hit list."

Priscilla's brow furrowed. "I told him the truth."

Wyatt spoke in a cold, accusing voice. "Well, Lee didn't hit himself with the oar. And you had it in your hand."

"Big Bill was merely speculating. Lee was drunk out of his mind. Anything could have happened to him both before and after his drowning. The mark on Lee's head is not from my oar," she said, her eyes blazing with anger. "Clint knows I'm innocent, and if you truly cared about me, you would believe in my innocence." She clenched her fist and struck his chest in frustration. "Why did you remain silent when the sheriff hurled accusations at me?"

He grabbed her by the shoulders. "Because I'm a federal agent. And I think you're guilty as sin."

She backed away and then collapsed onto a bale of hay, overwhelmed by a torrent of tears streaming down her cheeks. "I swear I did not kill him, and

I will despise you for the rest of my life for believing I could do such a thing." She spoke in labored breaths. "I thought you loved me, but I realize now that I was mistaken. It was all a ruse. You were merely gathering evidence. You want me in jail, don't you?"

Wyatt looked pained. "You couldn't be more wrong. I heard Clint go to your room last night and felt like I had a dagger in my heart. I was awake all night imagining you two together. This morning, I confronted Clint, and he told me nothing happened sexually, but you had a nightmare about Lee and hinted you'd killed him."

"Arrest me for having a dream," she said, jutting her chin.

"Stop it, Priscilla. I am trying to help you, but I need the truth because all the evidence incriminates you. When Big Bill questioned you about specifics, your responses were inadequate. He did not find you credible, and neither do I." He exhaled. "Honey, I want to help you, not hurt you." He leaned forward and extended his hand to offer comfort.

She swatted his hand aside, her tone sharp. "You believe a killer over me? Do you have any idea what it feels like to have the hands of a notorious killer around your neck? His hands are as large as dinner plates. I have no memory of what I said to him. I was too busy trying to stay alive."

"He's your cousin. You knew him. You could have recounted your side of the story and tried to reason with him. Instead, you spoke about your father playing the fiddle."

"A madman is not open to reason," she retorted, swiftly brushing him aside and saddling the black stallion. "I wanted to remind Big Bill of better days. He used to love to listen to my father playing the fiddle."

"What are you doing?"

"I'm going to practice my jumping. Not that it's any of your business."

Wyatt looked at her sternly. "You're in deep. Big Bill will not let this go. The whole town knows Big Bill and the sheriff are in cahoots, and he will pressure the sheriff to take you in."

Priscilla had had enough. "Do you know what I think?"

Wyatt shook his head.

"I think you're a sore loser," she said in a haughty voice as she led the horse out of the barn. "But I never thought you would stoop to this. My God—you want me to confess to something I didn't do?"

The stallion snorted as Priscilla mounted, sensing her anger.

When Wyatt grabbed the reins, Priscilla came down hard over his shoulder with the whip. She dug her heels into the horse and broke into a gallop.

Wyatt winced in pain. "Do you always attack when you're cornered, Priscilla? You can't run from the truth forever," he yelled. "Come back here."

Priscilla ignored his pleas and headed toward the jumps. Riding was the only thing that took away the stress and gave her back her power. Determined that Wyatt would not break her spirit, she rode hard—faster and faster, aware of Wyatt gaining on her.

"You're going too fast! You're going too fast!" Wyatt shouted.

The horse failed to clear the rails, and they flew as Priscilla landed on the hard dirt. She lay sprawled on the ground, her face smeared with blood and out cold.

Wyatt kneeled beside her, gently cradling her head in his lap. A stable hand rushed over. "Call the doctor," Wyatt commanded. He buried his head in her neck, his tears mingling with her blood. "I never intended to hurt you, Priscilla. I'm sorry."

She stirred faintly. "Get away from me, you bastard," she muttered, her voice slurred before she lapsed back into unconsciousness.

The doctor arrived promptly. While she sustained a bloody nose, scrapes, and bruises, there were no broken bones. Her physical condition was stable. But Wyatt was left emotionally shattered.

Foul Play

At the bow of Priscilla's boat, Wyatt observed the marshlands, attuned to the symphony of crickets chirping, frogs peeping, and grasses rustling. A Blue Heron flew overhead, and he admired its expansive wingspan. Despite the natural beauty surrounding him, Wyatt's purpose was not one of leisure; he sought evidence connecting Priscilla to the murder of Lee Dodd, intending to exonerate her, not condemn her.

He meticulously examined the worn gray oar for dents or chips, but found nothing abnormal. Running his hand along its edge, he stood and mimicked the sideways swing that Big Bill had described. The oar was too heavy for Priscilla to hold at the end and fling it. Wyatt deduced it was a sharp blow to the head from another angle. Wyatt peered into the dark, blue-hued water, its opacity hiding whatever lay beneath its surface. Lee's black hat was found on the riverbank, which had alerted the sheriff to foul play.

Relieved that he had found no evidence to prove Priscilla had killed Lee, he hopped out of the boat and stood on the sloping riverbank. He walked further, then leaned against an old oak tree and reminisced about the time he had lain naked with Priscilla. Her body had been flawless, and her innocence had astounded him. If only he could turn back time. That was when she loved him. Now, he saw only disgust on her face.

Sure of the implications of a third party, Wyatt proceeded to Belle's Saloon. If anyone knew what happened, it would undoubtedly be Belle. Upon entering the saloon, the gray haze and intertwining curls of smoke momentarily blurred his vision. Wyatt surveyed the room until his tired eyes located Belle at the bar, attired in a red satin, low-cut dress complemented by fishnet stockings. She acknowledged his presence with a wave and motioned for him to take a seat at the bar.

Her piercing emerald eyes quickly scanned the surroundings to ensure they weren't being overheard. She leaned in and said in a hushed tone, "Rumors are that some guys are getting together to take Big Bill out."

Wyatt wrinkled his nose at the overpowering fragrance of her perfume. "How do they intend to do that? He is the fastest draw in all of Maury County."

Belle signaled to the bartender for a bottle of the establishment's finest whiskey and poured him a shot, her diamond-adorned fingers dazzling. "They have devised a sure-fire plan. It will take the right place and time, but it will work."

"When is all of this happening?" he asked with unconcealed interest.

"Any day now," Belle said in a grave voice. "Priscilla can come home, and our lives can get back to normal. I've hardly had any time with her, and Martha misses her sister. The sooner we get Big Bill off the streets, the better."

"Sounds like you miss her bad," Wyatt remarked, taken aback by the depth of Belle's emotion; it was a side of her he'd never witnessed.

"I cried for two weeks when she left, but I knew she had to go," Belle said, wiping a tear away with a white bar napkin. "I would do anything for her. She's like the daughter I never had."

Wyatt stared at the white napkin covered with black mascara, thinking Belle and Priscilla were an unlikely pair. The woman had to be worth millions, but her profession could embarrass the family if Clint were to marry Priscilla. He downed the whiskey, enjoying the burn, and set his glass down for a refill.

Belle promptly filled it up. "I've got to go," she said. "My bartender will take care of you. Everything is on the house." She smiled the bright smile she was famous for. "Your money's no good here. Tell Priscilla her nightmare is almost over." She paused. "By the way, what brings you into town?"

"Just came into town to check on Priscilla's house and boat," he said casually.

A look of alarm came over Belle's rouged face. "You don't have to do that. My cook, Jake, checks the property every day. His property adjoins Priscilla's."

"He checks the boat, too?"

"Yes, and he checks for footprints to ensure no one is trespassing." She looked at him through narrow eyes. "You didn't leave footprints, did you?"

"Kind of hard not to in all that mud," he replied.

Belle's complexion paled, making her rouged cheeks stand out. "If I were you, I'd go back and cover my tracks," she warned. "Big Bill's got people around here riled. And the sheriff is looking for anyone he can find to pin Lee's death on."

Wyatt frowned, suspicious. "You know, Big Bill has accused Priscilla of flinging the oar at Lee and contributing to his death. Did Jake do something to that oar, Belle?"

"Why would he?" she asked. "Big Bill's word is worthless. Priscilla didn't hit Lee with the oar—he was staggering drunk when he left here. Whatever happened, he did it to himself."

Wyatt looked at her hard. "You would do just about anything for Priscilla, wouldn't you, Belle?"

Belle was blunt. "I would."

He lifted his brow. "Would you kill for her?"

"I didn't kill Lee, if that's what you're asking." She pinched his cheek hard. "You're sounding like an FBI agent or something." Then she walked away, the feather in her hair swaying with the swing of her hips.

He rubbed his reddened cheek, his thoughts racing as he attempted to reconstruct the crime scene. It struck him that someone could have trailed Lee if Belle or anyone at the saloon knew he was heading to Priscilla's. But the question remained: who? Was it Jake, Belle, or perhaps one of Belle's girls?

As Wyatt exited the saloon with a deliberate stride, he scanned the area for any of Big Bill's hoodlum friends who might lurk nearby. Big Bill wasn't dead yet.

He returned to the riverbank and covered his footprints. He scrutinized the oar with a new perspective, convinced that someone had already been there to eliminate any evidence. It was spotless. Belle had previously staged Priscilla's death to safeguard her, and it seemed plausible that she would go to any length to protect Priscilla. Belle, a wealthy woman with many unsavory connections, posed a lethal threat.

A Score to Settle

Priscilla struggled with paranoia, believing that Clint and Wyatt were conspiring against her. Pain radiated through her ribs, rendering her unable to enjoy her breakfast of Eggs Benedict and toast, which she pushed aside. In a hushed, raspy voice, she said, "The maid who brought my breakfast looked at me suspiciously. Do you think she knows what happened?" Without waiting for an answer, she blurted. "She thinks I'm a murderer."

Martha placed her hand on Priscilla's forehead. "You appear to be running a slight fever," she said, concern etched on her face. "It seems you may be overthinking the situation. All appears to be normal—or, at least, as normal as it can be within such an imposing mansion." She exhaled. "I find their demeanor somewhat pretentious, but helpful."

"You are mistaken, Martha. I've heard their whispers." She cast a wary glance over her shoulder. "Rumors travel, and it seems many believe Big Bill's lies."

"No one holds any ill will towards you, Priscilla. Perhaps the pain medication is affecting your judgment. If we were at home, I would prepare you an herbal tea," Martha said, pulling a thread on her worn gray sweater until the button fell to the floor. She picked it up and stared at the button. "I don't even have my sewing basket to sew this damned button on, and I'm hesitant to ask for things that I need. You're right—something is out of kilter. I don't feel welcome."

"If I am the murderer, then you are the accomplice," Priscilla retorted. "Even the help fears you, Martha."

"Me?"

Priscilla put her hand to her forehead. "Yes, you. And I'm to blame for all of it. God, how I wish I'd never been born. And I've drawn you into this." A tear streamed down her cheek. "Can you forgive me, Martha, for dragging you through this hell with me? You don't deserve it."

"I never thought I'd hear you talk like that. Blaming yourself and wishing you'd never been born won't solve anything. None of us was born with a silver spoon in our mouths, and complaining about it doesn't make anyone happier or richer." A sigh escaped Martha's lips—one that conveyed volumes about her emotional state. "You didn't drag me anywhere, Priscilla. I'm here because I want to be, but I'm willing to admit I made a mistake. I'm miserable. Let's go home where we belong."

"You're fortunate to know where home is," Priscilla lamented. "I've spent the last four years here with the Wilders and believed this was my destiny. The horses in the stables, who once meant everything to me, are part of this House of Cards that has collapsed. It's time, I admitted, my dreams are going up in smoke. It's all because Big Bill planted seeds of doubt. Clint and Wyatt are distancing themselves from me. Neither has been to see me this morning."

"You're young. You can start again," Martha encouraged.

Priscilla's demeanor changed from sorrowful to angry. "You're right, I'm not a child anymore, Martha. When I ran away from home, I had to grow up fast, and I've been running ever since. I can't keep living like this." She hugged herself. "I can almost hear the loons calling." She seemed lost in thought. "Their haunting calls have always struck a chord with me. Someone once told me that when they are silent, it means they are in God's presence."

Martha smiled. "Who told you that?"

"A wise man," Priscilla said with a wistful expression. "Get packed. We're going home where we belong."

Despite a burgeoning sense of relief, Priscilla wrestled with internal conflict. She'd once believed she had a future here. But everything changed last night, and she suspected it had to do with Lee's murder. Affection for both men ran deep, but her self-respect prevailed. She couldn't be where she felt unwanted.

She thought about Rosalee and how the tables had turned. Early this morning, she had declined Rosalee and Amanda's invitation to join them for shopping and lunch. The two women had cultivated a close bond, with Amanda securing a rental space in downtown Nashville for her dressmaking business, which included living quarters on the upper floor. Although Priscilla was happy about Amanda's new entrepreneurial venture, she lacked the motivation to get involved with the dust-laden premises that had once housed an antique shop. She told herself that Rosalee would be fine without her.

That afternoon, she and Martha departed, leaving a note. When she put the pen to paper, she remembered something her father had told her: never burn your bridges.

To the Wilder Family,

Thanks for everything. You've been wonderful, but it's time I fought my own battles. I've disrupted your lives long enough. Martha and I are going home to Mule Town, where we belong. Whether the town welcomes us—doesn't matter. I can no longer live in fear of Big Bill.

Please respect my wishes and don't contact me. I need time to heal.

Priscilla

Priscilla acclimated to the understated elegance of her childhood country home. The tranquility, coupled with the well-maintained household and Martha's unwavering dedication to cleaning and cooking, afforded Priscilla the luxury to focus on organizing and reading as her ribs mended. She slept, rising each morning with the rooster's crow. Two weeks later, she felt stronger than she could ever remember feeling.

Priscilla stood by a window and sipped a cup of hot English tea. The aroma of baked apple pie and homemade bread filled the air as she watched the red and gold leaves drift in the air from an old oak tree. A reminder that winter was coming and they would need firewood. She felt a pang of loneliness. Martha had baked this morning and then gone to visit her sister. She'd taken the horse and buggy they'd bought. It was a significant expenditure, but necessary so they could both get around town. Martha's sister only lived a mile away.

Stepping outside onto the expansive wooden porch, the air felt brisk. The light denim jacket and the scarf she wore didn't seem like enough. She took a long breath, delighting in the revitalizing smell of fall. The harmonious warble of a finch disrupted the tranquil atmosphere, only to be shattered by the sound of wood being chopped. Priscilla assumed it was a neighbor, but discovered that the noise was coming from the back of the house. She was startled when she came around the corner and came face-to-face with Wyatt, who was wielding a long ax. Dressed in faded blue jeans and a red plaid shirt, his rugged good looks made her heart flutter.

When their eyes met, he placed the ax aside. "I thought you might need some firewood with winter approaching."

Priscilla felt a flush of embarrassment, realizing she had fallen behind on her work. "Thank you. I appreciate it, but you didn't have to come all this way to chop wood. I've been meaning to get to it—we were going to ask Martha's nephew for help."

"I didn't come just to chop wood," he replied, taking a few steps closer. "I need to talk to you."

"Wyatt, don't make this more difficult than it has to be. I'm trying to get my life sorted out."

"Why did you leave?"

"I left because you think I had something to do with Lee Dodd's murder, and there was turmoil in the household. We couldn't stay." She paused. "I needed time to think. A lot happened that night when Big Bill attacked me."

"I didn't handle the situation well—I had to convince myself you were innocent. However, the crux of the matter is that despite my attempts to analyze it from various angles, I arrive at one unsettling conclusion: there was someone else with you on the night of Lee Dodd's death."

"No one else was there," she asserted. "What leads you to think otherwise?"

"Because I do not believe you're strong enough to strike Lee Dodd in the head with an oar and knock him off balance. I am convinced that a man murdered Lee."

"Have you forgotten he was drunk on moonshine? It wasn't the blow to the head that killed him. The medical examiner's report said the cause of death was drowning." Priscilla crossed her arms across her chest. "He was alive when I motored away. After I left, he must have slid down the muddy bank into the water and drowned. And he was too drunk to save himself."

Wyatt set his jaw. "I know you pretty well, Priscilla, and I think you're lying. Who are you trying to protect?"

The air was thick with tension.

Wyatt broke the silence. "It's pretty damned cold out here. Can we talk over a cup of coffee?"

"Of course. I owe you that much for cutting the firewood, though it wasn't necessary."

"I didn't come just to cut firewood," he admitted. "I have a message from Amanda."

Martha greeted Wyatt as they entered. "I'm so glad to see you! You're just in time for dinner. If I remember correctly, pork chops are your favorite, and I made mashed potatoes, gravy, and green beans."

"It sounds and smells wonderful," he said. "I'll go wash up. Is it okay if I use my old room?"

Priscilla hesitated, her chest tightening as she met his hopeful gaze. The sincerity in his eyes tugged at her heartstrings, drawing her closer to the comforting illusion he sought. "Of course," she replied, forcing a smile. "Everything is just as it was." Yet, beneath her heartfelt words lingered an undeniable truth; the air between them felt charged with unspoken tension. Though her tone was reassuring, she knew things had shifted. His lingering doubt had seeped into the core of her emotions, leaving a trail of uncertainty where once there was trust.

As they sat down for dinner, the warm glow of candlelight flickered around them. Their conversation meandered through the familiar territory of small talk, focusing on the unexpected chill that had set in.

"I appreciate the wood you chopped," Priscilla said, her voice warm with gratitude. "Martha was going to ask her nephew for help, but life got in the way, and we never found the time."

Wyatt looked into her eyes, a glimmer of uncertainty in his gaze. "I'd be more than happy to stay for a few days and help you get ready for winter," he offered, with a hint of determination in his tone. "There's so much for us to catch up on."

Martha cleared her throat, her expression serious. "Wyatt, Priscilla was ill for a long time. Her ribs are almost healed, but the doctor clarified that rest is essential for her complete recovery. I've been encouraging her to take it easy. So I would be grateful if you could stay for a few days and help."

Wyatt's brows knitted together in a deep frown as concern etched on his face. "Why didn't you call?" he questioned, his voice tinged with worry.

"There's no need to worry; I'm fine," she said with a carefree smile, her light tone almost melodic. "But can we change the subject? You mentioned you had a message from Amanda. What did she say?"

"If you don't mind, I'd rather save that for later," he replied, glancing away as if the message weighed on him.

"I'll serve the pie," Martha chimed in, noticing the sudden tension in the air. She moved toward the kitchen, her mind working to lighten the mood with the comforting aroma of baked dessert.

After dinner, Martha carried a tray of coffee into the drawing room, and Priscilla and Wyatt sat in front of the fire, a cozy ambiance despite the wall between them.

"How have you been?" he asked.

"It's lonely," she said, "But every day gets easier."

"I'm lonely, too, and I miss you like crazy," Wyatt confessed. "Can't we put this behind us and move forward?"

"The last thing I need right now is a relationship; it complicates everything. When I realized you doubted me and suspected me of killing Lee, it changed everything for me. And there's Clint to think about. He's my benefactor, and I care for him. Without Clint, I could very well become a woman of the night, or worse yet—dead."

Wyatt's brows creased. "We need to talk about Clint."

"Is he okay?" Priscilla asked, feeling anxious. His tone told her something was amiss.

"He's okay, but your note was so final, almost as if you were ending your relationship with all of us. After that, he and Amanda started dating."

Priscilla paled. It was stinging to realize that something so profound and conflicted had ended. "My sister wouldn't do such a thing. She knows I'm in love with Clint."

"Do you love him?" Wyatt asked. "Or is it gratitude for everything he did for you?"

Priscilla wanted to tell him it wasn't gratitude, and that she loved Clint, but her voice caught in her throat.

"I know it's painful," Wyatt said. "Clint loved you at one time, but people must move on with their lives."

Wyatt reached out and took her in his arms. "We got there, Priscilla. You'd be lying if you said we didn't."

"Maybe we did, but you doubted me," she said, her voice choked. "I did not kill Lee, even though the evidence points towards me."

Wyatt's voice was tender. "It doesn't matter what happened. I can't imagine my life without you."

Priscilla looked at him straight on. "It's too late. Your doubt killed everything I felt for you." Her voice cracked. "I don't care anymore. I don't care if Clint has discarded me for my sister. None of it matters."

Wyatt had a pained expression. "I've made mistakes in our relationship, but I love you. I was investigating to clear your name. All I've ever wanted is to protect and care for you."

Priscilla's voice was firm. "That's noble of you, but I can take care of myself. Besides, who would want a girl on a hit list whose friend owns a brothel? I'm not a good fit for you or anyone, so you'd best be heading down the road." She turned on her heel. "Goodbye. And you can tell Clint and my sister I hope they'll be very happy together."

Without warning, a resounding thud echoed as something struck the window. Priscilla stood up and approached the window. The sight of a lifeless black crow lying on the ground sent a chill coursing through her.

Wyatt joined her at the window, narrowing his eyes as he surveyed the scene. "It's a sign," he said.

"I no longer place stock in signs," Priscilla retorted. "If I did, I would think it was the devil himself telling me that Big Bill's malevolence and evil won, and I'll soon be dead as the crow."

"My God, you've given up hope," Wyatt said in disbelief.

Priscilla felt bitter, still reeling from the shock of hearing that Clint and Amanda were together as a couple, not to mention the sight of the dead crow. "Maybe I have given up hope. Everyone knows you can't win against Big Bill. He believes I murdered Lee, and he's hell-bent on destroying me."

Wyatt embraced her. "Priscilla, you're not alone. Don't push me away."

"You're far too young to be a widower," she replied. "Can't you see? It's me against Big Bill. I can't let anyone else get hurt." She bit her lip. "There's been enough bloodshed."

Wyatt met her gaze with unwavering resolve. "There's something you don't know. Big Bill's reign of terror is about to end."

Her voice brimmed with intensity as she asked, "How can you be sure that's the case?"

"Undercover agents got wind of it, and I've talked to Belle. There's a plan to take Big Bill down."

A glimmer of hope flickered in Priscilla's hazel eyes, yet she struggled to convince herself that her harrowing ordeal might soon end. "I can only hope they take action, as I am certain I am next on his hit list."

His gaze fixed on her with an intensity that suggested he was on the verge of asking something beyond her capabilities.

"Would you care for a shot of whiskey?" she asked, seeking to soften the blow of her inevitable refusal.

"Only if you will join me. I don't enjoy drinking alone."

"Of course," Priscilla said, proceeding to the cabinet to retrieve a bottle of Jack Daniel's. "My mother believed whiskey was a remedy for a variety of conditions: colds, arthritis, and high blood pressure."

Wyatt's gaze followed her every move, and as she extended the tumbler, their fingers made fleeting contact, igniting a spark of electricity that coursed through his body. He knew she sensed it as well.

Priscilla tilted her head back, savoring the burn of the whiskey, then refilled the tumblers. After downing her drink, she felt like she was on fire—not because of the whiskey, but because he was much too close, and his rugged good looks bothered her.

"Shall we indulge in a third shot to ensure our good health?"

When she extended the bottle for a third pour, he replied, "I've had enough, Priscilla, and I think you have as well."

She set the bottle down with a bit too much force, feeling satisfied that she'd enjoyed two shots of whiskey and was still in her right mind. Aside from the burn, she had felt little.

"You appear distressed. Whiskey can help, but it isn't a cure," Wyatt said. "The pain will still be present in the morning."

Her heart stung as she thought of Clint. She went to the piano, struck a chord hard, and listened to the sound echo through the room.

"Play for me," Wyatt asked in a gentle voice.

"No," she replied, her tone slurred. "I'm not in the mood for music."

Wyatt frowned. "I'd hoped for a serious discussion tonight to discuss our future, but I can see you are in no frame of mind for meaningful conversation."

"You are right," Priscilla said, her gait unsteady as she moved to the sofa and settled beside Wyatt. "I'm in no mood for conversation."

"If you tell me what's wrong—maybe I can help," Wyatt coaxed.

"The messenger brought bad news," she huffed. "My God, do you think it's easy to accept that my sister is having an affair with Clint behind my back?"

"Get over it," Wyatt replied. "They have every right to move on—you seem unable to decide anything." He set his jaw. "Triangles don't last, Priscilla." She inhaled. "I didn't ask for this—you made the first move, so don't blame me."

"That's not true," he said, compelling her to meet his gaze. "You were an open invitation that day in the marshes when you were naked. I was the perfect gentleman."

"You kissed me first," she lashed out. "That's what started it all. Otherwise, I would never have given you a second thought. You were using me as a ploy to get to Lee Dodd." Her hazel eyes flashed. "Don't deny it, Wyatt."

"I'm not denying any of it," Wyatt said. "And I sure didn't mean to fall in love with a brat."

"A brat?" she exclaimed, her voice laced with indignation. "I've worked hard, Wyatt. I've proven myself despite running from a madman for months."

"Who are you running from? Big Bill or me? I want the truth because my life has been hell without you."

His words melted her defenses. Her knees went weak. "Has it?"

His eyes held a somber intensity. "Yes, I can't eat. I can't sleep. And I can't stop thinking about you."

"That's what I needed to hear," she declared, catching him off guard with a fervent kiss. It was a defining moment as she poured her heart and soul into the kiss.

Wyatt nestled his face into her neck, relief washing over him.

"Priscilla, you must decide. I'm not playing second fiddle to my brother anymore."

A tear streamed down her face. "It sounds like Clint has made his choice. He saved me from a horrible life, and I will always be grateful and love him. But I love you, too, in the way I believe a wife should love a husband."

"And how should a wife love her husband, Priscilla?" he asked, his eyes locked with hers.

"Well, you're always on my mind, and I miss you when we're apart."

He smiled. "That's nice... but what about the passion? Is it my imagination, or do we share something special between us—warm, wonderful, and fiery?"

Priscilla blushed crimson. "All that and more," she replied.

He carried her into his old bedroom, and they fell asleep, dressed, wrapped in each other's embrace. They both understood they weren't over the hurdle. But it was a beginning.

Wyatt's words lingered in her mind the next day with an unsettling intensity. He had said, "Clint had moved forward." This left her with an emptiness in her stomach, for she was in love with Clint and convinced that he reciprocated her feelings. The alcohol had numbed her feelings last night, but she was in a fighting mood today, and her sense of betrayal was toward Amanda, whom she believed had instigated this rift. Not only had she experienced the loss of Clint, but Amanda's deceit compounded her anguish, leaving her in emotional turmoil. The only thing to do was to have it out with Amanda.

After dinner, she saw Wyatt off, then went into the drawing room and dialed the Wilders' number.

The maid answered the phone, and Priscilla felt a surge of jealousy as she detected laughter and animated conversation in the background. When Amanda came to the phone, Priscilla wasted no time. "Wyatt informed me you and Clint are now a couple," she said, her tone icy.

"I assumed Wyatt would mention it," Amanda replied. "And I knew you would be upset."

"Upset? I am furious," Priscilla retorted. "You are my sister; you knew I was involved with him. I feel as if you've stabbed me in the back."

"The reality is you've been in a love triangle for quite some time," Amanda clarified. "Everyone believed you had chosen Wyatt, but then you disappeared, and there was no communication from you. If your connection with Clint had been genuine, I would have expected you to reach out. Yet, you did not."

"Did it ever occur to you I might have other things on my mind? Like staying alive. Big Bill has already tried to kill me once, and he's miles from me. I'm a sitting duck." Priscilla's eyes glittered. "Did Clint tell you about my dream? And that he came to my bedroom to console me?" When she heard Amanda take in a sharp breath, she knew her words had cut to the core. That's what she wanted—to hurt her like she was hurting.

"Are you implying something occurred between the two of you?"

"Yes. He told me he loved me, and he does," Priscilla retorted.

"You can't have two men, Priscilla. I've always catered to you, but I'm standing my ground this time because I believe Clint loves me. Would you deny me a chance at happiness?"

"How is it possible for him to love you? You are a woman of questionable reputation—you consorted with John in New York," Priscilla accused.

Amanda gasped in disbelief. "You sound just like Mother, Priscilla. I loved you, cared for you, labored tirelessly, and sent you money to enable you to join me in New York and fulfill your ambitions. Do you recall our discussions about your aspiration to become a telephone operator?"

"How dare you compare me to Mother! How dare you!" Priscilla unleashed her fury. "I despise her. She claims to be a Christian while hiding your letters and pilfering the money you sent. If there is indeed a God, why did He take Father and leave me with a mother desperate to marry me off to Lee Dodd? Do you understand the lengths I had to go to survive after you departed?"

Amanda remained frozen in disbelief at the intensity of Priscilla's accusations.

"Do you have any idea how frightened I was? I worked in a kitchen at a brothel," Priscilla declared. "Belle even had to orchestrate my death. I was as good as dead—gone to my family and friends, forced to place my faith in a stranger."

"But it's all good, Priscilla. It all turned out."

"Did it?" Priscilla asked in a bitter tone, slamming the phone down.

The Duel

"Big Bill shot Solon Woosley in cold blood," Belle exclaimed when Priscilla picked up the phone. "A heated argument led to a duel on the street in Enterprise. He shot him five times and bystanders said he would have shot him more, but his pistol snapped. Then he said he was going home to get another gun and kill them all. But before that could happen, law officers descended upon the town and a manhunt began."

A chill ran down Priscilla's spine. "Oh, my God. The sheriff set him free to hunt down his next victim. He did. And I could be next," she lamented. "A revenge murder—the Wallace brothers shot Big Bill's brother-in-law four times, so he shot Woolsey five times. And what was Woolsey's crime? Testifying on behalf of the Wallace brothers. Did they catch him?"

"No," Belle said. "He ran into the woods, and they couldn't find him. He's still on the loose. Do you have your shotguns loaded?"

"Yes," Priscilla replied nervously. She reached for the shotgun in the corner and clutched it tightly as she peered out the window into the darkness. "Martha's sister is sick, and she's gone to take care of her. Wyatt was here for a couple of days chopping wood and helping us get ready for winter, but he went back to Nashville to take care of business."

"You shouldn't be alone in that country house," Belle warned. "Your neighbors are miles apart. Why don't you drive into town and stay with me? I have plenty of room."

"I don't want to be out at this hour driving on those lonely stretches of country roads," Priscilla argued. "I'll be fine."

But she knew deep down that she wouldn't feel safe alone in the isolated country house. Every creak in the old house made her jump, imagining Big Bill was sneaking in through a window. As she got up to get a glass of water, she couldn't shake off the feeling of being watched. She silently prayed for dawn to come quickly, knowing that she would never feel truly safe until Big Bill was caught or killed.

Two days later, she met Belle for lunch at the Saloon, grateful for a friendly face and some respite from her worries. They both breathed a sigh of relief as Belle informed her that Big Bill had finally turned himself in to the sheriff. However, the sheriff planned to release him to prepare for his trial. "This time, there were witnesses," Belle said, "and the whole town believes he'll be convicted and sent to the penitentiary."

Days later, as Priscilla was driving home from town, Big Bill passed her on the road, swerving recklessly in a "hell on wheels" old Dodge that belonged to his brother, Flourney. His brothers, Flournoy and Gillie, and a friend, Walter Graham, were with him. The threat of conviction and going to the penitentiary hadn't fazed Big Bill one bit. He was clearly drunk on his homemade moonshine and shouting obscenities at anyone who crossed his path. Fear gripped Priscilla as she spun the Tin Lizzie around in the nearest driveway and sped back home, breaking every speed limit along the way. When she arrived, she found Martha outside hanging clothes on the clothesline. Priscilla insisted she come inside immediately, for their safety. For hours, Priscilla sat at the window with a shotgun by her side, anxiously watching and waiting for any sign of danger. She blamed the sheriff for releasing him.

Suddenly, the shrill ringing of the phone broke through the tense silence. It was Belle calling, delivering news that sent chills down Priscilla's spine: "Big Bill's chickens have finally come home to roost," she said ominously. "The Cummins brothers ambushed him on Watt's Hill. He's alive, but barely."

Beads of sweat broke out on Pricilla's brow. Her voice trembled as she spoke, recounting her terrifying encounter earlier that day. "I saw them," she stammered, her words catching in her throat. "They were drunk, driving recklessly, and shouting obscenities. I was sure they were going to turn around and come after me." She closed her eyes briefly, trying to block out the intense memory of fear and danger hovering over her like a dark cloud.

"After Big Bill murdered Woosley, the whole town was scared, especially his enemies," Belle said. "His enemies took the fight to him. Reese, Jack, and Tommy Hugh Cummins, along with their friend Leroy Adams, laid an ambush for him on Watt's Hill. They had lookouts and knew he was coming. The old Dodge could hardly make it up Watts Hill, and they unleashed a barrage of shotgun blasts from both sides of the gravel road. They shot him to pieces."

Priscilla gasped in horror at the brutal scene described by Belle.

"His right arm was mangled and covered in blood," Belle continued. "His brother Flournoy was injured, but he's going to be okay." The two women fell into a heavy silence, each lost in their thoughts about the violent encounter that had taken place on Watt's Hill.

Upon Wyatt's return from Nashville that evening, she was still visibly upset. That night, as she cuddled against him, she expressed her relief. "I escaped Big Bill's wrath twice. I feel like a cat with nine lives."

Wyatt's deep voice broke through the tense silence. "If Big Bill wanted you dead, he would have killed you. As kin, your life held some value to him, and taking it would have sparked conflict within his family. No, I believe this was about power and control. In these rural parts, men often dominate and women submit without question - but you and Amanda refused to succumb. He wanted to punish you for your defiance, but not end your life." Wyatt's gaze was intense as he spoke, his words laced with conviction and reasoning.

The Reign of Terror Ends

The following day, they ventured into town to gather more information. The entire community was abuzz with talk of the attack. At the saloon, a group was wagering on whether Big Bill would survive. One man declared, "They have shot him to bits. He won't make it." Another countered, "But he's invincible. They can't bring him down." A third chimed in, "I heard he refused a transfusion from his brother Gilley because he ran away during the ambush. Can you imagine—he's hanging by a thread and has the guts to say, *don't put that coward's blood in me.*"

A heavy silence fell over the room. Some looked over their shoulder at Big Bill's gutsy remark as if he were still there. One of Belle's girls brushed a tear away from her eye, her expression filled with sorrow and fear. "A man doesn't become like that without some deep-rooted pain," she spoke up, her voice trembling. "I blame his daddy, Jerome Milton. He raised him to be ruthless and even put a gun in his hand when he was just a young boy." She straightened her back, determined to speak her truth. "I've been with him. He was bad, but there was also goodness in him. I saw it."

Priscilla and Belle exchanged a knowing glance, their eyes reflecting their thoughts on Big Bill. He wasn't a regular customer at the saloon, but when he came in with his brothers, trouble and chaos followed.

The young girl's voice was tinged with sadness and defiance as she defended Big Bill, her words ringing out in the quiet room. "You should stop bad-mouthing him," she hissed, her dark eyes flashing. "He was a hardworking blacksmith with a tight-knit group of friends who hung out together at the blacksmith shop. He was a devoted husband and father, always putting his family first." She paused, her mascaraed lashes shimmering with unshed tears. "His wife is a stunning woman, known for her devout faith and dedication to raising their children right." She pointed her finger at the crowd. "You all played a part in this. Your brutality and harassment drove him to become a murderer. You challenged him because of his size and skill as a gunslinger. There was always someone who thought they could take down Big Bill Thomason."

A gruff voice came out of the crowd. "How is it you know so much about him?"

She raised her chin with a defiant sparkle in her eyes. "Many years ago, way back when... we were neighbors. I was in love with him. I would have moved mountains to win his heart. But when he turned away from me, rejecting my affections, the pain twisted within me. In my anguish, I spun tales—lies born from heartbreak—that only grew more elaborate with each passing day."

The room fell silent as she spoke, her impassioned defense casting a new light on the man known for his hot temper and feuds that had plagued their small town for years. But everyone in town knew the roots of the feuds began with Jerome Milton Thomason, Big Bill's father, leaving Big Bill to carry out the vendettas on behalf of his family's honor.

One man spoke up, his voice a deep timbre. "Listen to this," he said, his voice filled with excitement. "It's fresh off the press." He read aloud from the headline: *'Thomason Better. Enterprise Blacksmith Shows Improvement After Ambush.'* A rustling sound filled the air as the man held up a newspaper, its thin pages crackling against his fingertips. *"Big Bill Thomason, Enterprise blacksmith who was shot in the arm by ambushers on Watt's Hill Wednesday morning, was reported much improved today. Blood from his son, Jerome, 16, was used in a transfusion administered to him just before his arm was amputated. He spent a restful night, and was able to eat today, and showed much improvement over his previous condition."*

"That proves his family loved him—his son gave him blood. It says right here in the Tennessean Nashville newspaper."

Belle leaned closer to Priscilla. "The Cummins brothers are going to be mighty upset when they read that," she whispered.

The atmosphere in the crowded saloon shifted, becoming charged with tension, and the air was thick with the scent of sweat and wood smoke, a familiar combination in Belle's saloon. Big Bill, the legendary figure who had been shot multiple times and survived, loomed over the room like a menacing giant. Belle's patrons couldn't help but shudder at what he might do if he found out they had been placing bets on his life. Despite their fear, there was a sense of camaraderie among them, forged through years of working together in this rough-and-tumble town. And most secretly wished for Big Bill's demise.

They got their wish. He died the next day at King's Daughters Hospital. At age 44, Big Bill's reign of terror had ended.

That evening, Priscilla set aside her anger and, feeling the need to talk to the family, reached out to Amanda and called.

"It's over," she said. "Big Bill has passed away. Now I can move forward with my life, no longer burdened by the uncertainty of when he might strike. He was larger-than-life, and it is difficult for me to accept that he is no longer with us. I still look over my shoulder."

"I heard about the ambush," Amanda said. "Any other man would have died on the spot, but not him. I heard about my cousin Gilly wanting to give blood, but he refused. I wish I could express my condolences for Aunt Vinnie's and Uncle Jerome's loss of their son. They have always shown us kindness. Mama will be there for them. Like always."

"I have not given my mother much thought. Given that Big Bill tried to kill me, I have no intentions of extending condolences to anyone."

"It's sad that everything turned out the way it did with both Lee and Big Bill dying horrific deaths. "

"Live by the sword, die by the sword," Priscilla said in a tone devoid of empathy. She exhaled. "I find myself at a loss for words. Our family went to hell in a hand basket once Daddy died, and Mama married Sidney."

"I've heard through the grapevine that our older sisters are supportive of Mama. They get together."

Priscilla rolled her eyes. "Looks like we're the black sheep of the family."

"It's of little consequence," Amanda said. "What matters is that we have each other. And we have a new family now—the Wilders are wonderful people."

Priscilla felt her heart soften towards Amanda and said, "That's true. I should show them more appreciation." Treading with caution, she said, "How is everyone?"

"Well, Wyatt called Clint and said you were back together. He's talking about a wedding. Wants us to have a double wedding."

Priscilla raised her brows in surprise. "He said nothing to me."

"Maybe I spoke out of turn. But I would love it. I could start making our dresses right now. I know where I can get exquisite fabric in New York."

Priscilla closed her eyes. Wyatt had yet to propose to her, though Clint had. A tumult of emotions surged within her, rendering her almost speechless. "I will need time to consider it," she said. "As I mentioned, Wyatt has not made a formal proposal."

"I am so sorry," Amanda said. "I just got so caught up in it, and I wasn't supposed to tell you, but Rosalee has already begun planning our wedding. She is brimming with excitement and is eager to see you. When are you coming home?"

"I am home," she said.

"Oh, you cannot remain there," Amanda insisted. "Our lives are with the Wilders now. We must leave Maury County and leave our past behind. The events of the trial and the murders will linger in the minds of the townsfolk for a long time. You cannot stay there."

"I'll think about it," Priscilla said, biting her lip. "I'll call you tomorrow."

"We all love you, Priscilla."

"I love you, too," Priscilla said, before hanging up the phone.

Then she covered her eyes with her hands and allowed her tears to flow. The memory of Clint's proposal was painful, and she had accepted. *Had he forgotten?*

The Silence of the Loon

As soon as Priscilla thought the chaos had settled, her phone rang. It was Belle. "Jake had a heart attack," she said with a heavy sadness in her voice. "He's barely hanging on and asked to see you."

Without hesitation, Priscilla grabbed her purse and headed out the door. She tried to persuade Wyatt to stay at home, but he insisted on accompanying her.

When they arrived at the saloon, she led them to the back room where Priscilla used to sleep when she worked for her. Jake lay motionless on the same cot that she had once slept in, his face pale and his breathing labored. She leaned over him, tears welling up in her eyes, and whispered, "It's Priscilla. I'm so sorry."

"Don't be sorry, baby girl," Jake rasped. "I'm ready to meet my maker."

Priscilla couldn't hold back her sobs any longer. "Are you okay about everything?" she asked gently.

"I've made my peace, if that's what you mean," he replied, his eyes barely open. "We weren't the only ones there that day. If you think way back — there was a loon."

Priscilla gently squeezed Jake's withered hand, offering comfort and support. "You don't have to talk about it if you don't want to," she reassured him.

But Jake's memories flooded back, fragile and vivid as ever. "I remember it like it was yesterday... the loon. After I did what I had to do, it gave a long, haunting cry." His eyes took on a vacant stare, lost in the past.

"And then everything went silent," he continued, his voice fading.

Leaning in closer, Priscilla listened intently.

"That's when I heard Him speaking to me. He said, 'Everything is going to be okay, Jake.'"

Belle, sitting quietly beside them, closed Jake's now vacant eyes. The weight of the moment was heavy on her heart.

Tears streamed down Priscilla's face as she broke out into sobs, overwhelmed by the emotions and memories shared between them. It was a bittersweet reminder of the most horrible day of her life and what Jake had to do to save her.

Wyatt stepped out of the shadows and wrapped his arms around her, pulling her close. She sobbed into his chest, releasing all the pent-up emotions. Jake had been her protector from the beginning - orchestrating her death upon her arrival at the saloon and later saving her from Lee at the riverbank. He had been her savior.

As the night settled around them, Priscilla found comfort in the warmth of Wyatt's embrace. She took a deep breath and began to tell him the story. "Lee came out of nowhere when I was headed towards the boat. He was stumbling, clearly drunk, and delivered a stinging slap across my face. I fell to the ground, disoriented and fearing for my life. He was on top of me, and I remember fighting like a wildcat and somehow freeing myself."

She paused, tears welling in her eyes as she relived the terrifying moment. Wyatt held her tighter, silently encouraging her to continue.

"That's when Jake appeared from the thicket," she continued, her voice quivering slightly. "He saw what was happening, and Jake grabbed the oar without hesitation and swung it at Lee's head with all his strength. The sound of impact echoed through the air as Lee stumbled back, stunned."

She closed her eyes, reliving the memory of Jake's fierce protectiveness and unwavering loyalty. The marshes swirled in her mind, a maze of tangled waterways and thick vegetation. "Jake told me to get in the boat and go deep into the marshes," she recalled, gritting her teeth at the recollection. "Lee grabbed onto the bow of the boat as I pushed off. I begged Lee to let go, but he cursed at me and tried to climb aboard." She paused, clenching her fists in frustration. "I swung the oar with all my might, hitting him hard and causing him to fall back. That's when he got stuck in the thick mud, sinking deeper and deeper."

Wyatt listened intently, his mind racing with each new detail.

"Jake told me to go, and I did. After I heard you calling for me, I came back. Lee and Jake were gone. My heart sank when I saw Lee's hat on the riverbank. I stared into the murky water, knowing Lee was there because he never went anywhere without his hat. Choices had to be made that day—hard choices. I silently vowed to keep Lee's fate a secret because I knew Jake and I would get into trouble. I'm pretty sure it was Belle who told Jake to follow Lee after the trial."

A thick silence settled between them, heavy with unspoken emotions. After a moment, Wyatt's voice broke through the stillness. "I suspected that someone else was involved," he murmured, his tone laced with disbelief. "But I never would have guessed it was Jake. I always thought it might be Belle or one of the other girls. You did nothing wrong, Priscilla. Thank God Jake was there to intervene."

A sense of relief washed over her. The weight of the situation lifted from her shoulders, and she was grateful for Wyatt's understanding and support. The events of that night seemed like a distant nightmare now, but the memory still haunted her. She had kept silent all these months, burdened with guilt and fear of being found out. But now, with Wyatt's comforting presence beside her, she finally felt free.

The Double Wedding

Priscilla and Wyatt, together with Clint and Amanda, celebrated their love with a grand double wedding at the stunning Andrew Wilder's mansion in Nashville. This venue exuded elegance and charm. Over five hundred guests filled the decorated halls, their laughter and joy creating a vibrant atmosphere. There was a faint smell of azaleas and magnolias from floral arrangements adorning the tables. Belle and her friends drew attention with their eye-catching, bright colored dresses and bold, dramatic makeup, yet the crowd embraced their cheerfulness. As the evening unfolded, champagne flowed, cascading like a sparkling river. A lively band played an eclectic mix of tunes that kept everyone dancing well into the early morning hours, ensuring the celebration was unforgettable.

The event was celebrated with congratulations, recognizing both the wedding and Priscilla's equestrian successes, including many horse-jumping wins and her "Horsewoman of the Year" title in Tennessee. Andrew Wilder took immense pride in his daughter-in-law, introducing her to his circle of friends and guiding her from one group to another until Clint intervened, leading her to the dance floor.

A smile played on his lips. "You're wearing the diamond necklace I gave you."

She dropped her eyes. "I didn't think you'd notice."

"I notice everything about you," Clint said as he whirled Priscilla around the dance floor. "Promise me you'll be my best friend forever."

"I promise," Priscilla said, her tone assuring. "I don't know how I can ever repay you for all you've done for me. I'll always love you."

"And I'll always love you," Clint said, his voice filled with a bittersweet longing. "You were never mine, and that only makes you more precious. I realized when it was time to step back to let you find your way. I could see the uncertainty in your eyes—you couldn't decide. So, I took it upon myself to make that choice for you."

"I'm so glad you did," Priscilla said, warmth radiating from her smile, relieved that it wasn't *because he couldn't get there with her.* That's what he'd told Wyatt. "Now we'll always be together, the four of us, and I can't imagine anything I'd love more. You're happy, aren't you?"

Clint grinned, his eyes sparkling with joy. "Yes. I've never been happier."

Wyatt cut in, his playful tone cutting through the moment. "What were you discussing with my brother?" he asked, a teasing edge in his voice. "You're making me jealous. Let's take a walk—get some fresh air."

With a flourish, he twirled her out the door and onto the patio, and into the shadows. He leaned in, kissing her, his lips lingering on her neck, sending shivers down her spine as he whispered in her ear, "Are you second-guessing your choice?"

"Oh, no," Priscilla replied, her heart swelling. "You were always the one for me. It's just that I will forever be grateful to Clint for everything he did for me. Had I not met him, we wouldn't have crossed paths."

"I offered to pay him back," Wyatt said with a hint of admiration. "But he refused."

As a tear slipped down Priscilla's cheek, she wiped it away, determined not to let sadness overshadow the joyful occasion. She reminded herself that today was a celebration, a new beginning.

She closed her eyes, nestling against Wyatt's chest. "I wish my father could be here," she remarked, her voice tinged with longing. "I miss him." At that moment, the melodious sound of a fiddle emerged, infusing the atmosphere with a cheerful, uplifting tune. "Do you hear that?" she asked, glancing up at Wyatt, her eyes shimmering with both laughter and tears.

His brows furrowed before realizing, "It's the fiddler. Your father is playing the fiddle." He gazed into the sky; his ears perked as he listened to the music. "Look, a falling star."

Priscilla put her hand over her heart, tears streaming down her cheeks as she watched the bright star falling from the sky. At that moment, she realized all her dreams had come true: she was married to the man she loved, and Amanda and Clint would be a part of her life forever. She had everything she'd ever wanted. And then she said the words she knew her father was waiting to hear.

"I believe, Daddy. I believe."

About the Author

MEG ANNE BRIGHTON is a former hospice nurse from Henderson, Nevada, who now resides in the countryside near Charm, Ohio. She cherishes quality time with her family and is passionate about home improvement projects. An avid collector of quilts and a frequent visitor to thrift shops, she refers to herself as a 'treasure hunter.' Meg spends much of her time in her extensive library, which boasts over five hundred volumes, diligently writing or researching her rich family history that traces back to Georgia and Maury County, Tennessee. Many of these ancestral figures have found their way into her literary works. Other highly acclaimed novels include *The Girl with the Golden Ribbon, Tess of Owl Creek, and Run, Susan Run.*

Cast of Characters

Priscilla Powell - A fictitious character inspired by my grandmother, the daughter of an evangelist, who married Lee Dodd Thomason, the grandson of a moonshiner/gunslinger, two weeks before her fourteenth birthday in Maury County, Tennessee. She settled for the 'arranged' marriage and lived a life of regret. In my book, she rejects Lee and flees, fighting for the life she dreamed of having.

Amanda Powell - A fictitious character who symbolizes the women of the 1920s who dared to speak up for themselves and others. She was Priscilla's older sister who paved the way for the women's suffrage movement. Outspoken and courageous, she is defined with no gray areas. As an opportunist, she follows the path of many women of her time—using her boyfriend, John, as a stepping stone to gain experience and improve herself. Once she joins up with Rosalee, she is unstoppable. She crosses boundaries and enters a relationship with Clint, blaming Priscilla for her lack of attention to him. Priscilla forgives her. (I had many ancestors named Amanda, and I love the name. I had no particular ancestor in mind when I created the character.)

Lee Dodd- An ancestor. A villain in my novel. He was my grandfather, whom I never knew. In my story, he drowns in the marshes at Duck River. In reality, he was pushed into the Tuscarawas River in Coshocton, Ohio, during a craps game that went wrong. The Coshocton Tribune reported that his black hat was found lying on the riverbank near the water. He had been married for seventeen years and died at forty-one, leaving my grandmother alone to raise eight children. Though my grandfather escaped death by gunshot like other gunslingers in his family, he was murdered and died a tragic death.

The black hat he wore is in my story because it was found on the riverbank. Law enforcement ruled his death a suicide, but word got back to the family that he had been murdered. He married my grandmother on March 16, 1921. He had been married twice before marrying my grandmother. At age 17, he married his first wife, Mary Lou Davis, on Dec. 28, 1916. At age 21, he went to war. After that, I can find no record of Mary Lou Davis. He served in World War I from 1918 to 1919 and was a POW in France, one of the deadliest conflicts in history. The Census shows Lee living in a boarding house on Screamer Street after his return from the war.

Raymond Holt also lived at the boarding house, and Lee appears to have met his second wife, Grace Holt, through Raymond. She was most likely Raymond's sister. Lee married Grace on May 12, 1920. The marriage was brief, as he married my grandmother the following year, on March 15, 1921. Lee is buried in South Lawn Cemetery in Coshocton, Ohio. His grave marker indicates he was a POW in World War I. There must have been children from Lee's first two marriages, but this isn't part of the family history. I believe I will find a DNA match someday on Ancestry.com. That part of his life remains a mystery, as does his biological father, who is thought to be named Dodd. He was a married neighbor of Lee's mother, Winnie Thomason.

Fannie Powell - An ancestor. My great-grandmother. An antagonist in my story. She was an evangelist and matchmaker with the best intentions. She used religion to manipulate and control her daughters. The 1920s were an era of change. The 19th Amendment was passed, and women earned the right to vote in 1920. World War I had ended, and the economy was booming. Amanda wanted more out of life and was determined to take Priscilla along with her. In my novel, a profound conflict between the two girls and their mother persists throughout the book. In truth, she was a highly respected woman loved by her children and everyone who knew her. She was often seen in pictures with a baby in her arms. She was a midwife in her younger days and was known for her nursing skills. She was known to be somewhat of a Queen of Hearts, often meddling in her children's and grandchildren's affairs. She remarried a man named Sidney Treherne, but divorced him because he didn't like her daughters visiting so much. She helped many ministers start churches in Coshocton, Ohio. One of her sons was a well-known evangelist in the state of Virginia. She died at her daughter's house in Coshocton, Ohio, at age 82 of heart-related problems.

David Powell - An ancestor. The fiddle player. Priscilla's father, whom she loved dearly. He was a telegraph operator who had previously worked in the coal mines. The coal mines led to black lung disease. His undying love for Priscilla continues throughout the novel. He is an ancestor who really played the fiddle and worked in the coal mines. He fathered fourteen children. Six with his first wife, Rachel Clay, and eight with Fannie. Rachel Clay died of tuberculosis.

Sidney - Fannie's second husband. Fannie divorced him because she said he didn't like that her children visited so often.

Big Bill Thomason - An ancestor. A villain. A shoemaker by trade, he was known as a notorious gunslinger and moonshiner from Maury County, Tennessee, whom I discovered while researching my family history. Standing at 6'8", he earned a reputation as the fastest draw in Maury County. Courthouse records in Columbia, Tennessee, and various newspaper clippings reported that Big Bill killed Solon Woosley in a duel in Enterprise, Tennessee. Allegedly, he took the lives of over six people in gun duels throughout his lifetime. He was a handsome man, just like all his brothers. Women were drawn to him, and many stories about his conquests circulate in Maury County—though I'm sure not all of them are true. He met his end in an ambush on Watt's Hill in Mt. Pleasant, Tennessee, at the hands of the Cummins brothers, who sought to end his reign of terror. That part of the book is factual. He is a legend in Mt. Pleasant. People still visit his grave. Big Bill died at age 44, after having an arm amputated and losing a lot of blood.

Gilly Thomason - An ancestor. Big Bill's younger brother. He ran during the ambush by the Cummins brothers. When Big Bill was on his deathbed, Gilly went to the hospital to give blood, *but Big Bill said he didn't want that coward's blood in him.* Because of this, I portray Gilly as a man who tends to *go along for the ride,* even though he often finds himself in the middle of trouble. Strangely, two years after Big Bill's death, Gilly was shot and killed by Big Bill's 17-year-old son, Jerome Milton Thomason, who was named after his grandfather. Newspaper clippings reported that Gilly was drunk and approached Jerome while planting potatoes in the garden. Gilly searched Jerome for a weapon. When he found none, he went into the house and began to harass Big Bill's widow, Janie. Jerome Milton followed Gilly, grabbed a rifle, and shot him. Jerome Milton was taken to jail. He told his story and was released. He died at age 36.

Winnie Thomason - An ancestor. Lee Dodd's mother. Lee was illegitimate, and his biological father was named Dodd. I call Lee—*Dodd* because he wasn't a Thomason. Dodd is a mysterious figure; I have not yet found him, but I'm still looking. He is, in reality, my great-grandfather. Winnie later married James Marion Fautt, a widower. He died at age 48 of gunshot wounds to the head, having been murdered by one of the Wallace brothers. That part of the book is true. At the trial, Big Bill was upset with Solon Woosley because he testified on the Wallace brothers' behalf. That led to the duel and murder of Solon Woosley. Three of her children died in infancy. She died at the age of 59 from a fall.

Jerome Milton Thomason -An ancestor. An antagonist. His daughter, Winnie, was Lee's mother. Jerome was a farmer, moonshiner, and gunslinger who constantly feuded with his neighbors. His children inherited old feuds that continued for years. The still he owned seemed to cause much trouble with his neighbors. He dodged bullets his entire life. He raised Lee as his own child. Lee was raised alongside Big Bill and believed him to be his brother. Many of his children were murdered, and his brother, Porter Love Thomason, was murdered by a man named Calvert and was convicted of manslaughter, serving only two years in the penitentiary. Jerome died of natural causes at age 71.

Vinnie Thomason—an ancestor. My great-grandmother was originally from Georgia. Her father, Lewis Riddle Powell, came from a long line of war heroes. William R. Powell (1772-1847) was killed in an Indian massacre. Capt. William Powell (1605-1695), her grandfather from Wales, is referenced in numerous historical books, including *The Powell Families of Virginia and the South.* They are descendants of royalty. She hailed from a respected family whose father was held in high esteem. It remains a mystery why she married Jerome Milton Thomason, who had a history of feuds; she suffered considerable heartbreak during her time with him, as many of her children followed their father's path and were murdered. She and Fannie's mother, Mary Elizabeth, were sisters, and Priscilla and Lee were cousins. She died of myocarditis at age 69 and is buried in Spencer. Hill Cemetery in Mt. Pleasant, Tennessee.

The Wallace/Fautt Trial. The trial is actual and took place in Columbia, Tennessee. It is said to be one of the most famous trials of all time in Tennessee, and the courtroom was filled. Six Wallace brothers, Jack, Rufus, Otey, Ollie, John, and Willis, were indicted for the murder of James Marion Fautt. The pistol, which was found lying beside the body of Fautt when the officers arrived, did not belong to the dead man. And the pistol holster, found buckled around Fautt's body, did not belong to him, but was placed upon his body after the shooting, before the officers arrived. It was found during the trial that James Marion Fautt was in the vicinity of the Wallaces 'still when he was shot four times in the back. His wife, Winnie, said he was trapping, but there was bad blood between the Wallaces and Fautt, and the Wallaces believed *he was up to no good.* Since a dead man tells no tales, the judge ruled in favor of the Wallaces. One of the Wallaces (the shooter) was charged with manslaughter but, to my knowledge, did not serve time in the penitentiary.

The Wilder Brothers, Martha, Blake, Rosalee, Andrew, Belle, the girls, and Jake are all fictitious characters.

Although many characters' names are fictitious, the Thomason name and its associated characters are authentic. They were my ancestors. The trial in Columbia, Tennessee, is also actual.

The Tennessean Newspaper

Nashville, Tennessee Saturday, March 17, 1923

Columbia, Tenn., March 16. The case against Jack and Rufie Wallace, charged with the first-degree murder of James M. Fautt, was given to the jury just before court adjourned late this afternoon. At 9 o'clock tonight, no verdict had been reached, and the jury was locked in until the opening of court at 9 o'clock Saturday morning.

All of today was taken up by attorneys in presenting the arguments. The speechmaking started with an address by W.S. Fleming, Jr., special prosecutor, who presented the theory that the killing occurred when Fautt surprised the defendants at the moonshine still. They followed him for a considerable distance up the hill and that Rufie Wallace, son of Jack Wallace, fired the four shots which took effect in the fack of Fautt's head, ending his life.

Speeches were to be made by General Job B. Garner, Pride Tomlinson, Tom Cotton and Major Leroy H. Hammond for the defense and by Judge S.E. Stevens for the state. Mr. Fleming closed for the state.

The oratory of the lawyers attracted an unusually large crowd to the courtroom, which was packed to overflowing during the arguments.

The theory of the defense was that the deceased, Fautt, cherished a grudge against Jack Wallace as the result of damaging evidence.

Columbia Tennessee Newspaper Clipping

Thomason Better.

September 14, 1930. W.J. (Big Bill) Thomason, Enterprise blacksmith, who was shot in the arm by ambushers on Watt's Hill Wednesday morning, was reported much improved today.

Blood was his own son, Jerome, 16, was used in a transfusion administered to him just before his arm was amputated, and he spent a restful night, and was able to eat today, and showed much improvement over his previous condition.

Note from the Author: Big Bill died on September 16, 1930, at 12:15 a.m. He was 44 years old.

Author's Notes

I wove this story together, using both truth and my imagination. It took five years of research, a labor of love, to piece it together like a patchwork quilt; every piece of the story had to come together.

Through the research, I gained a new understanding of my ancestors. I knew very little when I uncovered the secrets of my family, the people my mother had hidden, like Big Bill Thomason, born into circumstances over which they had no control. He inherited the feuds from his father, Jerome Milton. Big Bill, who was 6'8", led the Thomason brothers, most of whom were over 6'2.

Jerome owned a still, and their love of moonshine was their downfall. Big Bill's love for his family ends in his demise when he stands up for his sister, Winnie's husband, James Marion Fautt, who was shot in the head four times. Fautt was unarmed. They did not serve justice at the trial, and Big Bill took the law into his own hands, murdering Sam Woolsley because of his testimony at the trial. Then, he threatened to kill others. That's why the Cummins brothers did what the law could not; they ambushed Big Bill, bringing an end to his reign of terror.

He was 44, leaving behind a wife and two children. The feuds began long before Big Bill was born. He was big and bad, and some said he had the face of a choirboy. He is a legend who will live on forever in Mt. Pleasant, Tennessee.

About the Author

Meg Anne Brighton lives near Charm, Ohio. She is a former hospice nurse from Henderson, Nevada, and was nominated for Nurse of the Year in 1993. Other highly acclaimed novels include: The Girl with the Golden Ribbon, The Nephew's Proposition, and Susan's Mirror Image.

Also by Meg Anne Brighton

A gripping psychological thriller.

Susan's Mirror Image

Susan James, a librarian, flees her violent husband, Blaine, after she uncovers evidence that he murdered his first wife, and a psychic warns her that her life is in danger. After starting a new life with former FBI agent Derrick Hampton, she lives in the shadow of his deceased wife, Jenny. She feels betrayed when she learns Jenny is her mirror image.

Blaine is a ticking time bomb doggedly stalking Susan.He becomes a monster on a rampage.

A THRILLER LOVE STORY

The Nephew's Proposition

A Gatsby-inspired story that will hold you in its grip.

A captivating story about a charismatic billionaire, Charlie Dern, a Gatsby-like figure who convinces his hospice nurse, Anne Jones, to quit her job and help him complete his bucket list.

Charlie's love of danger turns his bucket list into a dangerous challenge, intensified by his old mob ties.

The greatest threat is Gray, Charlie's nephew, who tempts Anne with an alluring offer that sparks romance and adds a fiery edge to this dangerous and thrilling story.

www.ingramcontent.com/pod-product-compliance
Lightning Source LLC
Chambersburg PA
CBHW030112260626
47156CB00008B/2623